"I was there avoiding his question.

"What day?" he asked confused.

"When you received your medal, Lieutenant," she said calmly. She found his eyes again. "Quite an honor." Sam shrugged. "And then I just played detective. I do that when I find someone I really care about."

He stood not sure what to say. "I…I didn't know," was all he could come up with. "You should have told me."

"The medal ceremony? I felt I owed it to you. We all did." She let her gaze fall momentarily. "You were busy. We were just visiting, and I assumed your plate was full."

"Really. All of you came?"

She nodded, finding his eyes again. "Yes, Mortimer, Charles, Holly and me," Sam whispered then averted her eyes quickly. He thought they were moist. "It was a lovely ceremony. Your fiancé must have been so proud." She took a deep breath and smiled gently, touching his arm as she turned. "Good-bye…Lieutenant. I won't bother you again. Ever," she said softly adding a gentle, "Promise," she added, crossing her heart.

Shane stood staring after her. He closed his eyes and took a deep breath then pushed his beer back at the bartender. "Keep this cold for me, Kenny," he said trotting after her.

Praise for Kevin V. Symmons and...

SOLO:

"A true page turner... Once I started reading it, I did not put it down... A heart wrenching love story of two lightning-struck soul-mates unable to be together for many painful years because of the twists and turns in their lives. The heroine is written with strength and resolve from a devastating past. Her rise to fame and fortune is a tribute to those who have suffered a similar fate."

RITE OF PASSAGE:

"Bubble, bubble, toil and trouble... You will not find Courtney Wellington stirring Shakespeare's cauldron with this chant. But, as the world's most beautiful witch, she will spirit you away to discover the non-stop romantic adventure she has with the love of her life, Robert McGregor. ...[A] fast-paced modern world of ancient rituals, evil doings, and the other toils and troubles these two gorgeous people face."

OUT OF THE STORM:

"An action-packed page turner...This was a great summer read. ... The author gives you the details fast enough so that you keep turning the page but throws in red herrings that keep you guessing. A lot of action but still a fine love story."

CHRYSALIS:

"Hunks, Horses, and Cape Cod! Does anyone truly have everything? Chrysalis is a young adult novel by Kevin Symmons that confronts this question by examining the lives of an Ivy League golden boy and the privileged rich girl he desires. Teenage angst is skillfully interwoven with the stark realities of dark deeds and the ultimate payback."

Eye of the Storm

by

Kevin V. Symmons

Eye of the Storm

Cover Art by *The Wild Rose Press, Inc.*

The Wild Rose Press, Inc.
PO Box 708
Adams Basin, NY 14410-0708
Visit us at www.thewildrosepress.com

Publishing History
First Mainstream Historical Edition, 2020
Trade Paperback ISBN 978-1-5092-2974-1
Digital ISBN 978-1-5092-2975-8

Published in the United States of America

Acknowledgments

No one writes a novel of 85,000 words without some significant assistance. Especially if it delves into area of expertise for which they are not experts. *Eye of the Storm* has a great deal in it—terminology, acronyms, and protocols—in the field of technology that I needed much assistance with. My good friend and successful technology expert, Ken Palmer of Integrity IT Solutions of Cape Cod was happy and more than willing to spend more than a few afternoons tutoring me on things like TOR, Virtual Networks, Man-in-the-Middle Protocols, and the like. If I have somehow blundered with his information downloads it is my fault not his.

Several local Police Departments—Plymouth, Dennis and Hyannis were kind enough to answer a host of questions I asked them on frequent occasions as to procedures and methods though I was asked not to credit anyone by name.

Also, so many Cape Cod residents and businesspeople were very helpful in putting together much of the local 'flavor' and literary ambiance for *Eye of the Storm*.

And one final big vote of thanks… to my publicist Jeanie Flynn who has put up with all my moods and helped to bring me some modest success for the last five plus years. Review this again when you finished *Eye of the Storm* since Jeanie Flynn is the name of one of the main characters!

And thanks to all of you who have been such loyal readers and fans!

~*Kevin V. Symmons*
April 2020

Chapter One

August 29th, 2012—off Florida's West Coast

The water slapped at the fifteen-inch gunwales of the sturdy inflatable.

The Coast Guard Lieutenant and the young woman lay back, each huddling with one of the two children—a young boy and a younger girl. The children shivered, trying to find shelter behind the adults since the wind had picked up.

The officer wiped the stinging spray from his eyes, gently tightening his grip on the boy. The lingering storm clouds had begun to dissolve, and the sun rose slowly, peering over the four-foot swells that were building again. Clear skies and sunlight were a Godsend when he was on the Raymond Evans, the 154-foot Sentinel Class Coast Guard Cutter he served on. But not when floating alone on the Caribbean in a tiny raft with four cold, frightened survivors. The improving weather would mean stronger winds and heavier seas. It also meant exposure and dehydration if they were not found within a few days.

"My uncle," the young woman began, nodding toward the figure lying on the floor of the raft. "I don't know if he's going to make it," she reached out softly, touching the man . "He's swallowed a lot of sea water and the boom hit him. He's got a nasty bump on the head." Her hand rested on the man's damp cargo pants. "And he wasn't well to begin with." She took a deep breath, withdrawing her hand. Her voice was soft. Her accent British. She turned, brushing away dampness from her flushed cheek. The officer wasn't sure whether it was seawater or tears. "I begged him not to make this trip. Not in the Caribbean during hurricane season." She shook her head wearily.

The man groaned and opened his eyes. Dark lips parted and moved as if to speak, but he shifted and drifted back to unconsciousness.

"My name," the woman continued. "It's Samantha. But you can call me Sam." She closed her eyes and huddled closer to the little girl. "You're a lieutenant," she whispered.

"Yes, ma'am." He nodded. "You know your insignias of rank," he offered wincing. His arm throbbed when he shifted his position. "Shane. Shane Winslow," he volunteered. Somehow a handshake seemed rather anti-climactic.

"Yes, Lieutenant. My father, uncle, and grandfather," she paused, looking toward the unconscious man again. "Were all Royal Navy officers," she said, her slender frame shivering. She reached over and touched his sleeve gently. "You're hurt."

"I'm all right." Lieutenant Winslow shook his head. "Try and rest." He moved slightly, leaving the boy against the edge of the raft.

"Shane? So that's really your name, Lieutenant? Like the old western movie hero?" the young woman asked. "Maybe it's fortuitous," she said with a soft laugh, shaking her head, and closing her eyes.

"I promise we'll have a happy ending," he told her with a confidence he didn't feel. He'd remain positive and not show her any doubts. He had slipped his lifeline and fallen into the life raft while his Coast Guard cutter had been attempting to rescue this family from their foundering sailboat. Then they'd been swept away on the fifteen-foot swells and gale force winds. "I'll see what we have here for…" he paused, thinking better of using the word 'survival.' "To help us till the Evans finds us."

The boy looked confused and frightened but did his best to muster a smile, crawling toward the young woman.

"What's your name, son?"

"Charles, sir." The boy answered.

"Charles is my younger brother and Holly is my cousin," Samantha explained.

Shane nodded. "Well, I need some help, Charles. Can I call you Charlie?" he asked.

The boy nodded, shivering from the stiff westerly wind.

"Well, Charlie, there's a pail over there." He nodded toward the bottom of the raft. "Could you use it to get rid of this water while I check out what we've got in this bag?" He held up the large orange container that said, 'survival gear' and rations he hoped.

The boy looked at Samantha hesitantly then nodded. "All right, sir," he said as he took the pail and began to scoop out the water sloshing around the raft's floor.

Shane grasped the waterproof survival bag in his right hand. His left arm had been torn and twisted when he fell from the rescue ladder onto the foundering

3

sailboat. He watched the boy. Charles looked like a good kid—frightened but savvy. He waited for the raft to dip into the trough of a swell then systemically used the small pail to collect it and bail.

When he surveyed the contents of the survival bag his spirits lifted. The young woman said her uncle had been a naval officer. He'd done well equipping the bag. Food packets, water in sealed ration envelopes, an extensive first-aid kit, a flare gun, parachute flares, mirrors, and more.

"Well?" Samantha asked evenly as Shane pulled out several sealed 10 X 12 bags and a handful of smaller ones. "What do you think?"

"He did a good job. We should be fine," Shane explained, showing the shivering family a forced smile. "Here. These are thermal wraps. Let's open the packages. They're thin but waterproof and have a lining that helps seal in your body's heat. We'll use them till the sun is higher. Then mother nature can dry our damp clothes." He gave the young woman and each child one of the smaller packets. "These are water rations. Each envelope has a small screw-off top. We should all drink several swallows then close them. Samantha, help me with your uncle. We'll try to get him to drink some then cover him with a wrap."

While they lifted the older man's head Samantha looked at the Lieutenant. "What do you really think?" she whispered looking at the children.

"If any ship can find us it's the Raymond Evans. And she will," he assured her. "I lost a fifty-dollar bet to the Engineering Officer yesterday and he'd never let me escape," he said with a shrug and a grin.

"Seriously," she whispered. "*Please!* Be honest."

"I think we'll be all right," he told her in a hushed voice. "We need to make sure no one gets dehydrated and that we stay warm and dry at night. The canopy should give us protection and keep us from getting burned during the day."

She tightened her grip on his arm. "Thank you...Shane." She shook her head, rubbing the dampness from her flushed cheeks. "You saved Holly's life," she added. "I...I could never imagine going through this alone."

He gently squeezed her hand on his arm. "Sam, the most important thing is to stay positive. Can't lose faith—especially in front of the kids." He found her eyes. They were nice eyes. Large, soft, and an amazing mixture of brown and green. But they were overflowing with tears. "We'll be rescued. Soon," he told her crossing his heart and saying a silent prayer before adding. "Promise."

****

Dawn. Day four. The swells had subsided overnight. Good. Holly had been sick. Very sick. So had Charlie and Sam. But the young woman sharing his burden was no lightweight. She showed no weakness. Throughout their ninety-plus hours in the raft she'd always managed a smile. Samantha now held Holly while the girl dozed restlessly. She leaned into him and opened her eyes, showing him one of her engaging smiles. Her lips were cracked, and her face drawn and dried from the salt and wind. She still looked spectacular. At least Shane thought she did.

Of course, Shane knew better. He had to stay strong, not lose himself in romantic fantasies. This was no place to have thoughts about Sam, but she was *quite* a woman. He looked forward to the times when the kids and the older man were asleep. She would huddle close to him and they would talk, even laugh about how they were going to celebrate their rescue.

And when he looked at Sam or she showed him that soft intimate smile he saw when he closed his eyes, he could feel the connection. It could simply be the circumstances or the lingering possibility that they might die out here in the Caribbean. The long hours had grown into days. And as they did the small signs of intimacy between them were obvious. But knowing that survival was paramount Shane shook off distracting thoughts of affection and took a deep breath.

Despite their bouts of fear and the queasiness caused by the long rolling swells Holly and her brother Charles had been nothing short of heroic. Both had taken turns sitting next to the older man, helping to give him water and food from the ration packets. Mortimer, Samantha and Charles Uncle, had made a modest recovery. He now sat, awake, and propped up, under the raft's waterproof canopy.

Almost four days and they'd seen no sign of ships or aircraft. But Shane vowed to take his own advice and stay positive. He sat up and gently shook Sam, opening a second flap to have a look at the weather and sea conditions. The bright orange kite signal from the survival bag floated lazily on the modest southwesterly breeze thirty feet above the raft.

"Hi," he whispered, sliding over to the opening. "Looks like a flat day out there." He managed a smile. "That's good. The kids can use a break."

"Yes. They've had a difficult time," Sam whispered, running her tongue over her cracked lips.

But Shane let his eyes linger for an instant. For someone who'd been floating around in the Gulf of Mexico for almost four days she looked remarkable. Her eyes still glistened, and he swore her short mop of dark hair still held the faint fragrance of shampoo or perfume. He felt a smile cross his face. "You've been great," he whispered. "And the kids," he added shaking his head. "They're nothing short of incredible."

"Thanks. You're our hero," Samantha said, nodding with a smile, while she gently let Holly down to nestle on her grandfather's shoulder. "And yes, Charles and Holly *have* been wonderful."

"You're all amazing," the older man mouthed, letting Holly rest against him.

Sam slid toward Shane. "I managed to get a seasickness tablet into her," Sam said quietly. She turned toward the open panels in the canopy and studied the weather. "And yes, it does look calmer out there," she added leaning back, looking thankful and closing her large dark eyes.

He nodded. "I did a check on our supplies," he said, joining her in giving the sky and horizon a thorough search. "We'll be all right for a few more days. More than that. Not that I think we'll be here that long."

She laughed softly. "You get the optimist of the year award," she said wearily. "But you've thoroughly convinced me, sir," she added with a mock salute.

She was about to answer when Shane held his hand up. "*Shhh!*"

Sam sat up suddenly, moving next to him and searching the horizon.

"Sam, get me the flare gun!" he commanded.

She grabbed the survival kit bag, tearing at the zipper frantically.

"Slow down. There's plenty of time," he assured her, showing a calm he didn't feel.

Samantha took a deep breath and opened the bag, finding the flare gun assembly. She handed it to him. "Here," she said with hands that trembled.

He knelt in the opening and craned his neck. He wasn't imagining the sound. He looked back at Samantha hesitantly.

"I don't hear anything." Sam said, following his lead. She knelt and craned her neck, too. Nodding, she grabbed his sleeve, squeezing. Sam closed her eyes and crossed her fingers. She still heard nothing.

He took a deep breath and loaded the flare gun with one of their three flares, then pointed it in the direction of the distant sound and held his breath then pulled the trigger. A bright reddish-orange glow appeared a quarter mile in the air to the west.

The flare burned then began to sink toward the low swells of the blue-green Caribbean. Ten seconds— twenty—a minute now. He checked his watch. Ninety seconds! Could the aircraft have missed the flare? Not likely in these clear skies at dawn.

He was about to sit down and say something encouraging, when he heard it again!

Sam squeezed his sleeve harder. "Yes! *I hear something now*!" she whispered, looking at the children. "I'm sure," she said, her words sounding like a prayer.

He still hadn't seen anything. Could he be hallucinating? No! Not after only four days. Too early for that. Way too early…

Chapter Two

Forty minutes later Sam, the children, and her
Uncle Mortimer were safely aboard the Sikorsky MH-
60 Jayhawk helicopter that had found them ninety
minutes earlier.

Her uncle lay on an air mattress on the damp metal
floor that vibrated with the action of the copter's
powerful rotor. He reached up and squeezed
Samantha's hand.

"Please, Miss," the Coast Guardsman working the
hoist that had lifted them to safety said to Sam. She
nodded but continued leaning out over the open-door
watching Shane while he was slowly lifted aboard.
"Lean back," the man scolded. "Wouldn't want to lose
you and have to send the rescue swimmer back down to
pick you up."

She shot the man a stern look nodding again
compliantly. Sam breathed a sigh of relief when
Shane's tousled hair and tanned face appeared in the
doorway. "Sorry," she said in a hoarse whisper.
Samantha had become suddenly aware of things now
that they were safe. Her lips felt painful when she
spoke. She touched them and felt painful cracks. Her
eyes stung when she blinked. They were dry. Sam
rubbed them to help her focus.

Another of the copter's crew touched her arm
gently and offered her a bottle filled with a clear liquid.

9

"Here, Miss, drink this. Please" he told her firmly above the drone of the copter blades. "You need fluids and electrolytes," he paused. "I know you had some emergency supplies, but you're all still dehydrated and suffering from exposure."

Sam nodded, following instructions. The liquid had a mild sweet taste.

"Welcome aboard. Lieutenant Shane!" she said grabbing his arm tightly when he was inside the copter.

"A pleasure to be here," he offered above the copter noise in a scratchy voice.

"All right, everyone. Please take a seat and fasten one of the belts around your waist, so we can get you all back to civilization."

"Good thing you used the flare gun, Lieutenant," the co-pilot yelled over the engine noise and the thump of the massive prop. "We were about to head back to Clearwater," he added with a smile, giving Shane thumbs up.

The crew member who had run the hoist now finished fastening a safety net over both doors and nodded at the pilot. The helicopter swung to the left. The nose dipped down, and the craft headed forward speeding across the waves toward Florida's West Coast.

Samantha sat next to Shane, leaning into him while Holly lay with her head in her cousin's lap. "Thank God you heard something," she whispered. "I didn't. Not at first."

"I have twenty-twenty hearing," Shane said attempting to maintain a serious face.

"Oh, right." Samantha gave him a soft punch. "Twenty-twenty hearing," she said, shaking her head and giggling.

"No," he admitted with a smile. "Of course not. But I've always had unusually sensitive hearing," he explained putting his hand to his ear. "When I was a boy, I could always hear things on the water that no one else could."

"Well. Praise the Lord!" She sighed, closing her eyes.

Charles had fallen asleep with his arms around the Lieutenant after gulping down two chocolate energy bars and a twenty-ounce Coke.

The crew member who seemed to be in charge tended to Mortimer—who lay on a litter between them. They'd given Shane a sling and some morphine for the pain in his injured left shoulder and bicep.

"That arm. Doesn't look good, Lieutenant. Think you may need surgery," the chief told Shane, shaking his head and looking at the family that now dozed contented and safe. "There's a good chance they might not have made it without you, sir. We radioed Clearwater Operations we're coming in with the family from the sailboat. You're the talk of the fleet."

Sam opened her eyes lazily and smiled. "A very good chance," she whispered. Shane looked at the chief who smiled and stood, raising his eyebrows and nodding at Shane then Sam.

"You would have done fine," he said with confidence. "You kept your head and the children behaved like they'd been trained for this. Your uncle and your whole family should be very proud of you."

"Oh my God!" she said, staring up at him. "I just realized. We just spent four days together in a life raft and we're safe." She pushed back giving him a curious look. "Now," she began, "is your name really Shane?

Like the old cowboy hero."

"Yes, Ma'am," he began with a thoughtful expression putting on a thick western twang. "And if the food and water had run out, I would have opened up, told you my life story, and bared my soul."

"Go on!" She twisted and gave him another soft punch in the stomach. "I don't believe you" she protested with a gentle giggle, not fooled by his clumsy attempt at humor.

"No, but it sounded good."

"Well?" she turned and shrugged.

"Shane. Lieutenant Shane Winslow at your service."

"You're not teasing me, right? Shane?"

"No, ma'am," he said with the same twang, opening his shirt pocket, and pulling out a damp smudged ID card.

Sam shook her head, giving him an incredulous look. "This is almost spooky," she said with a soft laugh leaning into him. He smiled and showed her a comfortable look, snuggling close again.

Lieutenant Shane Winslow closed his eyes, perhaps able to relax for the first time in days. Samantha purred. She'd never felt so warm and safe. His face reflected a pleasant euphoria. *She knew the feeling very well,* Sam thought drifting into a deep sleep for the first time in days.

****

Samantha straightened the small pleats in her fitted designer suit while she studied herself in the full-length mirror of her suite at the Clearwater Beach Marriott. When she surveyed herself, Sam smiled. She liked what she saw. Samantha planned to visit Uncle Mortimer in the hospital then head to the Coast Guard Clearwater Air Station to find out information about her lost hero.

Thanks to Poppy, the name they called her grandfather, Lord James Edgerton; Knight of the Bath; Lord Temporal of the House of Lords; and a retired Vice-Admiral in the British Navy, she had found the Lieutenant had not been teasing her. His name really was Shane. He'd graduated top in his class from the Coast Guard Academy in New London, Connecticut and had a distinguished career to date. She smiled, shaking her head.

Samantha had spoken to the Base Commander's secretary to set up an appointment. She had been given an extensive debriefing, offered a concise interview, and then transcribed a written statement to the Coast Guard after they landed at the Coast Guard Clearwater Air Station. Of course, there were the endless interviews on CNN, Fox news, the Weather Channel, and numerous local TV stations. Surviving the sinking of a sixty-foot sailing yacht in the midst of a category four hurricane like Isaac was something worthy of note. Sam had received a call from several magazines and even a publisher who offered to have her story written into book form. One call was from none other than Larry Levinson, CEO and major producer of the Hallmark Channel. "The handsome young officer and the beautiful heiress—surviving one of the most devastating hurricanes of the young century!" It was the stuff that legends were made of, he insisted. Sam thought it was all ridiculous.

Her goal was to make sure that their handsome young knight-errant received the credit he deserved. And after the flurry of media coverage since their rescue four days ago she had no doubt he would.

But Sam was honest enough to admit—at least to herself—that she had an interest in more than Lieutenant Shane Winslow's positive press clippings. Sam's interest was personal. She wanted very much to see the handsome unassuming hero who'd shared the life raft with her. And Sam was almost certain he felt something for her.

She sat in the waiting room of the Coast Guard Air Station Base Commander's office, tapping her fingers on the wooden arm of the worn chair while she fidgeted with the single pearl that hung around her neck on a gold chain. Looking up she smiled catching the eye of the Commander's secretary.

"He'll be out in just a minute, Ms. Edgerton," the woman said with a nod. "Promise."

"I understand. It's very kind of him to find time for me." Samantha nodded. "I'm sure he has a lot on his plate."

"Yes," The woman paused and continued to watch Sam. "That was quite an…an adventure you and your family had," she sighed and raised her eyebrows. "I'm sure he'd like to hear all about it."

Sam shrugged. "Like nothing I could ever have imagined. I just thank God we had someone who was so skilled and knowledgeable. Lieutenant Winslow was nothing short of miraculous."

The woman was about to add something when a tall silver-haired man opened the door to the inner office. "Ms. Edgerton." He smiled warmly. "Welcome. I'm Captain Lane, the Base Commander. I was acquainted with your grandfather." He took a step and offered his hand then gestured for Sam to join him.

"Please come in."

Thirty minutes later Samantha shook Captain Lane's hand again and nodded before leaving the office. "Thank you, Captain," she said doing her best to mask her disappointment.

"The young officer you shared the life raft with assured me you were wonderful out there. Courageous, unselfish." the Captain shrugged. "I'm just sorry I couldn't be more help." He showed her a kind smile and shook her hand. "I'm so glad you and your family made it through that frightening ordeal."

"Thanks to Lieutenant Winslow," she whispered. That thought continued to run through her mind after Sam left the office.

Sam walked down the hall to the elevator, absently pressing the 'down' button. Stepping on it Sam pressed 'one', brushing aside a hint of moisture from her eyes. *You're being a ninny,* Sam scolded herself. *Get over it!*

She exited the elevator, nodded at the sailor at the desk in the entry hall, walked out shielding her eyes from the sun and into the September afternoon heat.

Samantha took out her phone and hit re-dial, putting it to her ear.

"Well?" her cousin and Holly's older sister Gretchen asked impatiently after the first ring. "Did you find your hero?" she added with a giggle.

"Yes and no."

"Why? What happened?"

"The injury he suffered to his arm. It was serious." Sam sighed. "Very serious. They shipped him off to have surgery."

"And that's it. Wouldn't they give you any information?" Gretchen sounded incredulous. "For goodness sake's, Sam. You two spent four days on a damn life raft! He saved your life. You just have to…"

"The Base Commander was delightful, Gretch. But he explained that the injury might mean his transfer to a shore assignment or even discharge from the service." Sam sighed heavily again. Tears cascaded down her flushed cheeks. "And I think he knew I wasn't there on a selfless errand of mercy."

"Okay. So. You were attracted to him. What's the big deal?" Gretchen continued. "You…you thought he felt the same way, didn't you?"

Sam arrived at her rental car and unlocked the door, brushing away the tears. She opened the door and let the heat dissipate.

"Yes. Yes, I did."

"So what? Does the Coast Guard have some ridiculous policy about non-fraternization after a survival adventure in the Gulf of Mexico?" Gretchen asked.

"No, dear. Of course not. But in this case the Base Commander thought it best to give him some privacy. And Uncle Mortimer is doing fine, by the way."

"I know," Gretchen said in a haughty tone. "Your Mum told me earlier after she talked to him. I'm not getting it. This thing about privacy?"

"It was his way of being kind." Sam sighed deeply and sniffed. "Of letting me down easily, Gretch."

"I'm still not getting this, dear," Gretchen repeated.

"He told me that Lieutenant Winslow would be heading home after the surgery for an extended leave. Explaining that the Coast Guard had to do a post-surgical evaluation of his injuries to see about his continuation in the service. Adding that it would give him time to see his family—and his fiancé." Sam stood in the open door while the heat from inside the car drifted by her. "Get it now?" she asked quietly, sighing and closed the phone.

Sam got into her rental car, letting the air conditioning fight to control the stifling humidity. Studying her image in the visor mirror she brushed aside the damp traces from her face with a tissue and put on a pleasant expression. Having spent her life as a hopeless romantic this wasn't her first disappointment. It would not be her last. But it *was certainly* the grandest to date!

Chapter Three

Memorial Day 2016

Ilya Petrova Romanov. His given name. Ilya, Slavic for the Biblical Prophet Elijah. Romanov, the name of the Russian royal family who had died on a dusty basement floor a century earlier during their Revolution. Few called him by his given names any longer. Ilya had moved on to a sad and different reality.

The passport he gave to the Customs Officer at Boston's Logan International Airport had the name Sergei Axelrod. He had documents that identified him as a wealthy Russian business executive who had lost his wife to cancer and come to the United States on a visitor's visa to rent a house on Cape Cod for the summer.

The officer studied Ilya closely. Perhaps that was normal for Americans. To view Russians with suspicion. He was the soul of courtesy and humility, standing at parade rest while the man scrutinized his passport and other papers. After a delay that seemed endless during which a queue developed in the line behind Ilya the Custom's Officer handed him back his passport and other documents and showed an indulgent smile. "Welcome to the United States, Mr. Axelrod. Enjoy your stay," the man offered quietly followed by a loud, *"Next!"* motioning the line forward.

Axelrod was the name on his papers. But Ilya had become Axab. A name he had chosen. It had a purpose—a deeper meaning. Axab—Russian for Ahab, the biblical King and Melville's tragic hero. It served a painful reminder of the tragic wound that refused to heal. Ilya used it. It stirred the hatred. The fire that had been burned into his soul like a brand. And like the relentless single-minded Captain that drove the Pequod on and on, Axe stayed laser-focused on his objective.

Large and muscled, Ilya was a formidable man. More than formidable. He had never been one to be trifled with. Even before *it* had happened. And now, years after the senseless tragedy that had cost him all he loved, all he held dear, he had adopted both the pseudonym and the fear it instilled in all those who had come to know his new persona.

Unlike the Biblical Ahab, Ilya had not possessed the malevolent and sinful nature of the character in 1st Kings. That was before. A lifetime ago. Before life, hope, and love had been torn away. In his other life under the other name. Now, after long years and endless miles, like Melville's tragic Captain, Axe was bent on one thing. Retribution!

His plan had begun slowly, taking shape, and forming in the tear-filled sleepless nights that had filled the darkness. But like a snowball rolling from the mountain top down the slope to the valley it had gained momentum and size...Untold hours of meticulous preparation and planning had paid Axe dividends while preparing to execute the task that would make him whole again. When it was over, he would be rich beyond anything a simple man could have dared to dream of. But that was insignificant—a mere by-product. Axe wanted something more. Closure. The word he had heard so often. The one his existence demanded.

Standing at baggage claim in Logan Airport's Terminal E, Axe pulled the pictures from his shirt pocket. Their pictures.

Even now he felt the tears when he looked at the photograph: Naina, Svetlana, and sweet little Stipan. The radiant smiles beamed back at him as his children stood, small arms clutching Naina's legs. No. He promised himself each time that the tears would not come but studying the photo with weary eyes Axe felt the dampness grow. He sniffed and swallowed quietly, putting his hand to his face self-consciously and wiped away the trace of moisture after replacing the poignant painful remembrance.

Waiting for his bags, he retrieved a second photo. This one of a young woman and younger boy. Both handsome and lovely. Both full of life and promise. They stood next to a tall, impressive-looking man. His arm surrounded them. He beamed a smile in their direction as one held a medal aloft. Yes, they were beautiful. They were also brilliant and talented. Axe knew because he had spent endless months studying them and their lives. Every detail. His jaw stiffened, and his hand shook when he replaced this photo in the pocket of his navy-blue blazer.

He excused himself quietly and smiled at the older couple in front of him after retrieving his two bags. Like everything he had brought on this solemn mission his bags were chosen to be non-descript. Nothing to attract attention or interest. One large and one smaller, standard American Tourister—black with a small red ribbon tied to each handle to help identify them. He maintained a quiet unassuming demeanor when he left the Lufthansa section and headed to find his ride.

In retrospect the Customs and immigration process had been simple. Almost too simple. The prosthetic limb he wore served to hide his loss and his identity. Good since a man with one arm would be pitied. Even worse he would be remembered. Fixed in the memories of those he passed. But of course, the well-intentioned Customs and Immigration Agents who staffed their small cubicles had no idea what he planned. Nothing he carried on his person on the flight gave the slightest hint of the plot he would execute when *they* arrived. His targets.

Chapter Four

The phone rang in Eric Montgomery's newly renovated office at the Southside Marina on Cape Cod's Bass River. He shook his head and grinned, turning quickly from the small beach where Kylie, his adopted ten-year old daughter, and two of her friends were working feverishly to get the mast and sailing tack properly installed on the fourteen-foot Argo sailing dinghy. Kylie had loved sailing and shown some talent, so Eric and his wife, Ashley, bought the Argo for Kylie on her tenth birthday. Though watching it occurred to him that their purchase may well have been a bit premature.

"Jamie. Can you keep an eye on our sailors!" Eric yelled through the open casement window, pointing to Kylie and her friends. Jamie was only seventeen, but he'd been a sailing instructor at the West Dennis Yacht Club for two summers. And over his first two weeks working at the marina he'd shown an unusual maturity and sense of responsibility. Eric felt confident leaving him to supervise. His grin grew into a broad smile.

"Got it, boss," Jamie said scanning the dock and yard. Seeing no other demands, he headed to his new charges. Eric waved, knowing Jamie had already become one of Kylie's favorites at the marina he and Ashley owned and managed.

After acknowledging Jamie, Eric double-timed it

across his spacious new workspace and picked up the phone after the third ring. "Hello, Southside Marina. This is Eric," he said with a deep breath. The caller I.D. had been blank. "Can I help you?"

"Hasn't that brilliant wife of yours installed some hi-tech caller ID system that will override my security protocols yet?" The rough baritone voice that asked was followed by a throaty chuckle.

"Well hello! And thanks for calling but no. I don't need any more life insurance if that's what you're selling!" Eric joked when he heard the familiar voice.

"Glad to hear that, Eric. After all your adventures, I think you'd be an actuarial nightmare!" the man on the other end answered.

Despite the eight-hundred-miles that separated them, Eric could envision the man he spoke to. Tall, husky, with a full head of salt and pepper hair, and a face that belied the stress he'd lived with constantly for decades. Eric and his caller were kindred spirits. Men who knew each other better than most. The man on the other end had been instrumental in saving lives—their lives in recent times—his, Ashley's, Kylie's, and his former mother in law's. It happened during a terrifying episode almost three years ago. Since then they'd stayed in close touch and helped each other when Eric's special skill set or a world-class hacker like Ashley was needed and anonymity was paramount.

The caller was known by many names and titles—the Admiral to his staff and many of his professional associates. Also known as Mr. Carson to others. Eric and Ashley now knew him by his given name—Brian Turner. He headed the nation's most secretive and anonymous intelligence operation. Its staff was small—

tiny when compared with mammoth sprawling organizations like the CIA, FBI, NSA, Homeland Security, and the thirteen others that comprised the country's collection of high-level intelligence gathering and security operations. Yes, the Admiral's group of less than three-hundred was diminutive but consisted of the brightest and most skilled operatives in any of the clandestine services. It carried the rather insipid title of National Investigation and Research Agency. The title intentionally carried the sound of something innocuous—like it was attached to the Smithsonian or the National Archives. The name belied its deadly record. NIRA, as its staff affectionately referred to it, had been intimately involved in many major intelligence incidents and outcomes in the last three decades. They included many high-profile operations: Osama bin Laden, the capture of Ramses Youssef, architect of the 1993 World Trade Center attack, and a score of other secretive arrests or eliminations that would remain ever-anonymous.

"What's up, Admiral?" Eric asked, sitting down and leaning back in the new ergonomic desk chair Ashley insisted he buy. Despite his own impressive military record Eric still felt uncomfortable calling their savior and friend by his given name. "Please. Tell me you're not still trying to bribe my wife into abandoning the good life in picturesque New England to join you in Washington to teach those sadistic sneaky bastards in the Intel community how to become better hackers?"

Eric had been a Green Beret Team Leader. He'd served three brutal deployments in the Middle East. After resigning his commission, Eric had come home to escape the endless cruelty and carnage he'd witnessed.

But in the chaos and savagery the millennium world had become some things were difficult. Others impossible. Eric discovered those truths in a tragic way. In a world reshaped by hatred and violence no safe haven existed.

"No, Eric. Just a favor. And a relatively simple one for a change," the Admiral explained. "And since someone once called you Cape Cod *royalty*," he paused doing his best to hide a laugh. "I'd appreciate it if you could play host to one of my closest and oldest friends." He paused. "James Edgerton *is* royalty. Real royalty, English style. I'll have Jeanie send you the details, but I guarantee he's first-class. A member of the House of Lords and a legit member of the peerage. We served together on several joint assignments for NATO. And by the way, speaking of that brilliant woman you continue to hold hostage from me, how is my favorite tech genius and that adorable daughter of yours?" he finished with another thick laugh.

"Ashley's great. So's Kylie. Thanks. When you emailed you'd be calling she wanted to be here but she's working with my old friend. He's the new Dennis Police Chief. She's been working on some crazy software project. Something that can foil a holdup using motion recognition and sound?" Eric explained, peering out to the marina to make sure Kylie and her friends hadn't fallen into the River or detoured navigation around the channel markers. "Anyway, they're doing a field test today, so she's completely absorbed in that."

"I'm almost afraid to ask," the Admiral paused and chuckled softly. "Will her new technology *really* do that?"

"I don't know. They talk on the phone three times a

day. Just when I think I've corralled her into really being my business partner and working on something that will help the Marina she wakes up with that look in her eyes. She swears it will be *transformational* to use her word." Eric sighed. "At least that's what she tells me."

"Well, I look forward to hearing all about it. But if you guys can help my old friend from across the pond—show him and his family around when they arrive—I know they'd love it and I'll be in your debt."

"Come on, Admiral. *Done!* No need to ask!" Eric said watching Kylie and her friends out the window. Jamie stood pointing and offering comments and laughing heartily while they worked. "We owe you more than we can ever repay," he added.

Silence.

"Admiral?"

Eric could hear measured breathing following the sound of his comrade clearing his throat. "Just spending time with your family has repaid me a hundred times," the older man offered quietly. "It brings back pleasant memories."

Eric suspected his friend's comments were more than idle flattery. The Admiral had never mentioned his family. Once when they'd visited his office in Washington, he and Ashley had seen a faded picture of the Admiral in a Commander's uniform beaming a proud smile standing behind a lovely woman and two small children. Since their frightening adventure against a domestic terrorist three summers ago the Admiral and the Montgomery family had become close. Very close. Not an easy task with a man whose entire life was spent in the battle to keep the country safe. Perhaps that was the answer. Had his family been collateral damage—casualties of the Admiral's chosen profession. Eric wondered but would never violate his close friend's private space.

"Tell me the truth," the Admiral asked evenly. "How are they *really* doing? Any long term after effects from three years ago?"

"Well," Eric began. The terrifying events of those days *had* left scars. Being kidnapped by a psychopathic terrorist, threatened with death, and then buried alive would leave scars on the most courageous and hardiest of souls. Deep *brutal* scars.

"C'mon, Eric. No BS." the Admiral paused. "And since we're talking. How are *you* doing?"

"You can't go through something like that and not suffer some after effects." Eric exhaled loudly. "After the life you've lived and the things you've seen, you know that better than anyone."

Silence, then, "I asked you a question, Lieutenant. How are they?"

"Kylie's okay. She was more confused than anything. When it happened, she was so young it all seemed like a bad dream. But Ashley. I worry about her. She had a shitty life for years before that bastard kidnapped them." Eric wondered how you get over losing your mother violently, make a hellish escape from life-threatening danger, have a miscarriage, then become the target of an insidious domestic terrorist and get over it? "You and I know what it's like," he added. "To be in the cross-hairs. To be a target."

Silence for a long minute. Eric knew they felt the same way. Like seeing the end of a movie or novel that takes you by surprise.

"Okay, son," he paused for a long moment, breathing deeply. "When Lord Edgerton—James—and his family arrive," the Admiral said, changing the subject. "I'm taking some long overdue shore leave," he added softly.

Eric stood and walked to the door of the ship store. Kylie stood laughing with her friends again while Jamie did his best to hold up the mast. He thought about his wife. Her strength. Her genius. Her beauty and resiliency. He thought about what he and Ashley had built since the terror of three years ago and shook his head.

"We're doing fine, Admiral. But we always look forward to your visits. To seeing you."

Eric waited. There was no response. Only the slight sound of the man who'd help save their lives breathing slowly and evenly on his end.

"Sounds fine. Like I said. Jeanie will send you the details. So. I'll see you soon," he paused. "Give them both a hug for me. A big hug!"

"Can you tell me about Ralph?" Eric's brother Ralph had worked in deep cover for NIRA for a decade. Eric had discovered his brother's real identity during the terrifying episode three years ago. Ralph had been instrumental in their rescue. After a brief reunion during Eric's long hospital stay Ralph had disappeared, vanished again into the twilight that surrounded covert operatives. And his undercover work made it impossible for them to keep in touch.

Silence.

"Admiral?" Eric pressed.

"I can tell you he's alive and performing well. He's imbedded in a high-level op somewhere in Africa."

"I understand," Eric knew pursuing it further would be fruitless and strain their friendship. He hit 'End' and put down the phone, then stepped outside and headed toward Kylie.

Chapter Five

Week of June 7th, 2016

Samantha Edgerton shifted uneasily, coming out of her sleep when the announcement came over the intercom.

"Good afternoon, again, Ladies and Gentlemen. This is Captain Hayward from the flight deck. We're beginning our final approach and will be landing in Boston's Logan International Airport in approximately fifteen minutes. The Flight Attendants will be coming through the cabin to pick up any trash and make sure that your seatbacks and table trays are…"

Samantha groaned. Shifting, she opened her eyes and rubbed them to erase the sleep. Her brother Charles reached down and shook her arm. "Wake up, sleeping beauty. Time to be kissed by a handsome prince," Charles teased with a giggle.

Leaning forward Samantha looked around. She, Charles, her mother, and grandfather occupied the second group of Club World seats in their British Airways' 747-400. They sat four across in the staggered seats in the massive aircraft's upper deck. Samantha sat diagonally behind her brother.

Yawning, she lifted the remainder of the water bottle she'd placed in one of numerous cubbies the Club World seats offered and took a deep swallow.

She'd taken a sleeping pill immediately after take-off. The inside of her mouth tasted like something was growing inside. Something very unpleasant. "Oh, my God." She tugged on Charles' sleeve. "What a hideous taste," she said, turning toward him with a shiver. "Feels like my teeth are growing hair!"

"Yuck," Charles began. Stowing his magazine, he made a face, turning in the seat that sat slightly forward of his older sister's. "Yes, dear. I can even tell from over here," he said smiling and offering her a breath mint. "Better give a chew before you kiss a prince."

"Thanks," Samantha took the mint, chewed it up and ran it around inside her mouth before swallowing. "Got another?" she asked.

Charles opened his backpack, reached over and back, giving Samantha the pack. "Keep them. I've got scads just in case you see someone you find attractive," he said giving his sister's arm a friendly push and smiling.

"Now children," said a booming bass voice from across the wide aisle. "Play nice." Her grandfather shook his thick mop of graying hair and leaned out into the aisle.

Her brother made a face and put-up smile, turning his head to look at Samantha and his grandfather. "All right, Poppy?" he said using their pet name for their adoring grandfather.

Smiling, Sam sat back and closed her eyes. She'd heard about sibling rivalry, but Charles was always her biggest and best ego-booster. And though he was not quite fourteen he was becoming a man too quickly, she thought. Far too quickly.

Shrugging again, Lord Edgerton stretched his six-foot three-inch frame and tapped their mother Millicent who, like Samantha, had taken a sleeping pill on take-off. "Hello, my dear. Time to wake up and greet the New World," he said with a cheerful expression.

Millicent yawned and stretched with a groan. "My goodness. Thanks so much. Feels like I've been asleep for a month," she added in a hoarse whisper.

"Well, looks like you're all set," the flight attendant said to Charles and Sam while gathering the dregs of the seven and a half-hour flight. "And you, sir?" she asked, turning to their grandfather.

"Yes, thanks so much." He showed the flight attendant his dazzling smile. Sam had seen him use it often. Despite his age, Poppy had kept his looks. His lean fit physique added to the appearance of someone ten years his junior.

The young woman smiled at her grandfather and touched his arm momentarily, continuing to hold her look till well past him.

Samantha and her current companions had travelled extensively thanks to Poppy's royal status, the family's worldwide business interests, and more recently, their athletic successes—Sam's at the international level as a world-class skier and Charles on the show-jumping circuit in the British Isles and Western Europe.

Sam waved and smiled at her Mum, mouthing the word, 'Hi.' She felt a chill course through her. Unlike her grandfather, her mother's health had left her looking a dozen years older. Sadly, since her father died four years past and her grandmother a year later, the four of them—Sam, Charles, Mum, and Poppy were often mistaken for a family unit.

With seatbelts, tray tables, and seatbacks in order, Samantha leaned back in her seat and closed her eyes. She'd only been to the United States a few times in her twenty-three years. Several years ago, Poppy had taken her and Charles to New York City for the New Year's Eve celebration in Times Square. Though he was concerned about their safety and wanted to watch from the shelter of their opulent suite, Sam would hear none of it. And when she wanted something badly enough, she took no prisoners. Throwing caution to the wind they left their hotel and mingled with the masses. And of course, she'd been right. It had been a complete delight!

And the following year there had been a star-crossed sailing adventure that had turned into a frightening fight for survival. Hurricane Isaac had suddenly emerged from the South Atlantic and almost taken her, Charles, their uncle, and her young cousin Holly to a watery grave. But thanks to Uncle Mortimer's preparations and a quiet, handsome, heroic young Coast Guard officer they had survived the ordeal. Later that year Samantha and her fellow occupants of the raft had returned to see the young officer receive a medal for his heroism.

And now she, Charles, Mummy, and Poppy came for…what? Sam wasn't sure. Yes, of course there were always the endless business dealings, speaking engagements, and public appearances Poppy had to deal with, but Sam felt this was something more. A reunion? That would be delightful. Lieutenant Shane Winslow. She'd thought of him so often in the four years since the stoic, but gallant young hero had helped her survive and stolen her heart. She shook her head and smiled self-consciously realizing this sounded like a scene from a romance novel. But no. She had no illusions. Sam only hoped he had found happiness and peace.

No. Sam wasn't sure, but she knew something awaited her here. Something that would change her life. A reset perhaps? She loved that word. Because that was what this trip was. At least for her. We all have those moments when we know something grand awaits us. Call it intuition. Call it foresight, wisdom—even clairvoyance? Samantha had never fooled herself. She was an incurable romantic. And loved being one.

Sam had made a detour when Malcolm came along. After their tumultuous fifteen months together, she was thrilled just to be free of his arrogance and selfishness. Before he came along Sam would have died rather than entertain the thought that her loving and devoted grandfather might have bought-off one of her beaus, but after her last few months with Malcolm, Sam would have groveled at Poppy's feet just to be rid of him. But rather than swear off love and affection Sam couldn't wait to find it again. This time with someone of quality. Malcolm had taught her a life lesson: it wasn't love that was flawed but the quality of whom we chose to love.

Recovering from the December training catastrophe at Chamonix had been endless. Or so it seemed. Malcolm's reaction and his well-timed exit not so much so. That had been more rapid than a run on an icy downhill. But his hasty departure had been perfect both in timing and in his convenient but well-thought out excuse. Malcolm was a pretty tot that Samantha had picked up along the line somewhere after the Italian Alps. A charming, tall, pretty trinket. *A delightful, polished man-child to bring her pleasure and keep her warm on those frigid evenings in the Alps*, she thought with a grin.

Samantha believed in hard work, study, and preparation. She had spent each evening after her grueling therapy sessions gleaning every detail about Boston and Cape Cod. Committing them to memory. Granted it was a touristy destination, but this fascinating place was more than Old Ironsides, Bunker Hill, and Plymouth Rock. And now it was time. Her time. *Time to put her life back together*, she mused hearing the wheels find the runway.

"Good afternoon, ladies and gentlemen. On behalf of British Airways let me welcome you to Boston's Logan International Airport. The local time is one-fifty-five and the temperature is a delightful seventy-six degrees. Please remain seated until the pilot has…"

Their 747 taxied for another fifteen minutes then came to a stop. She peered out the window, hearing the jetway being attached to the fuselage.

"Good afternoon, ladies and gentlemen and once again welcome to Boston," the purser said. "You may claim your bags at carousel number…"

Sam tuned out the rest knowing the three men and one woman who accompanied them for their protection would find them and put them in their vehicles. Until someone had attempted to kidnap Charles last year, they had travelled with only Poppy's man servant and personal assistant. That had all changed. And while Sam felt safer when they went through what the security men called high threat situations their presence also meant restrictions. And though none of them was the least bit forward or pushy Sam sometimes longed for the old days when she and Charles were footloose and fancy free! To roam, to explore, and get lost.

Sam turned her eyes toward the Boston skyline. The city looked small—almost tiny by comparison with London, New York, or Paris. But that was fine. She secretly loved the idea of coming here. Where so many dreams had come true and so many lives had been reborn. Sam was certain. It was her turn.

Chapter Six

The driver in the black suit, crisp white shirt, and burgundy Repp tie stood in front of the spotless Lincoln Town Car. Axe had dispatched the driver earlier that morning to meet the next member of the team that would bring his project to fruition.

The black suit hung loosely on the driver's slender frame. His name was Ivan and his chiseled features belied his Slavic ancestry. Ivan was Axe's younger brother and his reluctant partner in his older sibling's plan.

The sign he displayed to the passengers exiting British Airways had the name Murphy written in precise three-inch black letters. Ivan paced back and forth on the long walkway that paralleled the wide asphalt drop-off and pickup lane in front of terminal E at Boston's Logan International Airport.

Axe had filed the necessary paperwork that registered this vehicle as a limousine. That allowed Ivan to stop at the driver's lounge and pick up the ticket he placed in the front window. It permitted him an hour of parking time to wait for the man. Then he would bring his passenger to where he would stay on Cape Cod.

Ivan knew of his brother's extensive research and observations regarding Lord James Edgerton. The man arriving that morning would be a critical component in his brother's plan. Observing and following the Edgerton's would be this man's responsibility until Axe's plan was put into action.

Axe had explained that Dylan Murphy, the man who arrived on that morning's flight from London was a legend: a distinguished officer in Britain's Special Forces—the SAS—an elite commando regiment that was the model for the US Army's Green Berets. Since leaving the military Murphy had become another kind of legend. In a murkier world. A world that paid him far greater dividends for his highly honed skills. A highly sought-after mercenary, Dylan Murphy specialized in high-level adventures that brought him and his employers massive financial reward without causing any harm to their potential victims.

Ivan stopped for a moment, still holding the sign, waiting and checking his watch. His eyes surveyed the flurry of disembarking passengers arriving on Flight 213 from London. The 747-400 flight had been eighty-five percent full so almost two hundred travelers would be exiting the terminal. Passengers having claimed their luggage created a constant stream departing through the two sets of automatic double doors.

A thick-set man of medium build emerged and stopped, searching the row of shiny limos behind a set of expensive dark glasses. The limousines sat parked in an orderly queue reflecting the bright mid-day sun under the watchful eye of a Massachusetts State Police Sergeant. That officer and two others did a thorough job of monitoring the vehicles. Ivan had spent a few afternoons studying their behavior and making casual conversation with limo drivers under the guise of writing a piece for a university newspaper.

He learned from the experts. Stay unoccupied for more than a few minutes and you were ordered to move. Stay unattended for any longer and your vehicle was subject to being towed without warning. Like so many other friendly courtesies, the days when a State Trooper might let a driver doddle to use the facilities or take a smoke break got dramatically tightened after 9/11. They had disappeared after the Boston Marathon Bombing in 2013.

The thick-set man spotted Ivan and his vehicle, waving casually, and smiling broadly. He pointed to himself, then toward the sign Ivan held. The man pulled a generous spinner-style suitcase across the asphalt and carried a large shoulder bag.

"Good morning, sir." Ivan greeted his guest enthusiastically. He took three steps toward the man and held out his hand. "My name's Ivan." Having been a student in Boston for two years, he had managed to erase much of his Eastern European accent. "I'll be driving you to your hotel this morning."

"Yes, Ivan. I'm Dylan. Dylan Murphy." The passenger took the driver's hand, shaking it firmly. "I was told to expect you." He nodded at Ivan who took his suitcase and placed it carefully in the open trunk. The man waited while Ivan closed the spacious trunk and opened his door. "The Sox are having a great year, aren't they?"

"Yes, they are. They'll be sorry to see Big Papi retire, though," Ivan responded casually with the words Murphy had been told to expect. Ivan waited, glancing at Murphy.

"Yes," Murphy said, showing a wry smile, adding, "Isn't everyone?"

Ivan smiled and nodded in acknowledgement. "There's Fiji water, some candy in the armrest, and today's Boston Globe on the seat, Mr. Murphy," he volunteered pleasantly closing the door. He walked around the Town Car, giving the State Police Sergeant a friendly salute and warm smile and slipped in behind the wheel, started the car's quiet V-8, and carefully maneuvered it into the busy early afternoon traffic while he headed toward the airport exit and the Ted Williams tunnel.

Ivan watched his passenger in the rear-view mirror. He sat flipping through the headlines and sports section in the Globe. "What do you think about this Presidential campaign?" he asked glancing at the surroundings when they came out of the tunnel and proceeded onto Exit 24 and the ramp that would take them to the Central Artery, the Southeast Expressway, and Route Three south toward Cape Cod.

Ivan smiled at his passenger and looked in the mirror. "I'm trying to remain neutral. Right now, it seems as if both the major candidates have significant issues," he responded, turning his attention to the congested tunnel traffic, adding, "You had a good trip, sir?"

Murphy nodded. "Yes. A smooth flight and right on time."

"And no trouble at Customs?"

"No, told them I was visiting my sister on Cape Cod for a few weeks," Murphy said with the hint of a smile.

Suddenly, Ivan heard his phone buzz. Ivan had signaled his brother when his passenger had entered the limousine. He passed his phone back to his passenger.

"Good afternoon, and welcome to Boston," a steady baritone said evenly. "The driver is part of my team. You may report information to him about your flight," the caller instructed Murphy calmly.

Murphy whispered, "Understood." Then looked at Ivan and nodded.

Ivan had been watching him and showed a faint smile. "I'll be recording our conversation." It was a statement, not a question.

"That's fine. I understand. Cell phone communication is too easily overheard by the wrong people," Murphy agreed with a nod.

"You had a good seat?" Ivan asked quietly.

"Yes. World Club on the Upper Deck." The man paused and looked out at the traffic. "A little late for commuters?" he asked, checking his watch. He leaned back and pulled out a cigarette, holding it up and raising his eyebrows.

"Feel free to smoke. This vehicle is window dressing." Ivan nodded. "When we're done, it will be destroyed with all the other remaining evidence."

"Thank you." Murphy nodded.

"So. You spent time watching Lord Edgerton and his family in London. What was your impression of their security?"

The man took out his lighter and lit the cigarette he was holding. "Decent security for a family operation," Murphy offered thoughtfully. "Three men and a woman on their permanent staff. They add one or two more when a large crowd or congestion is anticipated."

"You said, 'for a family operation?'" Ivan queried.

"Two of the men are big. Bruiser types." He shook his head. "When the protection is hired by the

41

principal—someone like Edgerton—they tend to be. Big, I mean." He laughed softly. "Tends to make the ladies and kiddies feel safe to be surrounded by men who look like Schwarzenegger or Lundgren. Sadly, for the clients they're usually more muscle than skill. Look at the world-class security and intel operations. Most of their field agents are small or average size. Places like CIA, MI-6, Mossad, GRU are not populated by Sumo wrestlers," he laughed again more softly and shook his head. "Hard to tell about the woman. She never had an active role. May be there to make the mother and granddaughter happy." He shrugged. "But this group has one man—the body man—the one who stays glued to the grandchildren—that's tall but slender. He moves like a cheetah. No wasted motion. Lean and sinewy." Murphy raised his thick eyebrows. Leaning back, he added, "He runs the team. Looks quiet and thoughtful. He's the one I want to avoid."

"So, the one security person you mentioned is worth note?"

"Yes," Murphy offered quietly studying the traffic absently. "Our job—my job—is to make sure he's not a factor when we take action. Several ways I can do that. But it will take some time and observation to determine the best way to accomplish it," Murphy added with a thoughtful look.

Ivan listened offering only a nod. This man knew his business and he seemed intent on avoiding harmful confrontation. "Traffic will open up between here and the Cape. Cape Cod that is. Always gets mucked up at the lane drop ahead by Exit 15," Ivan volunteered

The man nodded slowly, lighting another cigarette. "You know the area pretty well?"

"Somewhat." Ivan looked in the mirror and smiled. "I finished my degree at Boston University last year."

"Really," the man said doing his best to sound casual, but he looked genuinely impressed.

Ivan allowed himself a faint smile.

"Mr. Axelrod explained. I'll leave you at a high-end resort hotel on Cape Cod's East Coast. The Chatham Bars Inn. It's a beautiful place often frequented by celebrities and high-end professionals."

"Yes. That's fine. Then I won't stand out." The man nodded with a wry smile.

"It's a luxury resort and should fit our needs nicely. We didn't want to attract any attention, so we've booked you a suite in one of the adjacent buildings that fronts on the water. It's self-contained. Like an apartment. There's no lobby or common areas. You'll have a great view and relative privacy for Cape Cod in the summer. And the hotel has a constant flow of activities and conventions." Ivan looked at the passenger in the rear-view mirror. "During most of your stay there'll be a cardiac surgeon's convention," he added. "So, you and anyone you use to assist you should be virtually invisible."

"That's good. My second wife always wanted me to be a doctor," Murphy said with a soft chuckle. "Away from the main buildings, no need to be seen mucking around, and during a busy time. Excellent. I'll be anonymous. I assume I can rent an automobile there?"

"They have a thorough concierge service who can take care of your needs. And once you and Mr. Axelrod are satisfied everything is in order you may join us at our location," Ivan explained. "But if all goes well that may not be necessary."

"Yes. So I understand," Murphy agreed. "I'll need something plain—non-descript for a few days. Then something else." He tugged at his chin and looked thoughtful again. "A lorry or van we can use. And then maybe something high-end." A faint smile played at his lips. "Not a toy," Murphy said. "But something I can use to make an impression on our targets."

This man seemed to know his job.

"I'll handle all the logistics relative to our targets and Mr. Axelrod has explained that he has a first-class technology person on the team, too," Murphy said, studying the sparse scenery looking unconcerned. "And here." He leaned over and placed what looked like a cigarette lighter on the passenger seat. "Press the bottom and you'll find a thumb drive that contains my observations on Lord Edgerton and his family and more specifics on their security."

"Yes, sir. You have some questions I can answer?" Ivan asked after a long silence.

Murphy shook his head. "No...Ivan. What our employer plans seems simple and well thought out. And for the record any scruples I once possessed have long since disappeared. Having been long lost after witnessing endless pain, brutality, and man's inhumanity to man," he said with a tinge of sarcasm. Even disgust. "But based on the outline I was given there'll be no need for any of that in this project."

Ivan watched Murphy smile, lean back, then let the smooth ride of the Town Car lull him in and out of a doze while he continued studying the scenery.

Ivan turned off the phone he'd been using to record the conversation. He glanced at the familiar scattered industrial and commercial surroundings while they slowly disappeared in favor of thick stands of pines and hardwoods as they approached the towns of Duxbury and Plymouth.

A month from now it would all be over. His brother would have the closure he so desperately sought, and Ivan would join Ilya in his celebration. Justice served. And yes, of course, they would be rich beyond their wildest imaginings. And perhaps, just perhaps, Lord Edgerton would be wiser, having learned that his arrogance and indifference toward his fellow man had a price.

Chapter Seven

Eric Montgomery looked around the meeting room of the newly renovated Dennis, Massachusetts, Town Hall. He lifted the mahogany gavel Ashley had given him at Christmas, bringing it down on the small sounding block.

"Do I hear a motion to adjourn?" he asked, glancing at his watch as the sounding block scurried across the polished wooden table. Eric surveyed the room and shrugged at his fellow selectmen.

"Motion to adjourn, Mr. Chairman," called out one of the long-time members who'd been struggling to stay awake during the ninety-minute meeting. The major topic of discussion had been the upcoming Town of Dennis Independence Day celebration. This was Eric's first foray into local politics. Ashley and his best friend and manager of the Southside Marina, Bobby Rodrigues, suggested he try it but after a few meetings Eric's initial enthusiasm for public service had waned. Now it was in downright free-fall.

"Second," said Angela Adams, his Vice Chairperson and one of two female members on the Board of Selectmen.

"All those in favor say, 'Aye.'" Eric stifled a yawn, looking at his fellow members.

When the other four all said, "Aye," Eric brought down his gavel again and pronounced, "Meeting is adjourned."

Several nodded back at him. Some smiled. "Well done, Mr. Chairman," called out Natalie O'Connor, a long-time friend who'd also been instrumental in convincing Eric to run for Selectman.

Eric smiled at her and nodded. "Thanks," he offered with a wave. "Let's catch up later for coffee," he suggested with a shrug.

"How's tomorrow about ten?" she asked. "Buckie's in Dennisport?"

He nodded. "Call me later to confirm." Eric tugged at his chin. "Left my book at the marina and something's nagging at me."

Natalie nodded and winked. "Will do. If you find out there's a conflict just call me."

Two others looked around, made a few comments, and nodded at their fellow selectmen and women. They made their way toward Eric at the head of the table. He was sure he knew what one wanted. Especially since the person had objected strenuously to the last order of business before the meeting adjourned.

"What time on the third?" Jonathan Wellman asked, referencing Eric and Ashley's annual Fourth of July cookout on the beach in front of their house.

"Six-thirty," Eric told him.

Wellman nodded. "See you then. Need anything?" he asked.

"Yeah," Eric joked. "A million bucks, a fifty-foot Cabo, and a house with three-hundred feet of frontage on Nantucket Sound!"

Wellman nodded again and grinned. "See what I can do," he said with a smile and a wave.

The remaining member of the Board stood silently

staring at Eric. "Guess you know why I stayed?" Asked Neal Lohan, the senior member of the Board and the other person who'd sought the Chairperson's job.

"I'm guessing it's about the Harbormaster situation?"

"Yep," Lohan agreed. "Look Eric, I know you think I was trying to undercut you when I objected to your appointment of Shane Winslow for temporary Harbormaster, but I wasn't. Swear to God."

"I understand," Eric said, packing up his shoulder bag with the endless papers that went with this voluntary position. "You think he's too young? At least that's what you said."

Lohan nodded. "It'll be two months before Buck gets back," he explained referring to the man who'd been the Harbormaster before he'd broken his leg in three places. "And we both know this is the busiest time of the year." He shrugged. "The fourth of July, kids partying on the beaches, Dennis Days Holiday Celebrations, and the fireworks at West Dennis."

Eric nodded, doing his best to remain courteous. "Yes, Neal. I know the schedule," he offered.

"I know you do and look, Eric, I know all about Shane. A Coast Guard officer, hero injured in the line of duty, saved four lives in the process, awarded the Coast Guard Medal and so forth," Lohan droned indulgently. "I mean, except for you I don't know anyone who has a more impressive resume and yes, he's done a good job as Buck's second in command, but he's only been on the job since the season began. What's that? Six weeks?"

"Yep. That's right. Six weeks. The appointment is *temporary*, Neal. Can you suggest another candidate?"

Eric asked looking purposefully at his watch.

"I know you're busy, Eric. But look—between resigning his Coast Guard commission and his fiancé's death he's not the same person," he paused for emphasis. "Everyone's seen it."

"Sorry. Look. I have an important meeting at one-thirty," Eric explained. "But I think he can be good at this." Eric slung his bag over his shoulder and gestured toward the door. "Shane's Bobby's nephew. You know that. I've watched him grow up. I know he's taken a couple of hits. Big ones. But I've seen him in all kinds of situations. When things get tough, he doesn't back down or wilt. Just the opposite, Neal. Some people can deal with difficult situations. Hell, you were the one who just said he's great when the pressure's on. I really think he can do the job," Eric added, sighing. "And that rescue where he got injured and saved those people made the papers all the way up and down the East Coast. They had him on *Good Morning America!*"

"Okay. No more about this," Lohan said. "It's just that things can get pretty hectic around here during the summer." He shrugged. "And being a hero doesn't necessarily equate with running a busy and sensitive town department with an office full of people clamoring for favors or complaining."

"The Harbormaster's office is next door to our Marina. They keep the town launches there. The last thing I want is to have something go wrong." Eric patted Lohan on the back while they headed toward the door. "I give you my word. Bobby and I will watch him. Any sign that the job and the people are suffering or that he can't handle the job, and I'll be the first one in line to ask him to step down."

"All right, Eric. You're the boss," Lohan said.

"Thanks, Neal and don't forget the cookout." Eric smiled when they parted company in the parking lot. "Six-thirty or whenever you can get there."

They each headed toward opposite sides of the crowded parking lot. This was the beginning of the busy time—beach stickers, launch permits, tax bills, and everything else you could imagine.

Eric smiled to himself whenever he thought about the metamorphosis that took place starting in mid-June every year. When the quaint, sleepy hamlets that comprised Cape Cod's fifteen towns and villages morphed into bustling mini-metropolises. Four to five million tourists and three months from now, in September, after another season in the sun and the waves the exodus would be over. Cape Cod would return to its core. The hardy residents comprising the two-hundred thousand die-hards who stayed would breathe a sigh of relief unless their livelihood was tourist dependent. Eric's smile broadened when he slipped into his pickup. There was nowhere else he wanted to be.

Chapter Eight

Week of June 14th, 2016

"Oh, my God," Samantha Edgerton shouted, emerging like a dolphin from beneath the brisk three-foot swells. She stood, shaking rapidly, shivering as the chilly salt-water flew in clouds around her. Sam didn't spend hours studying and admiring herself in the mirror. That wasn't her style, but she smiled while she brushed the cold sparkling droplets from her bronzed arms. Glad she still had good muscle tone despite the long months since the ski accident in Chamonix.

Shielding her eyes from the bright sun overhead, she scanned Nantucket Sound and the spectacular scenery that bordered it. The waves were perfection! Just large enough to be a challenge but not enough to present a danger. In her copious reading about the U.S. she'd read that the undertow could be dangerous at some places on the East Coast. Not today and not here. She had already fallen in love with this place—the Bass River—and the houses that lined it. Some crowded together closely, taking full advantage of the scarce waterfront footage, but virtually every property looked well-maintained. Very well. Most sported docks and a few had the luxury of private beaches.

The scenery wasn't the only thing that could be called spectacular. The day was downright scrumptious! Just a sprinkling of clouds and a light breeze. Sam beamed, remembering something she'd heard or read—where she couldn't recall. *This day was the kind God envisioned when he created the world.* Yes. After surveying the scenery again Samantha knew that description fit her surroundings to perfection.

Running through the shallows near the shore, she could feel the strength in her quads and lower legs returning. Sam loved the feeling of being fit and couldn't help but smile again when she turned and stepped onto the flat smooth sand left by the receding tide.

She saw her brother lying on an expensive beach throw. "Oh, my God, Bro! Are you ever going to get your cute little butt up and enjoy these waves?" Sam asked unable to abide her brother's tendency to veg at any opportunity. At least Charles had given his string of young teenage followers an afternoon off.

Charles just waved and called, "Can you give me more sunblock, Sam?" he asked, lifting his head and pulling off his designer sunglasses.

Never one to resist the chance to playfully harass her handsome and adoring younger sibling Sam stopped. She caught sight of just what she needed. She turned and smiled, calling, "Yes, of course, dear." She hid a giggle. "Be right there."

"Excuse me," Sam said quietly, approaching a small group of children working diligently at constructing a massive sand castle. "Might I borrow one of your pails for a few moments?" she asked showing the children a warm smile. "Just a short while. Promise," she added crossing her heart.

The two older boys, eleven or twelve Sam guessed,

stared up at her. The larger one nodded. "S…. sure," he stammered, continuing to watch Sam. "Take it for as long as you…you want." Sam smiled at the boy's admiring glance.

Her features had been described as soft. Even gentle. Men would often describe her as cute. But there was something, an indefinable quality about her looks that men found hard to turn away from. Sam had seen that for herself. Often.

She nodded. "Thanks, loads," she said continuing to smile. Sam gave her benefactor a soft pat on the back.

The boy watching Sam jumped up, almost tripping he dumped the pail, rinsed it quickly, and handed it to her as his face grew crimson. "You…you thound like you're from thomewhere elsesth?" he asked with a pronounced lisp as his eyes dropped.

"Why yes. How observant of you." Samantha beamed a smile the young man's way. "We live in Cornwall," she said while she surveyed the small group who'd gathered round her. Sam possessed the ability to draw a crowd. Always had. *You have charisma*, Poppy told her often. "Have any of you heard of Cornwall?" she asked the half dozen youngsters.

"Yep." One of the group nodded. "Isn't that in England?"

"Why, yes, dear." Sam shook the girl's hand. "When I return the pail, I'll give you what we call a quid—an English pound. In silver. How's that sound?" Sam asked with a shrug.

"All right, then," Sam said when the group nodded. She smiled down at the eight-year-old pigtailed redhead who'd been so knowledgeable about geography.

"And you'd be surprised how similar Cornwall is, but I must tell you your seacoast here is delightful. Downright *spectacular,*" she added.

The small group surrounding Samantha had grown to a dozen. She stood beaming studying each quickly. "Why back in Britain we even have a Plymouth and a Falmouth just as you do over here." She explained as one of the large men providing security since Charles' riding competition last spring headed her way. "But for now, I'd simply like to use your pail if I may?"

Sam glanced up toward Charles, Poppy, and the large fit strangers who had become their constant companions. She gave a subtle wave and beamed a smile. As the larger of the men headed toward Sam and her impromptu entourage, she took the pail. Smiling, she put her fingers to her lips and waved away the man from their security entourage. Unless one of the ten-year-olds was concealing a weapon in their bathing suit she was in no immediate danger.

Misha nodded to the taller man then returned Sam's smile. She liked Misha the best. He commanded their security team and had been an Israeli commando. Sam had watched him doing his workout on several occasions. He was an expert at something she'd heard about called Krav Maga. Though he was by no means the largest of the group Sam was in awe of his flexibility and strength, feeling confident and safe whenever he was in sight.

She'd wheedled Poppy into letting her accompany him to the firing range one day. He fired ten shots within two inches of each other. "Must have been the wind," he told her feigning anger then showing her a smile. Sam also liked that he kept his distance, was courteous to a fault, and showed her mother incredible courtesy and compassion that bordered on friendship.

"Thanks so much. I'll bring it right back. Promise," she repeated as she filled the pail. The combination of her gentle good looks; outgoing, ebullient personality, and her general love for life often gave those she met the impression that Samantha was a flirt. Even a show-off, especially when combined with her love of high-fashion clothing. Nothing could be further from the truth. Sam was not what she appeared. Poppy described her as an adorable, talented, and athletic young woman who valued reading, life, and everyone she met! Sam only prayed she came close to her grandfather's flowery praise.

The small crowd around Samantha followed her with their eyes. She looked at them putting her finger to her lips for quiet as a conspiratorial smile grew. Sam giggled quietly while she tiptoed the few yards to her family and her primary target.

She was about to dump her bucket, when a sudden reflection drew Sam's attention. It came from the River. Several small cruisers sat anchored off the beach where her family lay swimming and sunning. A small fiberglass launch had slowed, weaving in and out close to shore. Squinting, she tried to focus on it. A man stood in the center column runabout taking pictures. Sam thought the reflection had been caused by a camera or phone. An uneasy feeling crept over her.

"Poppy," she called to her grandfather and put down her bucket.

"Yes, angel," he answered looking up from the book he was reading. "What can I do for you?"

She pointed toward the River. "Do you see that

small launch going through the boats anchored there?"

He stood and shielded his eyes from the sun. "The one with the man standing under the canopy?"

She nodded.

"Can't say I had," he said then looked toward Misha. "Can you have a look?" he asked as the young man approached them. "That boat moving through the others. Looks like he's taking photographs."

Misha brushed some sand from his legs and crossed the hundred feet to the River's shoreline, taking a set of binoculars with him. Suddenly the small boat turned abruptly to port and headed upriver into the main channel as it increased speed.

"You get a good look?" Lord Edgerton asked.

Misha shook his head. He put down the glasses and returned to the group. "It turned too quickly for me to get the registration number but I'm betting it was a rental." He nodded. "I'm guessing he was just having a look at the tourists," he added in a low voice that Sam overheard. "Perhaps he was a reporter."

"All right but keep your eyes open," Sam heard her grandfather say evenly, taking a last look at the small boat as it headed upriver. "I don't think it's anything to be concerned about," he said to Sam.

She shrugged and stood poised to grab her bucket when another vessel caught her attention, this one a double-ended launch coming in from the Sound. The new bumpers lining the gunwales and the fresh coat of white paint reflected the sunlight. 'Harbormaster' was stenciled in large black letters on its pristine hull. Sam had seen it pass by before.

Bending to pick up the bucket she caught sight of a tall lean young man in a tan uniform when he turned toward the beach. He looked her way, scanning the numerous pleasure boats and bathers then back down river. Samantha stopped suddenly; her eyes riveted on the launch. She caught just a brief glimpse of the handsome young coxswain. Could her mind be playing tricks on her? Because for a moment—one fleeting instant—the young man looked familiar.

The launch and the young man piloting it turned heading away from her. Sam shook her head. A fanciful illusion? Wishful thinking? To think she'd find the hero from her frightening survival adventure here on Cape Cod. No. That was ridiculous! This wasn't one of those lusty romantic novels they sold at the airport. This was life. Real life.

She watched as the launch became a smaller image, shook her head again, then hoisted the small bucket and turned toward where Charles lay, eyes closed.

"Do you want something, Charles, dear?" Sam asked casually while she tiptoed across the ten feet of sand and stood over her brother.

"Yes, can you help me?"

"Why certainly. Since you haven't been in the water, I wanted to cool you off," Samantha whispered dumping the water from the large bucket on Charles. She doubled over with laughter. Since she'd made a rather obvious show of the whole thing soft rings of laughter went forth from her Grandfather, her Mum, and Ashley Jean Montgomery, who'd been their informal tour guide and frequent companion since they'd arrived. Even the security people enjoyed the comic theater.

"I'll get back at you. Damn you, Samantha!" Charles swore at his sister but even he couldn't avoid breaking into a laugh. He threw a handful of sand at his sister.

"I know you will, dear. Isn't that part of the great mystique of sibling rivalry?" Sam answered evenly. She seldom lost her temper. Returning the pail, she caught a final distant glimpse of the tall fellow in the launch. Samantha stopped for a moment, then turned and rejoined the children. She deposited the pail with one of her pre-teen admirers. As promised, she'd retrieved a silver shilling from her shoulder bag and given it to the youngsters.

Sam returned to their beach throws. Laying down, she closed her eyes.

She found herself wondering about the small boat with the man and the camera. Something about it sent shivers down her spine. Why? She put it from her mind, turning toward her delightful companion and surrogate tour-guide.

"Ashley-Jean," she began.

"You can just call me Ashley or AJ. Everyone else does."

"I know. You've told me that, but, well, would you mind if I continued to use both names?" Sam felt her face flush. "Frankly, there's something I enjoy about the two names together. Has sort of an anti-bellum sound to it. Scarlett, Rhett Butler, Ashley Wilkes, and all that," she added with a shrug. "And you know I *adore* your accent!"

"That's fine. Call me whatever suits you, *Ma'am*," Ashley nodded. "And aahs just love yours, too, darlin'!" she added pouring on an extra heavy dose of her Virginia drawl.

"Did you see that double-ender out there with the

spanking new paint and bumpers on the gunwales?"

Ashley lifted her head and squinted. "Yes. The one with the tall ruggedly handsome young man at the helm."

Sam shook her head good naturedly. "Yes. My goodness. Am I that obvious?" she ended with a soft chuckle. "He looked…familiar."

"Not a problem. And as fate might have it, we know that sturdy vessel's captain. He's our Harbormaster. You know, sort of like the police chief on the water."

"Really," Sam said, pushing up onto her elbows. "He looked rather young for such a responsible position."

"He actually has quite a resume," Ashley said. "And both he and his co-captain, an adorable little spaniel, will be at our 4th of July Eve cookout. Something I believe you and your family will attend?"

"Why yes, of course." Sam did her best to hide her pleasure then shook her head. "Of course, we both know I'm supposed to remain anonymous. Protected and surrounded like one of Mummy's prize Hummels." Sam shrugged as a frown crossed her face.

"I understand, Sam. But…" Ashley began then paused. She stole a look at the impressive young men serving her family.

Samantha caught the look. Her frown softened into understanding. "Yes. I understand. Poppy's been concerned with our safety since Charles' attempted kidnapping last spring. But we're young. We want to live!" she said throwing her hands in the air, shaking her head. Her frown grew into a scowl. "Safety serves no good purpose if it makes one into a prisoner or a recluse."

"You make a strong case, Sam. At least I'm convinced." Ashley nodded and pushed herself up, checking her watch, showing Sam a smile. "Give me a minute. I want to call Eric about something," she explained with a curious look. She brushed the sand away and took her phone. Ashley walked toward the breakwater that separated the pristine strip of beach they lay on from another that fronted on the Bass River.

Sam could see her new friend talking on the phone and nodding. Returning to their large beach throw she sat down. "I had something I wanted to ask him."

She turned onto her back as Sam propped herself up onto one elbow. "I know this is tremendously bold of me, but is there any possibility that the occupant of the launch might be—available? You know. Should I need some guidance or assistance on the water while we're here." Sam finished, raising her eyebrows.

"Oh, Samantha, I'm so sorry. I don't quite know how to tell you this, but the poor boy's been…fixed. You know. Taken care of," Ashley shrugged apologetically.

"Pardon me. Fixed? You mean like…?" Suddenly she saw the smile on Ashley Jean's face followed by an animated laugh.

"Well, of course I assumed you were referring to Joey, his co-Captain and the River's second favorite spaniel."

Sam gave her a gentle push and grinned.

"How about this?" Ashley Jean asked. "You're going to Brewster Woods, the stable on the north side of the Cape so Charles can look into some of their riding events this summer. And you volunteered to pick

Kylie up for her lesson. Right?"

Sam nodded.

"Instead of picking her up at our house could you stop by the Marina?"

"I don't see why not," Sam said. She laid back down on the throw. "I can ask Poppy."

"Great. If there's an issue just call my cell."

"Sure. But I don't see any issues."

Ashley Jean lay down next to Samantha and closed her eyes. Sam watched while her new friend grew another curious, almost mystical smile.

Sam joined Ashley Jean, dozing and luxuriating in the day and the surroundings, reveling in the June sun while a warm pleasant feeling crept over her. When Sam opened her eyes, Ashley Jean had left their blanket and sat next to Poppy. He talked with her and nodded several times in reaction to her comments. She made sweeping gestures toward Nantucket Sound while she spoke.

Ashley Jean stood and returned to Sam. "I had to ask your grandfather something," she explained.

"Anything interesting," Samantha asked.

"I thought that your family would enjoy a cruise around the Sound. I volunteered one of our large Whalers—it's forty-two feet long and downright scrumptious. Like a giant living room on the water but very powerful and seaworthy. It's the one we use for trips and entertaining, and I also volunteered an experienced tour guide," Ashley Jean said. "And your grandfather agreed. Said it sounded like a 'Spanking good show'."

"Oh yes. That sounds capital," Sam agreed enthusiastically.

As they lay down letting the sun do its work Sam heard subtle movement. When she opened her eyes the water from the bucket Charles held was on the way. He smiled with satisfaction.

"*Aaah!*" Sam shouted with surprise and laughter.

Charles walked back down the beach to the shore and left the bucket wearing a satisfied smile. "You know what they say about payback?" he called back with a giggle.

Sam joined in his laughter, turned over, and closed her eyes remembering the striking young man in the spanking new launch.

Chapter Nine

The long rambling house and large private lot had been selected with the utmost of care. Axe left nothing to chance. Certainly, not for his special project. No. Everything would be perfect. The local contractor he had commissioned would rough out a small basement room he would use to accomplish his plan.

That contractor and his workers? They should present no problem. Collateral damage if it came to that. But he saw no reason it should. As far as they were concerned it was simply a storage room. They should suspect nothing even after he had achieved his goal. At least he saw none when he stared out the window into the dense growth that surrounded the house a hundred feet from the back porch.

He thought with bitterness even irony how his family would have loved this beautiful place. The scenery, the weather, the spectacular views. The very place where he would balance the scales of justice. Find fairness for Naina and their children. He shook his head then returned to his sad reality.

He closed his HP Pavilion laptop after studying the notes from Dylan Murphy's observations of the Edgerton family and analysis of their security. Axe had done his own evaluation of their family over a period of many months. He believed in redundancy and was pleased that Murphy's and his thoughts agreed.

His musings returned to the workers. Having been a worker once—one with a family he returned to every night Axe would feel regret if they became collateral damage. But when he closed his eyes and saw his beautiful wife and adoring children boarding the ferry any hint of regret shrunk to *nichego*...nothing!

Independence Day. That was how the Americans referred to their massive fourth of July celebrations. A special holiday. A time of festivity. For them. For Axe, it would be a different kind of celebration. By the time America celebrated their holiday this year he would have repaid Lord James Edgerton for the thoughtless neglect that had caused Axe and many others such pain. Though he had kept the frightening details from his loyal and devoted younger brother Ivan and the other members of his team. What Axe wanted—had wanted for the years since that accident that had destroyed his world was justice. Not revenge. *Justice!*

The ringing of the bell followed by a knock at the door signaled another of his associates, the video and electronics specialist. A key person. He was a different issue. Axe had paid him a substantial retainer. And this man had a reputation. Axe usually had an answer for every question. A way to dispose of every problem. This man would certainly surmise what Axe had planned. And there were less than three weeks until he put his plan into action. This man had come highly recommended in the shadowy world Axe had occupied since he had re-made himself after losing his family. The man could be trusted and had never failed to complete the contracts he'd been tasked with. Currently, his strongest option was to simply pay the man the promised remainder of his retainer and if necessary, deal with him after the fact.

Axe was concerned that disposing of someone so highly held by criminal society might provoke retaliation from those who had used and recommended him. That was not what he wanted. Once the terrible thing was complete Axe wanted to be done with it and the scum he'd been forced to befriend during his unholy quest. He had done some immoral things—perhaps too many—in preparing for his crusade. They were necessary, but once justice was done, he had no intention of becoming a fixture in the criminal population he'd been forced to befriend.

He sighed when he walked through the large, well-furnished home. It all had to fit—his new identity. He had used a reasonable pretense—a wealthy businessman who'd lost his wife and decided to renew himself in the United States. To date, his recreated persona had fit. But this technician. He played on Axe's mind. He worried when he awoke early in the morning or during his long sleepless nights.

"Good Morning, Mr. Lassiter. Won't you please come in," Axe gestured toward the ample well-furnished kitchen.

"Beautiful place you have here, Mr. Axelrod," the man observed studying the surroundings. "I've driven by once or twice. Just to get my bearings."

Axe had learned to control his emotions and facial expressions, but something registered when the man said he'd driven by.

"Simply to make sure I could find it, of course. I'm not that familiar with Cape Cod. You *are* quite a way off the beaten track here." The man said holding up his hands when he realized that his client looked concerned. He studied the kitchen casually and peered out through the glass slider that fronted the pine forest and the Atlantic Ocean miles distant.

"Can I offer you a coffee or tea?" Axe gestured to the long granite countertop. "I have an espresso machine."

"No, I'm fine." The man nodded amiably while he studied Axe. "Shall we get down to business?" the man asked. "You indicated in your call that my work would take place here."

Axe nodded but detected a sudden change in the man's previously casual demeanor.

"I'll take you down to the special room. The one where I'll be housing my...my special treasures," he suggested. "It's not complete but you can determine the size. I assume that will be essential to your planning?"

"Yes, that's correct," the man answered.

They went to the basement, spending the next thirty minutes going over the size, dimensions, and other details of the space. Lassiter took pictures and measured. "Once my work is complete, these notes and photos will be destroyed." He walked around the small room still being framed. "Excellent. Two top-end remote controlled high definition cameras. Sensitive sound equipment to go with the cameras. And of course, I assume you hired me because of my special skill at keeping the signals hidden from the outside world?"

"Yes, that is correct."

"And I'm also guessing that what you'll be storing down there will require certain needs in terms of climate—oxygen, CO_2, humidity, all that." The man didn't look at Axe. He spoke evenly without facial expression. "And you will want the cameras to be equipped for night vision?"

"Yes, of course. My apologies, I was going to mention that." Axe nodded deferentially. "That's why I hired *you.*"

"No need to be concerned. I try to anticipate all my customer's needs," the man added almost casually.

When they returned to the upstairs, they went into the one room Axe had made his own. He called it his study.

"Mr. Lassiter, I've given you a generous sum of…"

"Let me be frank." The man held up his hand. "I don't care if you're keeping the Crown Jewels or the First Lady down there. I will guarantee you flawless performance. And yes, you've paid me generously and I'm sure you'll complete our agreement."

Axe stared at the man for a long moment. Someone he could respect and count on to keep his secret. "That is exactly how I see it. And you. Your installation should be completed and functioning before the last week in June. We will determine the exact date as we progress with the project. And unless your references exaggerated your skills, I will deposit the second payment in your offshore account the following day. You'll send me the number?"

The man nodded and took a card from his pocket. "Here it is. I only ask that if you're ever called to be a reference you permit me that courtesy." The man stood. "With complete anonymity, of course. And I'll move in here after I receive all the necessary equipment. And of course, *you* will also destroy any materials that I have provided." He nodded at the card with his account numbers.

"Of course," they shook hands and the man left with a small smile. "I look forward to your company," Axe added in an agreeable way as if they would be sharing a pleasant vacation.

Axe sighed. This man was a professional. His final concern had been satisfied.

Chapter Ten

Shane Winslow pulled the sturdy twenty-four-foot double-ended launch into the town dock with his usual facility. But then he'd been on or around the water since he was born. Almost. A faded picture of him sitting on his dad's lap at the age of two on an earlier version of the town dock sat framed on the bookcase in his family's home.

The town dock sat adjacent to the Southside Marina. Eric Montgomery stood, smiling while he grabbed the bow of the launch as Shane let the slight wind and current bring the launch into its slip.

"Nicely done, Mr. Harbormaster," Eric said.

Shane still flushed when someone referred to him by his new title. "Come on, Eric. I get enough teasing from the other guys. Not you, too," he said evenly. "Sorry," he recanted. "I know you needed someone and I'm glad you had faith in me," he added.

"Yes, Shane, we did. And no one has the resume you do," Eric told him tying the launch to a cleat. "Honestly, if you hadn't been here, we would have been hurting." Eric shook his head.

Shane jumped off the launch and hung his life jacket on one of the cleats on the dock.

"Come on, buddy," he said turning to his golden cocker spaniel, Joey. He'd been the family pet for half a dozen years but had always followed Shane around dutifully. In the years since Shane had resigned his commission then lost Emily, Joey had filled the role of best friend. He obeyed dutifully, jumping up and over the thickly bumpered rail then onto the dock. Shane bent and picked him up, nuzzling his damp snout gently.

Eric put his hand on Shane's shoulder, studying him. "You *know* we really needed someone to help us through the summer after Buck broke his leg." Eric repeated and released his shoulder, patting him on the back as they headed toward the aluminum gangway. "I've heard nothing but good things about you." He shrugged. "And everyone still talks about your heroics with the Coast Guard."

"Got it, Eric. I'm glad to help," Shane nodded. "Sorry," he repeated. "Don't mean to complain or get defensive. You, Ashley, and Bobby have been great. But my ambition is to get my Master's License."

Eric nodded. "I know the last couple of years haven't been easy but hang in there. All the summer kids look up to you. And between you and me I know the older guys may tease you, but they think you're doing a good job, too." Eric said as they stopped to talk to Shane's replacement for the four-hour shift from 4 p.m. till sundown. "Take my word for it."

"Hi, Owen," Shane said as they nodded to each other.

"What's happening, boss?" The young man asked Shane.

"Nothing exciting. A pretty peaceful afternoon for this time of year with so many early tourists," Shane told his relief. "Keep an eye on those lobster pots near the first buoys beyond the breakwater on our side of the channel." The Bass River was a major waterway that divided the Mid-Cape, separating the town of Dennis on the east from Yarmouth on the west. "I don't want to have to give Tim and his partner a fine, but I've warned them three times and I'm afraid someone's gonna catch a prop on 'em."

"Got it," Owen called back toward Shane. He and Eric headed off the slip toward the parking lot. "Are those big wigs still here?" he added.

Shane turned and shook his head. "I think so. But don't spend so much time watching them! Especially the girl," Shane added with a smile and a wave as Owen gave him a friendly salute.

Eric smiled at Shane's comment. "You've heard the story, right? About who they are?"

"A wealthy family. Lord something or other?" Shane shrugged. "Guess so. Did I miss some breaking news?"

"They're visiting dignitaries. And yes, the older man is a Lord. A member of British royalty who's over here for few months. He's doing a lecture series at Harvard this fall but he's never been to Cape Cod, so he rented a big house and brought his family," Eric explained. "His granddaughter is going to take some classes there Ashley tells me."

"That's what I heard but is it all right to give them a special space like that?" Shane asked.

"No." Eric shook his head showing a trace of a smile. "But if you go down that section of beach there's nothing to keep people away. No ropes or barriers. Look closely and you can see they just have a small rotating staff of security people."

Shane nodded. "Got it and you're right. When I

went by a couple of times, I saw a girl talking to a bunch of local kids."

As they got to the parking lot, Eric took Shane's arm. "Look, I know you just did a long shift in the launch, but could you come back. Say about quarter to five? There's something I need to talk to you about in the office."

"I'll come by now," Shane volunteered.

"No. Don't want to be a pain in the rear. But if you don't mind, I'd prefer four forty-five."

Shane checked his watch then headed to his jeep. Four-eleven. "Okay. You're the boss. I'll grab a quick sandwich." He nodded and gave Joey a pat. "Five it is."

Chapter Eleven

His assistant of more than a decade showed the Admiral a scowl. "It's the new agent working with Jim Merritt. They're doing the surveillance of that man Lassiter, the…"

"Yes, Jeanie. I know," he stopped her.

"Do you really need to talk to every field agent every day, sir?"

"Jeanie. I do not talk to every field agent every day and you know that." He leaned back as his desk chair squeaked loudly. "You know I have a special interest in the person Merritt and his partner are following. He's had his hands in a lot of dirty adventures, but yes, I do like to keep in touch with our people in the field. Especially top young men like Merritt's partner, Mendes."

Jeanie gave him a stern look and shrugged. "Yes, sir. Well, your *favorite* top new man is waiting for you on line four…sir."

"Thank you, Miss Flynn." He gave her an exaggerated smile and nodded. "I'll see you at the briefing at two," he added, checking his watch.

"Good morning, sir," Mario Mendes said. "Lancaster. That's the name he's using at the hotel in Hyannis." He and his partner were keeping a high-profile electronics specialist under surveillance. Originally trained as a specialist by MI-6 he had spent the better part of the millennium working for Queen and country. About six years ago he'd found the dark side—terrorism, kidnapping, and extortion was more to his liking. At least the pay was better. Much better.

"It sounds like we got lucky and caught a break, sir," Mendes added.

"Occasionally, we do catch one, Mario," the Admiral replied. He sat in an unassuming three-story brick building that housed NIRA. He scanned the four twenty-seven-inch monitors that faced him in a semi-circle while he listened to Mendes. *Study, preparation, and diligence.* The simple mantra that had allowed him to transform a sleepy, low-impact think tank into a diminutive but powerful force in America's front-line security umbrella. "But I like that old mantra that says good luck is the result of preparation."

"Yes, sir." Mendes said quietly. He sounded contrite.

"Not a reprimand, Mario." The United States had eighteen high level intelligence gathering and law enforcement organizations. NIRA had two-hundred eighty-seven operatives. The Admiral knew them all by sight and almost always used their first names.

"Yes, sir. I've read the file."

"Of course," the Admiral began feeling penitent. "We lost Lassiter for a while last year, but thanks to the Brits and their remarkable CCTV network they found him in Liverpool three months ago. Had eyes on him till he boarded a British Air Flight out of Heathrow ten days ago heading our way. We picked him up thanks to our new facial recognition software and tracked him through Customs and Immigration at Logan Airport..." the Admiral had been talking on a secure land line and stopped, putting his hand over the receiver. He nodded as Jeanie came in again and left a file on his desk and pointed toward it, mouthing the words *top priority*.

"Sorry," he added as he scanned it and nodded, then returned to Mendes.

Mendes waited, then asked "Intel says his real value could be in leading us to bigger targets?"

"Yes. It could. Because what he does is constantly in demand by the type of people it's our job to stop. His skill sets make him a magnet for them. But since he's done nothing we can arrest him for we'll keep surveillance on him and use him as an unsuspecting CI."

"Got it, sir." His subordinate agreed. "He's been meeting with a man at a local restaurant called the Riverway Lobster House." Mendes paused.

"Yes," the Admiral interrupted. "I saw that on your report. I've spent time on Cape Cod. I know the location." He smiled to himself remembering several meals he'd shared with Eric, Ashley, and Kylie Montgomery over the last three summers. Some at the popular restaurant Mendes had mentioned.

"Sir," Mendes prompted his superior.

"Yes. Mario. Apologies. I must be getting old," The Admiral admitted. "I allowed nostalgia to get the better of me."

"I've been told you scan each of the activity reports from your field teams before you leave for the day. That doesn't sound like someone who's getting old, sir."

"Don't suck up, Mario," the Admiral said followed by soft laughter.

Silence then, "I give you my word, I wasn't."

The Admiral liked this boy. A tall, hard, much decorated Special Forces fire team leader, weapons and commo specialist. He was fluent in Spanish, French, Farsi, and Arabic. And now he belonged to the Admiral and NIRA. "Don't worry, Mario. I was just joking. I don't recruit sycophants."

"Thank you, sir. Merritt and I sent the photos of the man Lassiter met with twice in the last three days. Their conversation seemed very intense. I don't think it was a casual social encounter."

"I'm sure it wasn't. I'll have Jeanie bring me your pictures ASAP. And by the way, I'm coming down there next week."

"Sir?" Mendes sounded tentative. Nervous.

"No, Mario. I promise. No kibitzing or looking over your shoulder. Even I take a day off now and then. Just visiting old friends I met on a major case three years ago."

"I've heard that story, sir," Mendes said.

"So, if our unwitting CI is still there and he may not be, I may want to check him out." The Admiral sighed then asked, "You planted the bugs on his rental car?"

"Yes, sir. Followed SOP. Merritt tutored me as to where and how to place the bugs and avoid getting caught," the young agent said with a trace of humor in his voice.

"Excellent," the Admiral complimented his new agent. "Now you'd better get back to work."

"I'm three car lengths behind our target..." he paused briefly. "The Allen Harbor Marina on Lower County Road. I'm leaving him in Jason's hands."

"All right. Sounds like you have everything under

control."

"I think so…" Mendes stopped. The Admiral heard him take a deep breath. "I have to thank you for letting me join your agency, sir."

"Mario?"

"I'm having the time of my life!" the new agent enthused.

"I'm glad to hear that, son. Our work is more than a job—a weekly paycheck," the Admiral stopped and took a deep breath. "And I agree. I think of it as a sacred calling!" he added as he hung up.

The Admiral stared at the phone thinking how his last statement sounded like a platitude. And of course, it did. No matter. He felt a smile cross his face as Jeanie knocked lightly and approached his desk with a handful of photos. He didn't care how corny it sounded. It was the truth!

Chapter Twelve

Eric Montgomery headed into the newly renovated ship store, nodding to a couple of long-time customers before sitting down in Ashley's office. She'd just returned from the beach where she'd been playing hostess to the influential British family the Admiral had asked them to look after. She sat in her desk chair skimming through the mail.

"Everything okay?" Eric asked showing her a mock grimace. "Can we stay open for another month?" he said studying her. Her expression held his attention. Something had happened. His wife, the brilliant hacker who could infiltrate the most sophisticated computer program within minutes, usually had a pleasant, downright upbeat demeanor. But as Eric studied her there was no doubt. The demure beauty that turned heads and teased him with her honey-smooth voice had vanished. She had morphed into the serious Ashley Jean Fitzhugh.

He rose. Ashley nodded toward the door. Eric understood and closed it quietly.

"I just got a call from the Admiral," she said.

"Did he call to see how his friends are enjoying their Cape Cod vacation with you acting as tour guide?" Eric asked, glancing out to the ship store to make sure the doors were closed. He walked across the office to their Bose radio and turned it on loud enough to mask their conversation.

"Yes, but," Ashley paused and shook her head. "There's something else. He's got something going on down here. His people have found a person of interest. A lot of interest from what he said. Obviously, he didn't go into details. But I can read him. Sounds like it could be something serious," she said just above a whisper then paused. Eric sat on the edge of the desk and took her hand.

"I'm surprised he shared that. It shows how much he trusts you." Eric shrugged. "Well, we've had peaceful summers since that business a few years ago." He squeezed her hand. "I assume that means he'll be dividing his time between us, the Edgerton's, and this situation. Anything he wants our help with?"

"No. Not yet anyway. He just wanted to give us a heads up." She stood and bent slightly finding his lips as they kissed softly. "Now. Hmmm," she purred, showing him the teasing look and dimpled smile he saw when he closed his eyes. "Where do I know you from?" Ashley asked, letting the tension drain from her shoulders giving him a soft punch in the stomach.

"I believe you came knocking at my front door one rainy night two—no—make that three years ago? Time flies when you're having fun," he said softly, pulling her back to him, and kissing her hungrily while they joined in a tight embrace. Three years since their meeting and Eric could imagine nothing more perfect than to spend a night curled up next to Ashley tasting her sweetness and inhaling the sensuous fragrance surrounding her.

"Best thing I ever did," she continued purring, finding his ear, and using her tongue and lips to nibble and tease it gently. "Did he say anything about…about Ralph to you?"

Eric pulled away. "No. No he didn't. But remember he told us at Christmas he was going back under deep cover and the Admiral confirmed that," he paused. "I assume he said nothing to you?"

She shook her head. Ralph was Eric's older brother. Ashley had lived with her mother and Ralph for years. He was a deep cover operative for the Admiral and NIRA. His cover had been as the Chief Steward at the Officer's Club at the Norfolk Navy Base. When Ashley's mother died suddenly, and he thought his cover had been blown, he sent Ashley to find Eric.

A knock on the door shook them back to reality as they separated.

"Come in," Ashley said, straightening her beach robe and pushed away from Eric who put his arm around her as they went to the door.

Kylie, their ten-year-old daughter stood in her riding clothes, hands on hips.

"Thanks, Lu," Ashley said waving at Eric's former mother-in-law.

"Always a pleasure. Got to get to the library. I'm hosting a talk for the book club." She waved and blew them a kiss. "Have fun, honey," she said beaming her adopted granddaughter a warm smile.

"Bye, grandma," Kylie beamed back and waved, turning to Eric and Ashley. "How come you guys are always kissing?' she asked wearing an expression somewhere between curiosity and frustration. "None of my other friends' parents spend so much time doing that," she added with a curious look.

"Well." Eric shook his head and gave Ashley a

quick squeeze. "What do you think? Should we try to curtail all this affection?"

Ashley giggled at his squeeze then did her best to put on a serious expression. "Well, Kylie. Daddy and I will try much harder in the future not to be so...so affectionate in public."

"Okay." He nodded. "Less kissing in public. That's definitely high on *my* agenda."

"So," Ashley said as they walked into the ship store. "You're all set to go riding with Samantha and Charles this afternoon?" she asked. "And we want you to introduce them to Rebecca?"

"Yep. They seem really nice." Kylie agreed. "I can't wait to see them again," she added. She hadn't stopped talking about Charles since they met for dinner two nights before. Kylie had begun riding lessons the previous summer and like her sailing, she'd demonstrated a talent for it. "I'm really excited about seeing Charles ride," she enthused with a flush. "His grandfather said he was a junior show-jumping champion last year."

"Yes. They say he's a wonderful rider. But remember, honey, Rebecca's stable is probably not set up so he can show off his skills today," Ashley said giving Kylie's polo shirt a straighten then gave one of her pigtails a tug.

Just as Eric checked his watch, they heard the clatter of riding boots as Charles and Samantha came into the ship store.

Sam had seen him. "I hope we're not late. Are we, Eric?"

A tall fit-looking man who Eric recognized as the main security person—the body man for the grandchildren—stood just beyond the open door to the parking lot. He nodded and gave a small wave.

Eric nodded back then turned toward Sam and Charles. "No, not at all. You're right on time."

"The rest of our gear, helmet's, gloves, crops, and all that are in our bags outside. We usually don't put on our boots until we get to the stable, but we thought it would save time and be all right since we're just picking Kylie up and it's so late."

"That's fine, Samantha," Eric said while looking at his watch. "You know Ashley asked your Grandfather about your family taking a ride on Nantucket Sound tomorrow. It's supposed to be a spectacular day…"

As Eric looked toward the door, he did his best to hide a smile. "Well, look who's here," he added as Shane walked into the room with Joey trotting behind him as his stubby tail moved like a pendulum.

Shane stopped suddenly when he saw Charles and Samantha. He stood, mouth open studying the small group when they turned. He took off his baseball hat and smoothed his thick blonde hair with a self-conscious look. His eyes were fixed on Samantha.

For a long moment they stood, staring at each other.

Eric stole a look at Ashley who watched the subtle chemistry.

She shrugged and raised her eyebrows.

Eric was about to introduce everyone when Samantha took a small step toward Shane and smiled timidly. "Well. Hello…Lieutenant Winslow," she whispered, then held out her hand.

At first, Shane stood motionless. A smile slowly crept across his tanned face. He grasped her hand and shook it gently. "Sam." He swallowed deeply continuing to stare at her. "How…how are you?"

"Well. *Quite* well," she paused still grasping his hand. "Thanks to you."

"Well. I see you two need no introduction," Eric said watching Sam and Shane, staring at each other as if they were alone.

"No," Sam volunteered then let her hand fall away. She took a deep breath. "Shane and I are acquainted. Very well acquainted," she added, her face flushing. "Aren't we?"

Shane stood, his hand still elevated, nodding.

"Oh! Oh my God, Samantha," Charles stood transfixed. "Hello, Lieutenant. I can't believe it's you," he said closing the distance between Shane and himself.

"Yes. This is *him*." Samantha nodded as an embarrassed smile and a crimson blush spread across her face. "The Lieutenant. Our Lieutenant," she added as Charles held out his hand and beamed a broad smile at Shane.

Shane smiled back at Charles pumping the boy's hand. "My God, Charlie! You've grown up since our time together!" he said, releasing Charles' hand laughing softly and shaking his head.

"Yes. Shane, Charles, and I spent four delightful days vacationing on a life raft after Uncle Mortimer's sailboat sank," she said with a shy giggle.

Eric stood as Ashley shot a look at him.

"*Oh my God*!" She put her hand to her mouth.

"Well," Eric began putting his hand on Shane's shoulder. "This is amazing. Actually, it's perfect. I was trying to figure out who we could get to help take you out on our brand new forty-two-foot Whaler." Eric gestured toward the dock system. "You're not on duty tomorrow, are you, Shane?"

"Aaah…no. I…I'm not Eric." He stood, continuing to show a shy smile. He glanced at Charles again, but his eyes quickly returned to Samantha.

The chemistry between Shane and Samantha was obvious. He recalled Shane's heroic act as a Coast Guard officer but hadn't remembered the details. Until now. Eric suggested that since Shane had the day off, he could pilot the marina's pride and joy—their brand new forty-two-foot Boston Whaler and take Samantha, Charles, their mother, and grandfather on a day trip around the Sound.

After he let go of his stare at Samantha, Shane cleared his throat and nodded. "Sure, I'd love to if they're okay with it." Shane bent and patted his canine companion who hovered around his ankles. "This is Joey, by the way."

Sam returned Shane's blushing look. "I have a feeling that would be fine," she said approaching Joey. She bent giving his neck a tickle. He responded by licking her hand and wagging his tail.

"Oh my God. He really likes you." Shane said with a broad grin. "He's usually very shy."

"Like his owner," Sam whispered and smiled when Eric suggested that Shane take them down to the dock and show them the Whaler, so they could see their chariot for the next day's cruise.

"Will it be okay? I mean with your boots on?" Shane asked.

"We'd be delighted to have you as our tour guide, Shane," Sam said standing next to him. She shrugged and touched the baseball cap he'd been wearing.

"Kylie, honey, you go along with them. I have something I need to talk to mommy about." Eric suggested.

"Okay. Do you guys need to do some more kissing?" she asked with her hands-on hips.

"Miss Kylie Lynn Montgomery," Eric said putting on his best angry face. "If you don't stop talking about that, you won't be able to sit on a saddle for a month!"

She stood flushing and looking embarrassed, knowing immediately that her attempt at being cute had flopped—big time. "Sorry, daddy. I was...well. I was..."

Eric put his fingers to his lips and just pushed her gently after the others. "It's okay," he whispered with a wink. "Now *go!*"

As they stood watching the young people the tall man who'd been standing in the doorframe cleared his throat and knocked lightly while he entered the ships store.

He nodded and looked at Eric and Ashley. "Hello. Excuse me. I'm Misha. I work for Lord Edgerton," he said with an accent Eric couldn't place. "We met the other evening."

"Hello again," Eric said looking at him. He gestured toward the man with a shrug. "Are you enjoying the trip?"

"The scenery is spectacular, and the family has been very accommodating. Thank you for asking," he said and walked across the ship store. He took up a position near the door. The man stood trying to look casual yet poised to move at the slightest provocation, scanning the yard and the docks like a hawk might search for prey. Eric noted the man's lightweight sleeveless vest with the subtle bulge in the back. It obviously concealed a weapon.

Eric smiled at the man. He watched the girls and Shane leave the ship store then went back into Ashley's office and closed the door.

"I love your idea, by the way," Eric gave Ashley high five. "But I had no idea about the whole life raft thing with Shane, Samantha, and Charles. What are the odds?"

"Neither did I but, I'd have to say the odds are pretty low." Ashley shook her head then shrugged. "I was living in Norfolk playing computer games four years ago. I barely recall seeing something about it on the news."

Eric shook his head. "Well, I've never believed in playing matchmaker. But there was definitely something going on between them. If they stared at each other much longer, we would have had to put out a fire. And I just remembered that Sam's Grandfather told me she had a vulture for a boyfriend who bailed on her after a ski accident when she really needed some support."

"Yeah. I remember him saying that." Eric nodded and turned toward Ashley. "By the way, Ash, it's not that unusual for a family that's wealthy or well-known to have their own private security," he said looking toward Misha. "I knew some veterans who worked for private security firms after they left the Special Forces."

"Maybe there's something going on with the family—something we don't know about. We can ask the Admiral when he gets here," Ashley said as the man walked through the door on the river side.

"Well, I have no need of Earthly riches, dear. I'm

wealthy beyond imagination with my beautiful wife and daughter," Eric teased giving Ashley a quick tickle.

Ashley giggled like a schoolgirl and pushed Eric away as they went toward the river door and watched the Edgerton's interacting with Shane and Kylie.

He stood back as they got on the Whaler. Shane pointed out various things on the Whaler then pointed downriver toward the Sound. They all laughed and asked him questions. Shane stood back, answering them.

Getting on the boat looked tricky as they moved around with their riding boots. They got off with Shane's help and spent another few minutes walking around the dock system asking him more questions. Samantha stayed next to him, reacting with interest and enthusiasm to whatever he said. Kylie included herself, pointing out things of interest to Charles, beaming at him and giggling while Sam monopolized Shane.

Misha stood at the end of the float where Samantha and Charles were getting the tour and cleared his throat. "Excuse me. We should really get going so we can get back for dinner by seven-thirty."

They turned and nodded, heading as rapidly as they could up the float toward him.

Just as they reached the asphalt that bordered the docks Bobby Rodriguez appeared. He waved to Shane as they all came up the ramp.

Eric and Ashley could hear Shane introduce Bobby as the Marina's General Manager and his uncle. Samantha introduced her brother and Misha.

The group came into the ship store.

"Well, what time would you like to go out tomorrow?" Shane asked.

"Would ten be convenient?" Sam asked looking at Charles.

"Ten's fine with me. You should bring a sweatshirt or something warm," Shane suggested. "You can never tell what it will be like on the Sound. I was thinking," he looked at Eric and Bobby when he made his suggestion. "There are always some amazing yachts in Hyannis harbor and that's only a few miles. And if you want there's a great restaurant called Tugboats we could eat at."

"That's a great idea," Eric said. Bobby nodded his approval. "And since my friend here," he said nodding at Bobby, "used to run their maintenance department he could call and get you a table on their private deck."

Eric shot a look at Misha and raised his eyebrows. The tall man gave a subtle nod.

"That sounds scrumptious," Sam emoted while Charles nodded. "We have to run, but you all continue to be so kind. I feel—we all feel as if we've been adopted." She giggled then touched her brother's shoulder.

"Amen," Charles volunteered enthusiastically. "Thank you so much!"

Misha cleared his throat and looked at his watch. His tanned face showed the hint of a smile.

Sam and Charles waved good-bye.

"We'll drop Kylie by your house on the way home if that's all right," Sam said looking at Shane. "It's *so* nice to see you again," she added. "So *very* nice."

Shane stuck out his hand. "Me, too," he said quietly.

Samantha stared for a few seconds, then shook Shane's hand again and headed after Charles and Kylie.

"Sounds like a plan," Ashley said as they all waved and smiled one last time. "Now you be a perfect young lady," she told Kylie.

Eric gestured toward the security man. "He never gets a moment to himself," he said shaking his head and trying to imagine what the man's life must be like.

Eric, Ashley, Bobby, and Shane stood at the parking lot door watching the Edgerton's, Kylie, and their security person as they turned one last time.

Sam's eyes were fixed on Shane. He sighed deeply and lifted his eyes toward the sun making its way behind the trees to the west. Turning away, he let his gaze fall.

Eric looked at Shane and gave Bobby a subtle nudge.

His friend shrugged and put his arm around Shane's shoulder. "What do you say?" He began giving his nephew a little push. "Sox and Yankees at Fenway tonight. Rick Porcello is going for his tenth win!"

Shane kicked the crushed stones at the ship store entrance. "It's Wednesday night. Thanks, but there's something I have to do."

Bobby looked poised to open his mouth but apparently thought better of it. "Oh. Okay." He patted his nephew's shoulder as Shane thanked everyone and headed off toward his Jeep.

Bobby shook his head.

Eric looked at his best friend. "Wednesday night?" He shrugged. "He has a big date on Wednesday nights or something?"

Bobby shook his head again. "Nope. It's something else he does every week on Wednesdays. His mother told me about it, but it's kind of private."

Ashley touched Eric's sleeve and gave him a soft smile and a knowing look. "Don't you remember? After he left the Coast Guard because of his injury?"

"Oh, God. Yes. The first summer he was home. But that was the summer we met, and I was recovering from a bullet wound." Eric nodded. "So, that—*it* happened on a Wednesday?"

Ashley and Bobby both nodded.

"He still hasn't gotten over her?" he said quietly, shaking his head.

Ashley sighed and put her arm around his shoulder. "We all have people. People who are special in our lives. People we loved and never want to forget."

Eric put his arm around her waist and pulled her close. "Point taken." He sighed. Eric of all people could understand. He had a ghost of his own he had never quite exorcised.

Chapter Thirteen

Axe sipped on a robust Cabernet, savoring the rich bouquet and deep fruity taste on his tongue. He sat in the wood-paneled study of the large rental house assessing the progress the contractors had made in the last two days. That work had gone smoothly. Seamlessly as the Americans like to say.

He glanced at the calendar. June 18th. Less than two weeks until they executed his plan and achieved the closure he sought. Murphy had been as good as his resume promised. The plan they had devised would be both simple and foolproof. Even Axe, always thorough to the point of pessimism, could find no flaws in it.

Placing the crystal goblet on the mahogany desktop the irony struck him again. Like so many other things, his taste for fine wine had been acquired only *after* receiving the seven-figure settlement from Edgerton's ferry company. The result of the tragic accident that had torn his life apart!

Standing, he walked down the long hallway to the country kitchen then out to the deck where Ivan sat with Nicolai, his brother's best friend and the final member of his team. Dylan Murphy had spent the afternoon watching and photographing Edgerton's grandchildren while meticulously noting every movement and behavior. Since his arrival, Murphy had spent endless hours being their shadow, committing their routines and activities to memory and his tablet, while continually looking for any flaws in their security. Now confident that he could immediately recall the most simplistic detail of their lives from memory, Murphy had begun to refine the details of their plan.

"Now that you have seen the photographs of these young people," Axe began, studying Ivan and Nicolai closely. "What do you think?"

Ivan and Nicolai glanced at each other.

"About what, Ilya?" Ivan asked. He still chose to call his brother by his given name. "They are young, handsome, full of life, and you have told us they are both extremely talented."

Axe shrugged. "Our associate, Mr. Murphy, has been refining the thorough profile of their behaviors, likes, and habits," Axe said looking back and forth between the two young men. "We'll wait and find a pattern from their behavior that will enable us to finalize our plans." He nodded and raised his glass motioning to his brother. He handed a dozen pictures to Ivan and another dozen to Nicolai. "Study these for a few minutes. Murphy took them over a period of several days. He selected these as the best ones for us to examine."

Ivan studied the pictures he'd been given carefully.

Nicolai did the same with his dozen photos.

Axe gestured with his hand to indicate they should exchange. He waited patiently while the two young men studied the second group of photos and then looked at him. "Now that you've spent some time reviewing Mr. Murphy's work which would you choose to use for what we have planned?"

Ivan shot a look at Nicolai. "Based on our limited

exposure to them and looking only at these?" He held up his dozen pictures.

Axe nodded. "Yes. Suppose for a moment that your future depended on it," he continued evenly showing a curious smile.

Ivan and Nicolai looked at each other again then Ivan volunteered, "The boy. The one they call Charles."

"And your reasons?"

"We watched them for a short time ourselves and after looking at these pictures he seems the most logical. I would call him flighty—immature." He held up his hands. "He would be the better for us to take since he will be more frightened and more easily given to plead for his safe release, making our task easier."

Axe stood just smiling. "And what about you Nicolai?"

"Sir, I would choose the girl. The one called Samantha." He explained with a thoughtful look, glancing at the photos once more. "Yes. She is older and more mature, but I think we could use those qualities to reason with her. Get her to speak with her family without hysterics. That would give them confidence she would be returned safely and encourage them to handle her imprisonment quickly without any outside interference."

"Interesting," Axe nodded. Both had made a good argument. Since the tragedy and his subsequent re-birth, he had become a student of human nature. People's movements, gestures, expressions, and the words they spoke. Each had a hidden meaning and Axe had made himself an expert, now able to read each subtle change when he watched people act and behave. "You've both made fine arguments for your choices.

I'll share your thoughts with Mr. Murphy. But as with all things, the final selection may be based on chance and time. Whichever of them presents us with the best opportunity."

****

The two younger men had ordered take-out and cigarettes from a local restaurant. Axe insisted that Nicolai visit no local shops or restaurants since he still spoke with a strong accent and had a habit of engaging people in conversation. Especially young women. He lay on one of the couches in the living room watching some mindless comedy on the 52-inch wide screen. Axe had been watching and when Nicolai dozed Axe gestured to attract Ivan's attention.

He offered his brother an American cigarette and gestured toward the generous deck at the rear of the house. Marlboro was the brand Axe had grown the fondest of. He gave his brother a light. Each inhaled, drawing the smoke deeply into their lungs.

"Nicolai came highly recommended." Axe said, exhaling. He fixed Ivan with a steady stare. "Especially by you," he added, turning back toward the distant Atlantic that hid beyond the thick growth of scrub pines and hardwoods.

"Brother," Ivan began. "I noticed your look earlier when we viewed the pictures." He put his hand on the railing then inhaled his cigarette.

"Yes," Axe said quietly while he continued to stare at the new moon as its reflection began to sparkle on the wave tops some miles distant. "He studied the pictures of the girl at length. Seemed almost reluctant when I asked for them back." Axe extinguished his cigarette, shook his head then added, "And he suggested we take her as our prisoner. I purposely left them on the coffee table and found him studying her pictures again."

Ivan nodded and watched his brother intently as Axe stared at the moon's distant glow.

"I become concerned with anything that may cause us a problem," Axe continued. "Anything that will interfere with the completion of the project. And so far, he has shown me very little, brother. At least nothing that would indicate he deserves his share of the ransom."

Before Ivan had the time to respond Axe turned toward his brother. "I know this man was your friend. But you know I have developed well-honed instincts. A sixth sense if you will. I must be sure that he doesn't think that our... guest is a plaything. Something to enjoy if or when we look the other way. Bear in mind that if he displays any behavior that suggests that, I will not hesitate to see that he becomes another victim of this event."

"I understand. Completely," Ivan assured him.

Axe nodded then patted his brother's shoulder, crushed out his cigarette, and carefully put the butt into the large tub filled with sand that sat near them. He nodded and turned, heading back into the house.

Chapter Fourteen

"You really had no idea who she was?" Eric asked, turning toward Ashley.

"Of course not. Why would I have kept somethin' like that a secret'?" she said putting her hands on her hips. "And how would I have known?" she added, frowning. "Computers I can read like a book, darlin'. But clairvoyance is not in my bag of tricks."

Eric sighed. "It wasn't an accusation, Ash. But my God. It is one hell of a coincidence." He shrugged.

"How could she have known?" Bobby interrupted quietly, following Shane with his eyes. "How could anyone? He hadn't seen her since they dismounted from the Jayhawk in Florida four years ago. When he came home for his convalescent leave Shane told me she tried to see him, but he came home to Emily and well…" he left the thought hanging.

Eric and Ashley joined Bobby watching Shane head to his Jeep.

****

Shane looked at his watch. Five-forty-five. "Come on buddy," he said giving Joey a nod and turning to give them a wave.

His golden cocker spaniel and best friend followed obediently at his heels.

Shane let him into the oversize cab, running his finger across the door when he closed it. "Time for a good wash," he said absently to Joey as he rounded the tailgate and got into the driver's seat.

The Jeep was a present from his parents when he'd graduated from the Coast Guard Academy. A proud day for them. It had taken a long time for his family to return to some semblance of normalcy after losing his older brother, Evan, in the Second Gulf War. Receiving the Medal of Honor posthumously did little to replace him at the Thanksgiving dinner table or on Christmas morning.

Shane's family was small but close. Incredibly close. His parents, Evan, and his sister Sue Ellen, who taught High School English in Sandwich, always spent as much time together as possible. Since Evan's death they'd grown closer.

Shane headed down Pleasant Street, turned right onto Route 28 for half a mile, crossed the Bass River Bridge and took the first right onto Uncle Barney's Road. When he reached a community called Wrinkle Point, he drove another quarter mile then turned into his family's driveway.

Shane sat trying to get his mind around seeing her again. Sam. He'd thought of her so often. Dreaming and fantasizing about what it would be like to see her. Be near her again. It had been four years, but she'd never left him. Samantha was always there, a lovely captivating ghost waiting for him in his imagination and dreams. He had no idea what to do or how to react. Yes. Part of him was thrilled at the prospect of seeing Samantha and spending time with her again. But seeing her again brought back another emotion. Guilt. An emotion he'd been carrying for four years.

The Winslow home was a long ranch with a

second-floor addition that spanned the main part of the house. More than half the homes in Wrinkle Point had been bought by affluent families who did a tear-down—completely knocking down their modest purchases and replacing them with mammoth two-story "trophy houses" filled with state-of-the-art technology and conveniences. But despite some concerns as the old houses fell one by one, Shane and his parents found their new neighbors caring and friendly for the most part.

"Oh, come on," he said to Joey when he opened the door. "I'm not going to carry you," he added doing his best to put his thoughts of Samantha and what it meant out of his mind. Joey followed obediently, wagging his stubby tail like a pendulum.

"I'm home," he yelled when he entered the generous kitchen that spanned the entire left side of the house.

"Either you or a burglar," his mother said appearing from the laundry carrying a pile she deposited in Shane's hands. "Glad it was you. Dad's shotgun's upstairs," she grinned, standing on tiptoes, and planting a kiss on his cheek. "You're going on your …," she paused, hesitating and backing away while holding her son's eyes. "Are you visiting her tonight?" his mother added quietly while she studied his face.

Shane nodded. "Yep," he said, scanning the kitchen to avoid her stare. "Then I'm gonna visit Cal. But I'll be back right after the Sox game. Okay?"

"Course," she said patting his back. "You're a big boy, son. I trust you. No need to give me your itinerary."

He mounted the stairs and put his clean clothes on

his dresser. He jumped in the shower, turning the water to hot and soak away the cares of the day. When he emerged, he spent five minutes with his electric razor then quickly changed into a pair of khaki shorts, a T-shirt from the Academy, his sandals then headed back downstairs. When Joey stopped eating and looked up at him, Shane shook his head. "No, buddy. I'm making this trip solo."

Joey stared up at his master with sad eyes then seemed to sigh before he resumed his dinner.

Shane laughed softly after leaving the kitchen. His mother relaxed on their broad deck with a glass of red wine. She sat west, facing the sun as it made its way toward the horizon. It was only a week before the summer solstice so sunset wouldn't occur for almost three and a half hours.

"I never get tired of this," she said, reaching out.

Shane offered his hand.

She took it and squeezed it tightly. "Your rose is on the table. I especially liked this one and kept it in water since I cut it after lunch from the trellis next to the garage." She took a deep breath and released her grip on his hand. "If you don't mind, I...I'd like to come with you one of these nights."

"All right," Shane agreed as he followed her eyes and watched the boat traffic passing lazily by. The neighborhood dock was home to two dozen boats a few hundred yards to the west. He and his siblings had been so fortunate. Growing up in this spectacular place with so many remarkable views and things to occupy them. Shane gave thanks every night for his good fortune. The sun's orange glow still hung about twenty degrees above the expensive homes that lined the Yarmouth side of the river. But as Shane sat down, he saw it begin to work its way into the evening clouds that hung, hiding just above the treetops.

His mind drifted back to late afternoon again, recalling his reunion with Samantha. If that was the right name for their meeting. She seemed just the way he remembered her: bright, full of life, and cute. *Very* cute. And she'd been so attentive.

Yes, Shane knew that she had tried to find him. Perhaps to thank him. Perhaps because of their obvious chemistry. But when Shane closed his eyes his mind turned to something else—the vivid recollection of a February night. The February night when he'd lost *Emily.*

His mother touched his arm. "You okay?" she asked, looking at him.

"It's probably just my motherly instincts, but I worry about you sometimes."

Shane stood and nodded. "Thanks, mom." He touched her cheek gently. "No need. I'm fine," he assured her. He took the rose from the small vase, holding it as if it was fragile—that it might break if he held it too tightly. A delicate treasure for her. "Fine," he repeated to himself, turning and heading around the house to his Jeep.

Fine, he sighed and repeated the assurance to himself.

Chapter Fifteen

Early Evening—NIRA Offices, Washington, D.C.

The Admiral stood behind his mammoth desk, studying the four twenty-seven-inch monitors that faced him. The mahogany that had once shone brightly now hid, dulled and cluttered beneath piles of folders and his state-of-the-art technology array, its surface marred by scars, stains, and discolorations from a decade of constant use.

Two of the monitors showed the latest news feeds from across the world: CNN, Fox News, MSNBC, Sky News, Al Jazeera, and others. The screen on his extreme right displayed information from news outlets the US considered friends or allies, the one on his left the opposite. The incoming feeds were monitored twenty-four hours a day by the NIRA's communications team housed deep in the bowels of their headquarters building.

Each communications team consisted of at least three members—a team leader and two technician-analysts. When a crisis occurred, the teams might swell to five or more. Displays in the Admiral's office could also be shown in split screen—divided into quarters if the situation demanded.

Their sophisticated software, extensive training, and years of experience was used to analyze the constantly incoming news feeds, prioritizing it so that a new display could appear every thirty seconds. The Admiral had the ability to freeze any feed using voice commands or a remote. This luxury was an option available on the monitors of all the NIRA's regional team leaders, his Deputy Jon Milton, and his Executive Assistant, Jeanie Flynn. The feeds and attendant stories they showed could be immediately downloaded, stored, or recalled from one of three dedicated servers within twenty seconds—again using either verbal or manual commands.

NIRA was divided into seven separate work groups based on geography—one assigned to each continent. Approximately half of their staff was assigned to work on specific assignments—shadowing persons of interest, following leads from other intel agencies, or performing research. The remainder were assigned to their general geographic areas. Agents and the teams they formed had regional field offices and headquarters on six of the seven continents. Antarctica being the one exception.

One of the two remaining monitors in the Admiral's office was reserved for communications directly from the field. This was also filtered through the NIRA field communications team in the sub-basement four floors below. Their work area looked like a cluttered version of the mission control set in a sci-fi movie or a political thriller. And while this information was filtered and prioritized to *some* extent using technology, the use of humint or human intelligence gathering as it had been known for decades was by no means dead. NIRA team members were not zealots who prayed at the altar of technology. They were schooled tirelessly in the most advantageous way to combine and best utilize state of the art electronics while never losing sight of the value of a well-honed agent's intellect, experience, and sensory input.

The fourth screen was reserved for the Admiral's agency communications. He received endless emails and communiques marked 'Classified' or 'Top-Secret.' While he had the option to view these unilaterally, he opted to allow his Deputy Director and his Chief Assistant to share in their receipt. He trusted both implicitly—with his life if it came to that. Though in the ugly, often dysfunctional political climate that currently filled the Nation's Capital during this election year, the danger was far greater from those intent on attacking everyone and anyone in power.

Their office sat in an inconspicuous three-story building less than a mile from the White House. The location was chosen since the Admiral and his staff sometimes needed personal access to its occupants at all hours of the day or night at a moment's notice. This was to be expected when you led the incredibly talented three-hundred men and women of the country's most clandestine intelligence operation. They were not the largest. Far from it. They were diminutive when compared with the vast size and resources of the CIA, FBI, NSA, and several others. But in the rare and frightening case that the President and Joint Chiefs raised America's threat level to Defcon One—war status—a state of the art tunnel stretched the fifteen-hundred yards between the NIRA offices, the White House, and its Sit or Situation Room. While the Admiral and other top members of his staff *had* used the tunnel to quickly gain secret access to the President and members of his staff on occasion, he gave thanks every day that they had never used it for its ultimate purpose.

Unlike many of its grander and more notorious siblings NIRA never found itself in the public media. The Admiral and his staff did everything to avoid it. He had once observed he would find it difficult to lead a truly covert organization effectively if they found themselves named and critiqued in the NY Times and Washington Post several times a week. The evolution of the twenty-four-hour news cycle dramatically increased the public exposure of those larger agencies exponentially, often inhibiting their ability to perform their primary task effectively in secret. The Admiral had observed it would be difficult to maintain a clandestine presence when you're constantly being thrust into and second-guessed in the public eye.

The Admiral lifted his attention from the monitor when Jeanie Flynn entered his office. She was his confidant, most trusted ally, and best friend within the organization. Like most of the senior staff, Jeanie entered without knocking. She and the Admiral had the kind of working relationship seldom seen but always sought in any place of employment. Even more essential since their job involved the integrity and safety of the United States.

Jeanie glided in and out of the Admiral's office casually, taking advantage of the latitude. A slender brunette with dimples carved into her cheeks, Jeanie's abbreviated haircut sported a collection of small wispy curls that covered her sculpted ears. Despite the long hours Jeanie spent at the Agency, seeing her was always a pleasure for her co-workers since her good looks and glowing personality never failed to draw attention or bring a smile. At thirty-eight, she was fifteen years the Admiral's junior. Divorced with no children some mused that she actually lived at a hidden location within their offices since her hours seemed endless. Jeanie seemed to appear instantly when the Admiral called regardless of the time.

The Admiral had assumed command and revived NIRA after it had suffered a slow decline, becoming a sad and unproductive enclave for researchers and over-the-hill agents who had migrated after falling from grace at one of the more public and high-profile Intelligence Services.

After evaluating what he'd inherited, the Admiral had cleaned house. But rather than let the state of the NIRA bring on frustration its new chief had brought in fresh talent from the country's most prestigious schools and think tanks. Confidence and pride grew. The Admiral had a hands-on management style, an uncanny, almost psychic ability to assess threats, and an equally uncanny ability to find fresh talent and get the most out of it.

Within three years the success his new talent and management style engendered had made the organization the envy of the other seventeen intelligence agencies and guided it deftly through three diverse administrations. Yes, NIRA had grown and prospered in a way no one could have imagined two decades earlier. And in doing so the agency had gained the respect of the three Presidents they'd served.

"Anything worth note?" Jeanie asked, though the Admiral was certain she had seen the same scarcity of anything significant on her screens.

He flopped down into his chair. "My damn back is killing me. Does that count?" he asked shaking his head.

"No, sir, it doesn't" Jeanie offered when she put his evening coffee on his desk. "I'm your Senior Assistant not an ER doctor," she added, hiding a coy smile.

"Maybe I get confused because you fawn over me like a damn grandmother. Why do you do that?" he asked, nodding toward the steaming cup. "I worry that a couple of these hotshot young women from the Ivy League will appear outside my office picketing, accusing me of being a sexist who dwells in the past."

"Don't worry. They already know you are," she said evenly showing him a blank expression. She raised her eyebrows placing a Tramadol prescription bottle on the desk. "Take one," Jeanie ordered, adding as conversation returned to business, "Still a lot of activity in France and the low countries after the terrorist attacks. A lot of busy chatter after Brexit. Santos is still trying to work a deal in Colombia; Russia, Assad, Syria…"

"I've read the feeds. Is it possible the world will take a vacation, so I can enjoy Independence Day with the Montgomery's and the Edgerton's?" he asked with a smile. "Still nothing new on our old friend Lassiter?" he said watching Jeanie sit gracefully in one of the stiff visitor's chairs.

She shook her head. "Is Cape Cod really the place a world-class operator like him would be working?"

"I don't know," the Admiral answered thoughtfully. "I had the same question," he said after taking a small sip from his coffee cup, popping the Tramadol in his mouth while smiling. No one could make his coffee as well as Jeanie. "You wouldn't think so, but don't forget three years ago—the adventure we had with Eric and Ashley. Who would have suspected that a major domestic terrorist would end up *there?*" he offered, glancing back and forth at the screens. "Don't forget what we've learned the hard way. The old paradigm no longer applies," he added shaking his head. "Every time we think we've figured out how the bad guys work they invent a simpler better way to spread terror and destruction."

"You're right." Jeanie nodded. "Almost five-million people cross the access bridges to Cape Cod every summer. That's one hell of a target population."

"It is, but I still don't know. You said it earlier. His style doesn't lend itself to mass terror," The Admiral said raising his eyebrows. "He's into more focused things. I don't see his talents being utilized for a terrorist event. And the only person he's seen since he's been on the Cape—outside of the few incidental conversations at his hotel—is that man." The Admiral nodded toward the pictures that lay in his in box. "And I can't tell who he is by these pictures. We've had no hits on facial recognition software." He sat down heavily. "I'm going down there and check him out in person. Remember I'll be there taking my first vacation in four years."

"Yes, you are," Jeanie said with a frown. "Can't leave the bird-dogging to Mendes, Merritt, and their team, eh?" She shook her head. "That's some vacation."

"Yes." He found her eyes. She began to speak but he held up his hand. "Before you tell me I shouldn't be out doing field work with two-hundred-eighty plus professionals sitting out there," he began. Standing he went to the foggy window that offered views of the Capital. "I know we have a good team watching him. Merritt's proven himself repeatedly. And this young man Mendes. I like him. A lot. Not one of these recruits who want to be the next Jason Bourne or James Bond," he added with a hint of pride.

When he turned, Jeanie's face showed frustration. Anger perhaps? "Damn it," she said crossing the office to the door, shut it quietly then turned to face him. "You take too many chances, Brian," she said in an annoyed whisper. She never used his first name. "We don't want to lose you or see you get injured again when one of our agents could do the job." She sighed deeply. "*I*...*I* don't want to lose you or see you injured."

The Admiral continued holding her eyes. She had such wonderful eyes, he had thought so often. "You worry too much." He shrugged. "You know somehow I managed to take care of myself for almost a decade before you arrived on the scene," he said letting a smile creep across his face.

"No. I don't know that," she said, sighing deeply. "Actually, you were wounded three times and thrown from a moving train. That little adventure gave you the bad back you take Tramadol for. Once you were in Intensive Care for a month. Correct, Brian?"

He had no idea how she knew things that took place fifteen years ago or more.

"Fine! Go ahead," she continued, her cheeks flushing. "Take your working vacation. Just remember. If you *do* get hurt, do *not* expect me to come, visit you in the hospital, and hand you more pills while you're recovering!"

He shrugged. "You know I'll be on Cape Cod anyway visiting the Montgomery's and one of my oldest friends, James Edgerton."

She twisted her mouth into a pout. "Yes, sir," she said loudly. "Since you'll be leaving in two days, I'll be taking my vacation, too. I have eight weeks accumulated leave." She shook her head. "And unless you object, I'd like to start tomorrow morning." She stood fixing him with a stare that said what? Concern. Friendship? Even affection?

When he said nothing, Jeanie headed toward the door. She stopped before she opened it. Her face flushed. Her lip trembled. "Have a safe trip, *sir*," she said in a whisper.

"You, too, Ms. Flynn," he said in a weak voice.

The Admiral was tempted to follow her. That would have been a mistake. Wouldn't it? He sat down and took a deep breath watching her slender figure retreat through the door. He thought the world of Jeanie. Had for years and not exclusively for her professional expertise. She was lovely, brilliant. Yes, Brian Turner, aka The Admiral, had feelings for his prim dedicated assistant despite the years that separated them. Strong feelings. But despite her constant attention and the things she did to spoil him he never dared imagine she might feel affection. Care for him. Part of him was thrilled, flattered that this younger woman had shown him she did. That her feelings went beyond their professional relationship.

He sat transfixed, staring after her. When he'd lost Ellen and the children, he'd steeled himself. Become hard, burying his emotions. He'd promised himself he would let this job, this place, and the holy quest he'd embarked on consume him. Suddenly the dam broke at Jeanie's show of concern and affection, propelling him into a whirlpool of conflicting feelings. A new and different reality. Yes. Part of him was thrilled. Another part was terrified!

Chapter Sixteen

The Tahoe Samantha and Gretchen rode in pulled into the Montgomery's driveway at six-forty-five. Sam dismounted as Kylie got out of the back where she'd been sitting next to Charles. She and Charles walked with Kylie up the long gravel walk to the front door. Kylie looked at Ashley and waved with a broad grin.

"Oh my God, Charles is such an *amazing* rider," Kylie enthused to her mother.

"So I've heard," Ashley nodded. Their ever-doting grandfather had spent much of their first dinner together extolling Sam's excellence on the ski slopes and Charles' in the show ring. "How long did your grandfather tell us you've been riding?" Ashley asked Charles.

"Since I was four," Charles said quietly, averting her eyes, and flushing as Samantha put her arm around his shoulder with a proud smile.

"Charlie is very dedicated and *very* driven. He loves to compete and wants to be perfect every time he gets into the saddle," she said as they reached the front porch. "Lives for it. Don't you, little brother?"

"Please, Sam." Charles admitted as his flush grew crimson. "Yes of course, but you're embarrassing me," he added in a whisper.

"Daddy, we're home," Kylie said through the screen door. Turning to ask Charles, "How much time do you spend training every day?"

"Please Kylie. I told you earlier. Call me Charlie," he insisted. "And as to my training," he paused and grew a thoughtful expression. "Probably five to six hours, but that includes working out and time spent working around the five mounts we have. My favorite is Romeo—a wonderful thoroughbred I often compete on," he said, smiling at Kylie who couldn't take her eyes off him.

Ashley nodded. "I hope you had a good time," she said standing in the doorway.

"Wonderful. Kylie was a delight," Sam said with enthusiasm. "And for someone who's been riding for less than two years she's a fine rider. Downright amazing."

"She's just being nice," Kylie said, shaking her head. "But mommy, you should have seen Charlie. He looks like the riders I've seen on TV at those fancy riding competitions."

"Charlie, eh? We're getting very informal, Aren't we?" Ashley asked.

"Oh, please Ms. Montgomery. I insisted she call me that." Charles explained.

"Well. Do you want to come in?" Ashley asked gesturing to the door. "Maybe Misha would like a drink or snack."

Misha stood ever attentive a few paces from the Tahoe. He waved off her offer.

"No. Thanks very much. We really must get back and get cleaned up for dinner. Poppy's quite the task-master when it comes to eating dinner on time." Sam grinned. "Must be the sailor in him. And by the way, thank you for arranging the cruise tomorrow." She enthused. "We're looking forward to it so much."

"Oh my God. Who would have believed that you, Shane, and Charles knew each other?" Ashley shook her head. "That's just plain other-worldly!"

"Completely other-worldly." Samantha managed. "So." She stood for a minute.

Charles shook hands with Ashley then turned back toward the Tahoe.

"Oh, Ashley Jean," Sam said softly, closing the space between them. "I was wondering…"

Ashley came out onto the front steps. "Sure, honey, do you need something else?"

"Well. I have a question." Sam said standing in front of her. She looked down at the steps. "I…I was wondering. About Shane?"

Ashley looked curious. "Yes. About Shane. What can I tell you? He's such a wonderful young man." She sighed and touched Sam's shoulder. "Sort of a local hero. But I assume you of all people must know that he was awarded the Coast Guard Medal?"

"Yes, I know he was. We were all there. Charlie, me, Uncle Mortimer, and cousin Holly." She gestured toward Charles who nodded. "Though he didn't know it." Sam blushed. "When you spend four days in a life raft with someone you get to know them. Or at least you think you do," she added with a gentle laugh. "There's something I'd like to know."

Ashley shrugged as Kylie stood next to her.

Kylie put her arm around her mother's waist.

"All right," Ashley agreed. "What would you like to know?"

"Perhaps I'm intruding. He's delightful, charming, handsome—" Sam shrugged. "But not quite the way I remember him. He seemed very—shy. Distant perhaps?" Sam asked, feeling her face flush. "After we were rescued, I tried to find him. To thank him for—" she let the thought hang in mid-air then added, "But, well, his commanding officer told me he was getting married."

Ashley shifted her eyes toward Kylie. "Honey, could you go inside and get daddy," she said giving her daughter a squeeze.

Kylie loosened her grip and nodded, scampering off into the house.

"Yes. You're right, Sam." Ashley began not sure what and how much of Shane's life to share with her new friend. "Shane's had his share of sadness," Ashley said evenly while watching the door. "More than his share, I'd say," she paused. "His family lost his older brother, Evan. An Army officer killed in Iraq. Shane resigned his Coast Guard commission because of his injury and after he came home there was a…a terrible accident," she finished in a whisper.

Kylie came back out with Eric. "Here he is, Mommy." She grinned with satisfaction.

"Tell me, babe. Samantha was asking what time they'll be back, tomorrow?" Ashley asked Eric subtly nodding in Kylie's direction.

"Ah, yes. I wanted to go to Chatham. I've heard they have some delightful places to shop there," Sam understood and played along with the charade.

"Oh. Well, if Shane is any kind of a tour guide you should be back by mid-afternoon and most of their shops are open well into the evening this time of year," Eric explained.

"Well, it's been another scrumptious day. And you

continue to treat us like family, don't they Charlie?" Samantha said touching Ashley's forearm. "So." She sighed. "Have a nice evening and we'll see you tomorrow!"

She and Charlie walked quickly back to the Tahoe. Sam mounted the running board and settled into the front seat while he took the seat behind her.

Both waved and smiled as they pulled out of the driveway.

"What were you trying to get at?" Charles asked, touching his sister's shoulder gently.

When she twisted around, he showed her a puzzled expression.

"Just a question. Something I wondered about Shane," she answered thoughtfully.

Charles bent forward and put his head on the seat back smiling softly. "You're very fond of him, aren't you, Sam? Always have been."

She knew he'd heard what Ashley had told her about Shane. Sam assumed from Ashley's behavior there was more. Whatever it was she didn't want to share it while Kylie was within hearing distance.

"Bye. See you soon, Kylie," Sam called out loudly, opening her window and waving again to the little girl who stood in the door

Charles waved as well and yelled out a hearty, "Bye!"

Sam put her head back on the seat rest. "You heard her. His life has had more than its share of sadness and tragedy."

"Well, it was obvious that he was delighted to see you again, Sam." Charles patted her shoulder softly. "Maybe you can help change that." He sat back, fastened his seat belt, and closed his eyes.

"And yes. I liked him very much. You know that. Shane was a dream. As handsome and charming as anyone I've ever met, Charlie," Sam said softly fastening her own seat belt, studying the scenery as they passed Nantucket Sound. "And that's so sad about him leaving the service." She put her head back and glanced at Misha who showed her a smile. *There was something deep and mysterious behind those tempting eyes*, she thought while she yawned. *Yes. Definitely deep and mysterious, but there was more than that. Much more. There was deep sadness there, too.* Sam mused, yawning again and closed her eyes.

****

A deep sadness and something more. Something Sam couldn't begin to guess. Something Shane had never shared with anyone...

Chapter Seventeen

Axe sat at his desk reviewing the plan he'd been working on for many months. Endless days and sleepless nights while he studied the Edgerton's, planned his actions, and envisioned justice. That decision—the one to find closure following the tragic loss he had suffered six years earlier came while he recovered from his injuries. But the plot he envisioned needed funds. Significant funds.

He had waited patiently through the endless litigious process until the penalties, fines, and eventual settlements were paid by Lord Edgerton's company. After the initial verdict ruled in favor of the plaintiffs—or victims—the anticipated appeals were short. They lasted only fifteen months. Perhaps because the fault was so clearly beyond debate. Nineteen deaths, sixty-seven serious injuries, and more than one hundred hospitalizations. All because of outdated, poorly maintained equipment, non-existent safety procedures, and violations the company had regularly paid government inspectors to overlook.

Edgerton had made the expected appearances offering tear-filled public apologies and heartfelt condolences to the victims. Though it represented a mere fraction of his enormous business empire and he was not found personally culpable in any way, Edgerton pledged to personally supervise discharges, guaranteed improvements, and made promises to correct all the problems with his ferry company. Despite his apparently sincere anguish and regret over the tragic accident within a few weeks, rumors began to circulate that Lord James was not the bastion of honor and selfless commitment he appeared.

The plan Axe looked at was for a small room the workers were roughing out in the basement of his rented house. It would be 10' wide by 12' long by 8' high. It would be an airtight, soundproofed cell. A prison for one of Edgerton's grandchildren. He or she would be sealed into the air-tight chamber and left there while the electronic equipment Lassiter installed displayed their plight to the family. Most especially their grandfather. Lassiter would not only install the state-of-the-art video and sound systems but would make sure that the transmissions were sufficiently scrambled, so they could not be traced.

And of course, the standard age-old threat would be present: any sign of involvement by police, the FBI, or the private security the Edgerton family now employed would result in a terrible fate for the captive. They would be left to die of slow suffocation in the air-tight prison while the family watched his or her desperate struggle. Though he would not tell the Edgerton family Axe had a small air fan to supply and circulate the air in the chamber in case the family had difficulty raising the substantial ransom he would demand. Yes, despite the Edgerton family's substantial assets raising millions of US dollars in a few days would be a difficult task.

Axe put down his plan for the small room and surveyed the accompanying document for the hundredth time. It's title: *The Results of Long-Term Oxygen Deprivation and Buildup of Carbon Dioxide*. It was a scientific paper describing in graphic terms how long a person could live with a limited supply of breathable air and the subsequent increase in deadly carbon dioxide.

While he stared lost in a cruel reverie his cell phone buzzed. Axe pushed talk.

"Hello," he answered in a quiet tone. Lassiter. Calling after only a few hours. Axe hoped this meant good news.

"Hello. I'm sorry to bother you a second time today but I knew you'd want to hear the good news. My supplier called to tell me he'll be bringing material for your new storage room tomorrow," he explained. "I still have three small pieces that he has yet to deliver. Can I store what I have in your garage while we wait for the final components?" Lassiter asked.

Of course, the conversation was veiled and vague in the unlikely event that someone was listening. Though Axe felt certain that a top-level operative like Lassiter would insure that did not happen.

"Certainly, Mr. Lassiter," Axe agreed amicably. "We have plenty of room and my guests and I don't use the garage except to store our bicycles. There is some heavy shelving and two cabinets. The men working on the downstairs were using it, but they've removed their materials, so it's all yours."

"Fine. I'll call you about an hour before I'm coming by," Lassiter told him.

"Excellent. And of course, we have strong locks and the alarm system is tied into the doors and windows out there."

"All right then. See you tomorrow. I'll be here all day. And thanks." Axe hung up the phone. "Ivan," he called out to his brother on the back deck.

"Be right there," Ivan answered.

When his brother came into the study, Axe pointed toward the garage, visible through the large bay window. "Make sure the workmen downstairs have removed all their building materials from the garage," he instructed. "And also make sure the shelving and cabinets are cleaned. We have a delivery coming tomorrow and the equipment is sensitive. It cannot be damaged."

"Yes," Ivan said and nodded.

"Where's Nicolai?"

"Oh…he went to the store to buy more beer and snacks," Ivan said as he headed toward the basement door.

"Wait a minute," Axe said angrily. "I told you that I do not want him going to the store. He has an accent. A strong one. He also has a long stringy beard and his arms are covered with offensive tattoos that will draw attention…"

"I know. But we thought that he could frequent several different stores. Then no one would become suspicious. You know if they only saw him once or…" Ivan stopped in mid-sentence as Axe stood clenching his fist and pounded the mahogany desk so hard his pen and letter opener fell to the floor.

Axe shook his head and closed his eyes. "The next time one of you disobeys my instructions there will be…*consequences!*" He said the word as though it were profane. *"Do you understand?"* he thundered then crossed the room and closed the thick six-panel door.

"Do you think I spent years planning this and studying the Edgerton family so an imbecile like your friend could *fuck it up*?" He asked keeping his anger contained so as not to make too much noise while the workers finished below. Fortunately, their hammering and sawing served to mute his outburst.

"N...no, brother," Ivan said backing away trembling.

Axe turned around and fixed his brother with a damning look. "I warned you about him a few days ago. This is my last admonition."

Ivan nodded and held up his hands. "I understand. I give you my word," he whispered adding, "I'll speak to him again."

"If *I* have to speak about this again, I will have—" Axe stopped closing his hand tightly around Ivan's arm. "No! *We* will have to deal with him!"

Ivan nodded and opened the door backing out. He almost stumbled when he pulled away from Axe.

"You should begin finishing the room tomorrow morning. It will be sealed, and you will soundproof it with the materials in the basement," Axe ordered, regaining his composure.

He stood cursing his own stupidity. After all he had done to plan this project, he had been a fool. Despite all the study, research, and observations his one mistake, his blind spot had been trusting the only family he had left—the younger brother he loved so desperately. The only tie that remained to his former life.

Chapter Eighteen

"Mommy, can I go next door to Lola's?" Kylie asked looking back and forth between Ashley and Eric. "I want to tell her who I went riding with this afternoon."

Ashley looked at her watch. "Sure, sweetie. Just be home by eight o'clock."

"Thanks." Kylie nodded and took her plate to the kitchen sink. She came back and gave each of them a quick kiss. Her face grew a curious look. "Are Sam and Charlie…royalty?"

"No," Ashley told her when she'd finished her last bite of barbecued chicken. "Their grandfather is a Lord. I think he's an Earl which is pretty high on the chain of English royalty," she explained. "Maybe you and Lola can Google it and tell me when you come home. I probably should have done that, so I don't look like a dummy in front of our guests."

"No one would ever mistake you for a dummy, *dearest*," Eric offered with an unctuous grin.

Ashley shook her head and threw her napkin at him.

"Okay, sounds good. Thanks. I'll be home by eight-fifteen," Kylie said with a broad smile.

Ashley enjoyed that Kylie always laughed at their playful antics. She shook her head and held up eight fingers, mouthing the words, "*Eight o'clock.*"

Kylie screwed her face into a frown but then laughed and ran off and out the kitchen door.

Ashley waved and smiled broadly shaking her head. She gave thanks every day that her daughter had so many advantages. Advantages she'd never had as a little girl: a boat of her own to sail, a home fronting on Nantucket Sound, horseback riding, a great school, and wonderful collection of friends. But they did have one thing in common. Kylie had demonstrated from an early age that she'd inherited Ashley's other-worldly abilities with anything electronic.

"Eric," Ashley said after she heard the screen door slam shut and Kylie's footsteps grow faint.

"What's up?" he asked looking up from his cell phone.

"You know you spend hours looking at that phone every day now?"

He reached over, took her hand, and squeezed it showing her a shrug. "Hmmm. Who insisted that I run for selectman and then become the Chairperson? Let me try to…"

"Yes, all right. I did," Ashley interrupted, pulling her hand away roughly and holding it up. "But you can put some blame on your BFF Bobby, too,"

"Okay," Eric leaned back and looked out at Nantucket Sound in the distance. "Sorry, but another few months of this—this petty personality shit and I'm going to pass the torch on. I agree. This is consuming my life. Our lives." He touched her arm gently. "Now. What did you want to talk about?" he added as his tone softened.

"Sorry. And touché." Ashley shook her head then reached for his hand. "Truce," she said with a gentle smile. "I was thinkin' about Shane," she began quietly knowing she might be going into dark territory.

"Okay. Is there a problem?"

"Well, I'm not sure." She shook her head. "I know it's been three years since he lost Emily. And everyone thought—hoped—he'd move on."

Eric sat back turning toward her. His face showed no emotion. "All right. And?"

She sat searching his face—his eyes—knowing the subject was sensitive. "I like Shane a lot and it's obvious Samantha seems interested in him. Very interested," she repeated looking out to Nantucket Sound.

"I could see that," Eric agreed. "That's really amazing about them knowing each other from the hurricane four years ago. Like something out of a novel. But since you say he should move on I'm not sure why that's a problem. My God, Ash. She's talented, brilliant, and beautiful. Her family is English royalty. And the fact that she seems to really like him a lot is certainly a plus."

"That's all true, Eric. But Sam comes from a different world." Ashley knew she had to tread lightly. This was sensitive territory. Déjà vu again for Eric. He'd lost his wife, childhood sweetheart, and their unborn child in an auto accident the year before they met—eerily similar to the way Shane had lost his fiancé Emily. She also knew Eric blamed himself for the tragic accident that took the life of his wife and unborn baby. "Look, darlin' if this is someplace I shouldn't go you have to…"

He leaned forward and took her hand squeezing it. "Ashley. It's all right. I moved on." Eric found her eyes and showed a gentle smile. "I never told you this. Never told anyone." He took a deep breath. "It took me a long time to realize it. Elaine was wonderful. She was beautiful, sensitive, and so damn smart. But I came to realize after—after *we* found each other that, well...despite all her wonderful qualities we were different. Very different."

Ashley leaned toward him, caressing his hand. "Different. How?" There were times when she looked deep into his eyes and surveyed Eric's perfect face that she still wanted to grab him and beg him to ravish her. Or vice-versa.

"I came to realize that we'd found each other in middle school. The cutest cheerleader and the captain of all the sports teams. So naturally, we gravitated toward each other. It was never that we really had common interests." He raised his thick eyebrows. "I mean it was easy to want to be with her. I assume it was the same for her."

"I don't want to disparage your memory of Elaine, darlin' but..." Ashley twisted her face into a frown. "Can you get to the part where you tell me that what we found together was...was better? What you'd been searching for your whole life?"

He smiled broadly. "I was just about to. And you were. You are." He stood and pulled her up putting his arms around her. "I don't want to resort to cliché's but you're my soul mate, Ash. It's like we think each other's thoughts."

As he leaned toward Ashley's lips, her cell phone buzzed. "Shit!" she said. Ashley looked. It was Kylie.

She mouthed the word 'Kylie,' pressed talk, and backed away from Eric. "Hi, honey." She listened and then smiled broadly while she nodded. "Okay. But be home by nine-thirty. You're helping us at the marina tomorrow. Be good. Say hi to Mr. Goodwin and thank him."

"They're going for ice cream," she told him with a grin that teased. "Okay, getting' back to Shane and Sam, I'll play along and pray that they have fun and that well, maybe Sam can bring Shane back to the world again." She raised her eyebrows and sighed. "I think she may be the cutest thing I ever laid eyes on."

"Oh! My goodness, Ms. Fitzhugh." He closed the two feet between them. "I thought I was the cutest thing you'd ever laid eyes on."

"Oh, my God, Mr. Montgomery. Something happens when you use my maiden name." She showed him the most delicious smile she could muster and batted her lashes. "And no, Eric. You're strong, handsome, and the sexiest man I've ever met but cute? No way!"

"How long 'fore Kylie gets home?"

"At least an hour." She smiled broadly.

"Well," he said pulling her close and found her lips. "Yummy. You taste delicious. Just like barbecued chicken and corn on the cob."

"Let's go upstairs. I'll brush if…"

"No need. They're my favorite foods and besides, I can't wait that long!" Eric took her by the hand, and they headed upstairs…

****

…Kylie had called from Lola's when they returned from getting their ice cream and asked if she could stay overnight. Ashley insisted she come home and take a shower since Kylie had been at the marina and then at

126

the stables most of the day. She agreed and after Ashley gave her a backpack with shorts, T-shirt, toothbrush, and a few other essentials Kylie gave Eric and Ashley a big hug and scampered off next door with Lola who had waited for her on the front porch swing.

Eric gave Ashley a brisk tap on her bottom, bit her neck quickly, and then headed upstairs with a wink. "I'll be upstairs…reading—*Inferno*—that new Dan Brown book," he said in a whisper raising his eyebrows.

Ashley caught his drift and smiled back at him with a wink of her own. "Gotta do a quick clean up from dinner," she said in her best teasing voice. "But…I think I can be up there in fifteen minutes."

He stopped on the stairs and leaned backward. "Throw them in the sink and we can clean up together and have our nightly cigarette on the back porch," he offered.

She laughed tenderly. "Go take your shower and I'll see you in fifteen," she promised flashing her fingers three times.

Eric made a grand gesture of sighing then grinned and padded up the stairway.

Twenty minutes later Ashley started up the stairs then stopped abruptly. She'd heard the shower running but now she could hear him gently snoring. Ashley tiptoed up to the hallway and sneaked a look into their bedroom. It was a spectacular night and the light sheer curtains flopped listlessly as a faint breeze blew in from Nantucket Sound. She crossed to their queen size bed and bent, putting a quilted throw on Eric then bent and kissed his damp hair.

He let out a small groan but turned and pulled the

throw up tighter.

Ashley smiled and went back down the stairs. She'd promised herself she'd find out more details on the Edgerton family. The new project she was working on had kept her preoccupied when they'd arrived, but she'd put that on hold for a couple of weeks.

She flipped on her laptop and waited the few seconds while it booted up. Then she went to her email account and seeing nothing of import went back to Google Chrome. She typed in Lord James Edgerton and waited while a dozen links appeared: Things about his military service, his record in the House of Lords, several appointments, some sub-cabinet positions, a quick glance at his Wikipedia page then onto the next display.

Twelve more links, each with diminishing import, frequency of inquiries, and relevance as was the search engine's protocol. Suddenly, near the bottom of the second page of links she spotted it: *"Distinguished Lord Tarnished by Accusations of Negligence and Wrongdoing in Tragic Ferry Sinking..."*

Chapter Nineteen

Shane knelt with his eyes closed. He held the rose his mother had given him, feeling the sting of the thorns when he tightened his grip. A punishment of sorts? A sweet fragrance floated toward him from the wild flowers and bouquets that populated several of the nearby headstones. He opened moist eyes as the long rays of the setting sun played through the groves of pine and birch that stood watching over the scattered clusters of headstones where she lay. Her stone read…

"Emily Danielle Lindquist, Born September 21st, 1992, Died February 11th, 2014…"

The polished rose-colored granite reflected the fading sunlight. In eight months, it would be three years since her accident, he thought gently placing the single red rose in the vase they had buried in front of her marker—Emily's father, Calvin, and him. To Shane it seemed like an eternity. Something that happened in another lifetime.

Her mother had died when Emmy was in kindergarten. And she'd been an only child. So, when he left the cemetery Shane would drive up to Route 6A and head toward the Brewster-Harwich line and the pristine white cape on the small side road where Emmy and her dad had lived. Shane and Emmy had been a couple since they were in the sixth grade and he was almost as fond of Mr. Lindquist as his folks.

Closing his eyes again, he prayed in whisper. The prayer was not a long one and Shane no longer attended the Covenant Congregational Church in Dennis. It wasn't that he didn't believe. We all had to believe in something—that there was a God. A heaven. Something more than the few tenuous years we spent on this Earth. Shane was certain if there was—a heaven that is—Emily—his Emmy, would be an honored citizen.

"*I'm sorry*," he whispered standing to leave. "So sorry." Shane repeated his words while he brushed the moisture off his flushed cheeks.

****

They sat on the screened-in back porch that faced Scargo Lake, watching the Red Sox-Yankees game. Shane and Mr. Lindquist. They had long since dropped the formalities. He called the man who would have been his father-in-law by his first name. The small lake hid two hundred feet to the south, screened by the growth of small shrubs and weeds that had taken control. The waning moon was visible in the calm waters of the lake through the errant growth. They'd turned up the TV since the sounds of nature weren't intimidated by the cheering and sounds of the television from the porch.

Shane took a quick glance at his watch.

"Shane. You don't have to keep me company if you've got a—date," Mr. Lindquist said softly.

It occurred to him that in the long guilty months since Emily's accident Mr. Lindquist had never used that word. "No, Cal. Got no date," Shane assured him. "I have to be up a little earlier tomorrow. It's my day off, but Eric asked me to take some friends—important visitors from England—for a tour of the Sound. You know, maybe over to Hyannis so they can drool over the hundred footers at Hyannis Marina or Osterville to see how the rich and famous live," he added with a weak smile. "But I don't think they'll have anything on these folks."

"Sounds like a good gig," Cal Lindquist agreed. "If it's not prying who are the people?"

"No, not at all," Shane answered with a shrug. "An English big-wig who's a Lord and his family. His daughter, a couple of grandkids, and their security detail."

"Wow. A Lord with a security detail." Cal gave a small laugh. "Shane, my boy, sounds like you're moving up into the big leagues." He raised his eyebrows. "I'm impressed!"

Shane nodded and smiled politely. He wasn't about to tell his one-time prospective father-in-law that a member of the tour group was a beautiful and wealthy young woman, the one he'd spent four days with in the survival situation that had taken his career and more. Especially since he was sure Samantha had an interest in him and, heaven help him, Shane certainly had an interest in her.

Shane knew that at some point he had to take hold of life again and that meant finding someone to care for. Sam's sudden appearance here—where he lived—had shaken his insular little world and threatened to breach the thick wall he had built around himself. He shook his head and focused on the Red Sox.

After Rick Porcello pitched them to victory Shane checked his watch again then stood. He often stayed and spent time with Cal after whatever sporting events they watched together ended. Not tonight, he thought stifling a yawn.

Cal walked with him to the front door, asking, "Can I ask you a personal question?"

"Sure."

"You tell me about your jobs, your family, discuss current events, the Sox and the Patriots, but you never talk about your...your personal life, Shane," Cal said, looking concerned.

"I'm not sure what you mean," Shane said with a shrug.

"Come on, Shane. I'd like to think we're close. That despite the age difference we're friends," Cal began. "I've known you for what—fifteen years? Maybe more. And I know how much you and Emmy loved each other. Do you think I expect you to be celibate and spend your life in mourning?"

Shane studied the hardwood floor. He felt uncomfortable. "No, of...of course not."

"Good," Cal said. "'Cause I don't."

When Shane raised his eyes, Cal had tilted his head and stared at him, wearing a gentle smile reminiscent of Emily's. "I know this may sound strange coming from me, but I worry that you're hiding. You've done so much to respect Emmy's memory, Shane. No one could have done more." He continued to study Shane. "I like to think of you as the son I never had. Emmy died three years ago come next February. She adored you, son. And I knew her very well. The last thing she would want is to have you spend your life in mourning. Okay?"

Shane smiled back at Cal and lifted his hand.

Cal took it and shook it then pulled Shane to him

and hugged him tightly. "Time to live again, son," he whispered. "We both went through hell when we lost her, Shane. You more than anyone." Cal backed away and held Shane's eyes. "You've had more than your share of tragedy in the last few years. Your brother, the accident that cost you your career, then losing Emily." He shook his head. "But it isn't ordained anywhere that you spend your life in a cocoon. Insulated from affection, intimacy, and love."

Shane backed away with a sniffle. "Thanks," he managed. Turning he walked to his Jeep looking up at the blanket of stars overhead clumsily wiping the dampness from his cheek for the second time that evening.

How could he explain it to anyone? To Cal? To his folks? To Bobby? He wasn't just being loyal to Emmy or her memory. No. Shane was paying a penance. He had been for two years and four months.

Chapter Twenty

The Edgertons sat on the screened-in porch of the massive seven-thousand-square foot house they rented on Pleasant Street in South Yarmouth. The street held what locals referred to as estates though none compared with the massive edifices in Britain that boasted dozens of rooms and were surrounded by grounds that covered dozens of square miles. Notables from all across New England lived in these luxurious homes, some for the summer and others had retired here and used them as their year-round residence. Affluent business executives, two attorneys known for their high-profile courtroom theatrics, a retired President of the Massachusetts State Senate, and a former Boston Bruin's all-star were among the residents. They enjoyed their luxuriant life-style, frequenting the quaint shops, restaurants serving seafood you could see being unloaded on local docks, and of course the coffee shop on the corner of Old Main Street and Route Twenty-Eight.

The Edgertons fit well into the dignified but relatively low-key social activities on the street. But Sam had never been a party animal. For her part she much preferred the daily sorties to the cozy little section of West Dennis Public Beach that fronted on the Bass River and perusing the interesting little shops with their quaint cubbies that hid everything from candy to conch shells.

She and Charlie sat with Poppy and Mummy. Misha sat in a long plush settee that sheltered the family from the backyard. Sam looked in his direction, wondering again what it must be like to never have a moment to yourself. A brief respite when you can completely relax and let your guard down. She inhaled, taking a deep drag from her Benson and Hedges—the high-end British cigarette she preferred. Sam had followed in her mother's footsteps—and despite her dedication to a world-class fitness regimen she'd been a smoker since her early teens. Her mother had been forced to quit after suffering a stroke following her dad's death in a small-plane-crash years earlier. But her health problems and the endless warnings had yet to deter Sam from the habit.

"The bribe is now twenty-five thousand pounds," Poppy said, staring at his granddaughter.

They looked at each other and laughed out loud.

"You know from experience, Daddy, that you have to want to quit or be scared into it," Millicent, his daughter and Sam's mother said. "Bribery never worked for anyone. Not in the long-term."

"Yes, darling, I know. It's my little tease to let my beautiful granddaughter know that I continue to worry about her and disapprove of the habit." He shook his head turning in Sam's direction.

"Sam has promised me she'll quit when she reaches twenty-five," Charles said, beaming a smile her way. "And I believe her!" he added nodding vigorously

"Sounds good, Charles," he said shifting his gaze toward Sam. "But what about this marvelous young man you two were so revved up about when you arrived home. You've spoken of nothing and no one but Shane for the last three hours, Sam. Your hero from the life raft. My God, even Charlie here seems completely entranced by this fellow," he paused shrugging. "Would he approve of your distasteful habit?"

Sam crushed out her cigarette and returned the shrug as she stood. "Hard to say. It is possible he might not. In the life raft it wasn't something we discussed was it, Charlie?" She smiled and made a pleasant face. "I'll quit before Shane and I go on our honeymoon. Promise!" Samantha added with a broad smile and crossed her heart. "I'm going down to the dock," she said, nodding in Misha's direction.

The lead bodyguard stood and nodded. Smiling, he then followed Sam. They walked down the granite stairs and the crushed stone path, casually crossing the hundred feet to the small stairway that led up to the elevated dock.

They fell into step next to each other. Samantha stole a glance at her tall escort. "I love him," she turned and looked back toward the screened in porch. "But he does get a bit overbearing at times."

"Perhaps I shouldn't say this, but he loves you both very much, Miss Samantha," Misha said quietly looking toward her. His words held the trace of an accent Sam couldn't quite place. "It is a beautiful evening. Isn't it?" he asked, shifting to a neutral topic.

"Sorry, Misha. I understand that you'd feel uncomfortable talking about my family's petty feuds." She smiled and did a spin as they reached the dock. "And yes, the evening is spectacular and so is this place."

Misha smiled but stayed several paces behind her.

She wondered again what it would be like to spend all day, every day in a constant state of high alert. "Can I ask you something...personal?" Sam ventured.

"Of course, Miss Samantha."

"Do you enjoy the work?" Sam asked not sure whether she had crossed that invisible line that separated clients from comrades.

He stepped forward, his eyes surveying the Bass River. "In a word, yes. Very much." He turned and looked at her, adding. "Your family is special. Keeping you all from harm is a pleasure."

Sam studied his face. It was what she would have expected. Misha's physique spoke to his strength and fitness. He moved slowly but gracefully. Sam felt safe with him. But his face looked young, almost innocent.

He stood watching her. "I know that I gave what you would call the textbook answer," he showed her an uncharacteristic smile. "But it's true. Life is about purpose and years ago I discovered mine was keeping people—good innocent people like you and your family—safe. Protected from the evil that lurks out there in the darkness." He nodded.

Sam found herself feeling almost moved by his simple but touching answer. She took out another cigarette. Turning she offered him one. "It's all right. I've seen you smoke when you're alone."

He shook his head then retrieved a worn lighter from his shorts, lighting her cigarette. His eyes remained sharp and alert.

"May I?" she asked reaching for the lighter. "I promise not to tell my grandfather you helped me continue this evil habit," she grinned.

He hesitated then offered her the lighter. In the dim

lights from the house and the Halogen spots that illuminated the dock she studied it. Turning it in her hand she found an inscription: *To Misha. Our Captain, leader, inspiration, and special friend.*

Samantha slowly lifted her eyes, gently replacing the lighter in Misha's hand.

Misha nodded and took it back, glancing at it before replacing it in his pocket.

Sam had always felt safe in his presence. Secure, knowing nothing and no one could harm her. The inscription supported her emotions. "Thank you for letting me read that. It's beautiful," Sam said handing it back.

He nodded.

They stood in silence smoking their cigarettes.

Misha continued surveying the river, the yard, the thick pine groves that separated the estate from its neighbors, eyes alert and vigilant.

As Sam took a final drag and went to crush it out, Misha held out his hand. He took it from her and pulled the paper from the remainder as Sam watched curiously.

"It's called field-stripping, Miss Samantha. A habit I picked up in the military." He shrugged.

"Sounds reasonable, Captain," Sam said repeating the title she'd gleaned from the lighter. "Probably time to head…"

Suddenly the night erupted. Loud bangs echoed from near the house. Samantha was sure it was gunfire. She'd heard that noise before. Poppy had gone hunting and let her tag along. And Misha had taken her to the range. This had that same sound! Yes! This was gunfire!

"Down, Samantha. Lay down on the dock!" Misha said loudly focusing on the large screened-in porch. He crouched, automatic weapon suddenly in hand, straddling Sam with his long legs while he scanned the woods and twisted to make sure no threats existed from the river behind them. "When I nod, I want you to run, staying low and behind me," he commanded. His voice sounded remarkably calm. "For that stand of three large pines out of the light. Understand?"

"Y…yes," she whispered watching Misha just as screams emerged. The loud voices sounded like Charles and her mother as more bangs echoed across the lawn, sounding much louder.

A bright flash ignited the right side of the house and another the back yard. Samantha dove behind the trees Misha pointed to. He knelt in the firing position she'd seen him take at the firing range as running figures appeared beside the house…

Chapter Twenty-One

Joey let out a low bark as Shane's cell buzzed for the third time. "Thanks for the wake-up call," he managed, raising his leg and moving Joey off him as the spaniel grunted irritably. "Sorry to disturb you," Shane muttered, annoyed and trying to focus while he looked at the digital alarm clock lying next to his bed.

His night had been restless. His talk with Cal. And of course, there was Samantha. Yes. Samantha. He'd seen her on the beach all week never realizing she was his partner and companion from the life raft. They'd only met that once but since he'd seen her yesterday, she was there again. Filling his thoughts and seeing her in his imagination when he closed his eyes. But Shane had never been able to forget her. Not really. He found himself thinking about her as he'd done so often in the months after the life raft. The way she looked, her sexy accent, the intoxicating laugh, and that haunting smile...her face, her figure! He'd finally fallen into a restless sleep sometime after 3:00 a.m.

Now he groaned, reaching across the night table and groping for his phone. Its face glowed in his darkened room. 7:13 a.m.? The caller I.D. said Eric Montgomery.

"Hel...hello," he said. "Eric?"

"Yeah. Hi, Shane. Look, I'm sorry to bother you so early. Guessing I woke you, but something's happened…"

****

The Admiral walked into his office and put his briefcase next to his desk. He went behind it and studied the screens: Concern over Russia's continuing interference and support of Assad in Syria, Brexit backlash and angst in the U.K., the constant back and forth in Central and South America—Colombia and Panama of note but for at least another night the world had managed to stay in one piece. He knew when a crisis occurred, he'd be one of the first to hear about it.

He sat down gently, rubbing his aching back. A small note slipped under his folio said: *Your Tramadol is in the lower right-hand drawer....J.* Perhaps it was his imagination, but the Admiral swore the brief note held a hint of the heady fragrance Jeanie always wore.

Looking out toward the commotion and the attendant chatter that always existed beyond his office door he sighed, knowing there'd be no special coffee the way Jeanie prepared it this morning.

Shake it off, you old fool! He told himself. Perhaps it was Jeanie's sudden and unexpected display the day before. He'd had a restless night. Jeanie had sent him an email confirming what she'd told him yesterday afternoon. She was taking a long overdue vacation. But while he mused about how he'd deal with her absence and what they would say to each other after the tense but revealing moment the day before he looked up. She stood in front of him.

For an instant he thought he was still in bed. Dreaming a pleasant fantasy perhaps? But she was no dream, and this was no fantasy.

"Good…good morning," he greeted her clumsily,

stumbling over his words. Gunfire, terrorism, and devious spy craft he could deal with. This surprising unexpected reunion with Jeanie left him tongue-tied. "I didn't expect to see you this morning. You were supposed to be…"

"Excuse me, sir," she began. Her face showed concern. Even anguish? "I remembered that I'd left the extra bottle of your back pills in my desk and stopped in here on my way to National. I couldn't resist checking the feeds and I saw this from the team on Cape Cod." She handed him an intercept. The kind they received when one of their teams had gone to high-alert status.

He felt his stomach churn. The way it had the afternoon he received the information that his family had…

"It's about your friend, Lord Edgerton, and his family." She explained, finding him with her enormous eyes. "Something's happened to them. Something serious."

The Admiral read the terse communication. He was about to pick up his hot phone. The landline that got him any of the field teams within thirty seconds.

Jeanie closed the distance between them and put her hand on his while she gently guided the receiver back into its cradle. "Sir. I've spoken to Merritt. I'll give you all the details en route."

"En *route?*" he said looking up at her.

"I took the liberty of calling Andrews. They have an Osprey fueled and ready for us. Your car is waiting downstairs to take us there. I've already given the driver the emergency bag you keep in the closet. Anything else we can buy on the Cape."

"Us…we?" he shrugged. "I don't understand…"

She interrupted him for the second time smiling softly. "You may not remember but you hired me because of my field work. It was excellent," she whispered, flushing crimson. "At least that's what you told me. I love working with you here—in the office— but I'm getting rusty. I think I need a refresher. To get back in the field and well, get my hands dirty." She continued flushing and tugging his arm gently. "Come on. They have my bags, too. I may have overpacked since I was about to visit my sister in San Diego but hell. I'll be the best dressed field agent on Cape Cod."

He stood and smiled at her, nodding his approval. "Field agent Jeanie Flynn. I like the sound of that." And he did. Very much. "Let's go," he added as they double-timed it through his office door.

****

Ivan stood looking out toward the beach and the distant bay straining to find his brother. "Damn!" He sighed heavily then turned to see Nicolai enter the room.

"Do you have any idea what happened?" his friend asked in a shaky whisper as he studied the mahogany decking. "Any idea at all?" he repeated, raising his eyes to find Ivan's.

Then two of them stood quietly for a long moment, glancing back and forth at each other. Ivan ran inside and returned quickly with a high-powered pair of binoculars. He continued to shake his head.

All this time. All the plans and money! Would it all go up in smoke? Did Ilya have a contingency plan if the initial plan fell apart? Ivan wondered while he moved the field glasses back and forth searching the beach and the narrow trails that lead to the back yard.

Suddenly he stopped. Axe walked slowly up the closest path, shaking his head and speaking on a cell phone. But to Ivan's surprise and complete confusion his brother showed no sign of irritation, anger, or frustration. When he finished speaking, he smiled pleasantly and looked up at them nodding and waving.

"Oh, God," said Ivan in a whisper, turning toward Nicolai. "He hasn't heard the news." Ivan added, placing the binoculars gently on the wide porch railing watching as his brother casually mounted the dozen steps that brought him from the backyard onto the deck.

"Ilya. Brother," Ivan began shooting Nicolai an urgent look. "I...we need to tell you something that happened last night. Something that may change the project that we have planned."

Axe shrugged and looked back and forth between them. "I'm guessing you're referring to the attack on the Edgerton family?" he asked with a curious, almost amused expression. "Apparently you've heard or seen the local news this morning?"

Ivan looked at Nicolai then back at his brother. "Yes."

Axe nodded. "Yes, Ivan. I know all about it." He shook his head and broke into a grin.

Ivan stood looking at his brother. He was incredulous! Had his beloved brother Ilya finally gone over the edge. After all the years of planning and anticipation had this shocking news—news that might signal the need to rethink if not abandon his long-sought plan for revenge—finally pushed him past the breaking point?

Axe laughed out loud. "Fear not, my young friends.

This was not a surprise to me, actually," Axe added, putting an arm around each of them. "A rather inventive solution for what might have been the major impediment to our success."

He held up his hand and left the thought hanging then gently turned them back toward the house. "I don't indulge in alcohol often but if—make that when—the next part of the plan is successful I will ask you to go out and buy the most expensive bottle of Champagne you can find, and we will toast our success!"

Ivan had no idea what his brother was talking about but if there was one thing this project had taught him it was that Ilya left nothing to chance and that he surrounded himself with those who knew their business! And knew it well. Very well!

Chapter Twenty-Two

Shane pulled on a pair of Docker shorts, a clean Polo shirt, and his top-siders. He ran a comb through his thick hair, gave his teeth a thorough brush and headed for his Jeep in less than fifteen minutes.

"Shane, *honey*. It's only seven-thirty!" his mother said in her husky early-morning whisper. "I thought you were taking some visitors on a tour of the Sound this morning." She shrugged. "Aren't you a little early?"

He nodded. "Yeah, mom. I was," he began, grabbing his keys off the rack that hung next to the door. "But something happened to the people I was supposed to take on the tour. It'll be on the news I'm sure."

"Can't I fix you something? Toast or coffee? At least have a glass of orange juice."

"Thanks, but no. I want to get to the hospital and see how Samantha and her folks are."

He'd explained about the trip on the Sound, the Edgerton's, Samantha and who she was when he came home from Cal's house.

She frowned but patted his shoulder and finally showed him a reluctant smile. "Okay. But let us know what's going on." She turned and headed to the radio to turn on 95.1 FM. "Maybe I can catch some news." She shrugged again as Shane shut the screen door quietly, so he didn't wake his dad…

…He parked in the endless parking lot of the Cape Cod Hospital. At seven-fifty in the morning the visitor lot was sparsely populated, so Shane found a spot only fifty feet from the main entrance. Eric said that Samantha and her mother had been taken there for treatment. There had been an attack at the Edgerton's massive rental house on Pleasant Street. Between Eric's quick phone call and the news on 95.1 and 104.7—both popular FM Cape radio stations he'd gleaned no added details on what Eric had already told him.

What concerned him was that the radio confirmed that at least two women had been injured and taken to the Cape Cod Hospital. That also agreed with what Eric told him about who'd been injured. Shane had no idea how seriously they'd been hurt, but he headed to the hospital to find out in person. He reacted very quickly. Too quickly Shane told himself. He knew why. Their four days in the life raft had developed a bond. At least that's what he told himself when he found himself worrying about Sam. But somewhere deep inside Shane knew what he felt was more. Much more.

What had happened to Samantha and her mother was of concern, but the bigger question—the one that bothered Shane since hearing the news was who had attacked them and why? He ran across the parking lot and headed inside the main entrance when a large Sergeant from the Dennis Police suddenly stopped him. He was immediately flanked by the tall slender man from the Edgerton family's security detail. The one who seemed to be in charge.

****

Samantha lay on her bed in the Cape Cod Hospital

Emergency Room. She had closed her eyes, trying to doze when she heard voices near the privacy screen that separated her from the confusion and bustle beyond. Something serious had taken place. Something no one understood. She heard Misha and another man raising their voices. Misha warned the second man in a soft but commanding voice that Samantha was not to be disturbed.

She smiled. That was his style. And to date she had never seen anyone debate him. He lowered his voice, addressing the second man as sergeant as they spoke softly.

But there was another voice. Familiar sounding. Sam couldn't quite place it. They had given her several medications. Strong enough to relax and sedate her though she thought it completely unnecessary. And as Misha warned her adrenaline had kept her awake.

"Hel...hello," she managed in a hoarse whisper when she heard the familiar voice again. Suddenly it registered. "Shane? Isth...isth that you?" she asked. Sam tried to sit up but fell back as a nurse came into her small space.

Perhaps she was having a pleasant fantasy brought on by the OxyContin and Valium they'd given her. Could Shane be here? And if so, why?

"Yes, Samantha. Is that you?" It was Shane. Really! *Why was he here*? she wondered again.

"Yesth, it's me," she said, though her words came out slurred.

"I...I got an early call from Eric saying you people had an emergency. That you'd been *attacked!*" Shane said in a voice filled with concern. "And I heard the same things on the local news station." Misha pushed aside the curtain and let him in to see her. "I guess I wanted to, you know, to make sure you were okay," Shane stuttered.

"Oh, missth," Sam said trying to muster her strength. "Can you help me. Tho I can thit up?"

"Of course, Samantha." The nurse nodded. She pressed a button on the electric bed Sam lay on. Her head slowly came to the upright position. She tried to smile despite the throbbing pain in her ankle.

"My goodnessth," Sam said with a pronounced lisp. "Itsth tho nice of you to thstop by and check on me. Thorry. I meant on usth, of courseth."

Shane flushed and tried to hide a smile. He couldn't.

"Are you laughing at me? At the way I'm thspeaking, Lieutenant?" she asked, being equally unsuccessful at hiding her smile.

"I'm really sorry, Samantha," he continued smiling broadly, blushing brighter. "Actually, it sounds kind of cute. Really," he confessed, closing the three feet that separated them and standing next to her bed. "So," he fidgeted. For a moment he seemed to be reaching for her hand then took a step back quickly. "You are okay? Right?"

She lay looking up at him. The way she had been in her delightful daydream. Of course. They were supposed to go onto Nantucket Sound with him today. This morning. Sam felt her smile widen after she twisted slightly to see him more clearly.

"Samantha?" he asked, looking down at the soft cast on her left ankle. "You are all right, aren't you?" he repeated.

"Yesth. I'm fine," she whispered finding his eyes.

"I tripped when Misha pushed me behind him. Think I tore or thstrained thomething. In my ankle," she explained, wincing when she raised her leg to show him her walking cast. "I wasth a thskier. On the European tour and I had a therious athident and hurt my left leg laststh winter. I think from what the doctor thaid I may have tweaked it again."

"Okay, but why were you hiding behind him?" he asked moving closer. "They said something about gunfire on the radio?"

She shrugged. "The policeth aren't sure. About the gunfire, I mean." Sam shook her head. "At firststh they thought it might have been thomeone pulling a prank. That it might have been fireworksth."

"So…so everyone's okay and I assume they caught whoever did it?"

Sam twisted her mouth into a frown. "Well, Misha wasth sure it wasth gunfire. Tho wasth Poppy—my grandfather—and the policeth found thome shell casthings near the houseth tho now no oneth sure what happened."

"But I juststh tripped over my own big feet. And Mummy fainted. Shesth thstaying here for the day for obthservation." Sam shrugged again. "Thorry I can't give you more information."

"I'm sure it was something crazy. There are a lot of high-profile people who live near the house you're renting," he said, closing the final two feet and standing next to her bedside. "But we don't get many things like this down here. Even in the vacation season. I'm just glad everyone's all right. That you're all right," he whispered, letting his eyes fall away.

He smiled in the gentle way she'd seen the night

before and when they'd made the long trip home in the rescue copter. It was shy but so inviting Sam was certain she could look at it endlessly.

"That you're really all right." Shane repeated. It was his turn to shake his head. "You must think I'm crazy. I mean coming down here when we've only just—"

"Shush," Sam interrupted in a whisper. She reached out and touched his hand gently. "I think itsth very...very thsweet tho pleaseth, Shane. Don't apologizeth. You alwaysth theem to be there when I need thomeone. I'm juststh tho glad to...to thee you," she managed, tripping over her words and feeling a flush in her cheeks.

"Ahem. Excuse me." The nurse stood pushing aside the curtain that separated Sam from the other beds. "I'm sorry, but the doctor needs to check Miss Edgerton one last time." She paused. "And I have some paperwork that she needs to sign and a couple of prescriptions to give her before we discharge her."

"Sure. I'll leave you now," Shane said backing away from her bedside. "Like I said, I'm just glad you're all right."

"Oh, Shane," she called as he turned to go. "Maybe you could call later and come by. For a visthit? If I remember correctly thisth isth your day off."

He stopped and found her eyes, nodding. "I'd like that if you're up to it."

The nurse stood giving Sam an impatient look.

"Heresth my number," she said handing him her phone. He put her number into his contacts then handed it back, beaming a warm smile.

Samantha leaned forward, following Shane with

her eyes till the curtain draped shut. She caught the nurse watching her. "Do you know him? Shane, I mean."

"Yes, Miss. I was on duty the night his mother delivered him," she told Sam as the doctor appeared. "He's a fine boy, miss." The nurse smiled. "You couldn't find any better. A *fine* boy," she repeated walking away.

Samantha had only spoken to him twice since their perilous adventure in the Caribbean, but she agreed she thought when she lay back and closed her eyes. Yes. *A very, very fine boy*, she mused as fatigue and the drugs finally had their way with her.

Chapter Twenty-Three

"I just spoke to the Admiral," Eric explained to Ashley when he returned to the ship store. He narrowed his eyes, setting his jaw as he gave her a look that said frustration. "Can you believe this? The one time he asks us to do him a favor and something like this happens."

"Hey, take it easy. The Edgertons aren't our family." Ashley put her hand on Eric's shoulder, caressing it gently. "Chill out!" She turned toward him, looking hesitant. "This has nothing to do with us, darlin.'"

"Yeah, I know, Ash. I get it, but it makes us all look so damn impotent, so helpless!" he added angrily.

"*Impotent? Helpless?*" Ashley repeated angrily and gave him a push. "Oh my God. Come on, Eric. Is it our fault that someone decided to harass or attack them? Jesus," she continued. "I'm angry and frustrated, too, but no one knows what this was or why it happened."

"Okay. It's just that when the Admiral asked us to play host to the Edgertons I never thought they'd be attacked for God's sake!" He turned away. Was he really so concerned about impressing their high-profile guest?

"Okay, but should I remind you that this lovely hometown of yours is full of stories?" She took his chin and turned his face toward her. "Didn't they call you and your high school friends 'the wild bunch'? For all

153

we know this was just some high school kids letting off steam."

"Yeah. We did some crazy things when we were kids, but the head of their security—Misha—told me he heard gunfire. He's pretty savvy. A pro. And *he* doesn't think it was a couple of kids playing a prank." He stopped and looked at the tile floor. A smile softened his expression. "I guess it's just that I didn't want to disappoint the Admiral." Eric shrugged, waving at Kylie and her best friend while they struggled with the sails on her birthday present again. "He saved our lives, and he's never asked anything in return until this summer."

"Darlin', he'd never think we're to blame. No one has any idea what happened yet," she repeated. "Did it occur to you that if Lord Edgerton has a staff of professional bodyguards there may be more to their situation than we know?" She gave his shoulder a squeeze. "After Kylie asked about them last night, I felt guilty—thinkin' I should know more about them—so when she went to Lola's and you pooped out on me, I Googled Lord Edgerton."

"Really? I don't remember you do—"

She held up her hand as a coy smile crossed her face. "Well, dear, like I said, you were too—spent from our earlier activities," she added with a soft smile. "Anyway, he's got quite a social media presence. It was interesting. Lots about his Naval service, awards, political affiliations—you know, the usual you'd expect from a person of his stature. Then I checked some of the other links and he's had a couple of things in his business life that have been a little," she paused and gave him a thoughtful look. "Not sure how to describe 'em?"

Ashley sneaked a look around and continued. "There were some minor accidents, injuries, and even lawsuits against one of his businesses—his ferry company. Then in two-thousand and ten somethin' really bad happened. A tragedy. The story said his family had owned the ferry company for decades. They did runs across the English Channel and had a branch that served several cities in the Baltic. They'd had some minor problems before, but like I said, this one in two-thousand and ten was big. More than a hundred injured and about twenty killed. There were the usual accusations and lawsuits—blame thrown around, fingers pointed but rather than fight or deny anything Edgerton made huge payoffs to the victims—out of his own pockets. He offered a public apology, made pledges to correct deficiencies and flagrant safety violations."

"And…?" Eric shrugged.

"More than a hundred people killed or seriously injured, the man who owned the company making big settlement payoffs to victims and tear-filled public apologies." Ashley took her arm from Eric's shoulder and walked a few steps and sat in one of the deck chairs on display. "Do you think that might be a reason for someone seeking revenge?" She asked with a sigh. "Maybe why he's got a world-class security team?"

"Jesus. I don't know." Eric looked incredulous. "Would the Admiral be close friends with somebody who's responsible for innocent people's deaths?"

She shrugged and shook her head. "I'm not sure how to ask. But I have another question," Ashley continued. "If their security is so damn tight and well-trained how did someone get inside that compound they're renting?" she asked. "It has a metal fence, and didn't they tell us it was equipped with sensors and camera surveillance?"

His expression said he'd been wondering the same thing. "I don't know that either." He shrugged. "Misha looks pretty savvy, but he's not doing the job alone. I've seen the rest of their team but never talked to any of them," Eric added shaking his head.

Ashley reached out and took his hand. "You never told me what the Admiral's reaction to all this was."

"Hard to judge," Eric began while he studied the activity on the docks. "He sounded concerned but almost… upbeat?"

"Upbeat?" She asked. "I know he loves visiting us and he was lookin' forward to seeing his old friend but that does sound kinda strange, especially when he heard about what happened."

Eric raised his eyebrows. "Maybe it has something to do with the agent he brought with him."

"Really? He brought a field agent with him?" She asked. "He told me he had a team down here surveilling someone."

Eric nodded. "He called her an agent. It's the woman he's mentioned before. His top assistant, Jeanie Flynn," Eric explained, looking curious.

She nodded. "Oh my God. Jeanie. Yes! He's talked a lot about her." Ashley squeezed his forearm and grinned. "Is it possible that he's…" her words trailed off.

"I guess we'll find out soon. They landed at Logan thirty minutes ago and should be here in a couple of hours."

Chapter Twenty-Four

"So," the Admiral began. "No one knows what actually happened. This may turn out to be nothing serious. A false alarm," he said, putting his arm on Jeanie's shoulder as they dismounted the Osprey. "I'm sorry if that's how it turns out," he added, looking back at their aircraft, thinking again that Ospreys resembled a giant praying mantis.

A Marine Sergeant had taken their luggage from the aircraft, after hoisting it onto a utility cart he nodded at them.

The Admiral waved toward the Tahoe that awaited in the private parking lot hidden behind Logan Airport's International Terminal 'E.' The Terminal building served as a screen for several military runways. When the spotless black vehicle came to a stop in front of them, he turned toward Jeanie. Feeling torn, he touched her right arm. The last thing he wanted was to have his old friend's family assaulted or threatened, but the last twenty-four hours had brought a surge of long dormant emotions. Emotions that lay deeply buried had surged to the surface. Jeanie had shown him that she had feelings for him. Far more than the loyalty and friendship of their workplace relationship. And if he'd had any doubts her insistence on making this trip had put them to rest.

"I'm glad we had the chance to travel here

together," he began pushing aside his disappointment. "But since we can't be sure if there's any crisis—at least not one that would demand *our* expertise I assume you'd like to get back to your vacation," he said gently feeling like a school boy. He hadn't felt this way since he'd courted Ellen. But as his eyes lingered on Jeanie's he wanted to call forth so many rusty phrases that now dwelt in the dim corners of his memory.

"Well, sir," Jeanie cleared her throat and turned looking shy, like a schoolgirl, hesitantly giving his hand a gentle touch. "I've never been to Cape Cod. Always wanted to see it. I remember the way you always spoke about it." Her face flushed and her gaze fell to the tarmac. "Would it be…awkward or uncomfortable for you if I stayed. Perhaps tagged along for a couple of days?"

He felt his own face flush while he stood then gently taking her chin in his hand. "Upset? You think I'd be upset with your company?"

"I…I don't know, sir." Jeanie shrugged. "Couldn't we say that I'm here in some capacity as your assistant?"

"First, I liked it when you called me Brian the other day." He mustered his best smile. "Since we're no longer in the office, could we return to that?"

She nodded, letting her eyes find his again. "Yes. Fine…Brian," Jeanie added softly.

"Fine." The Admiral agreed. Letting his hand fall away, then put it on her shoulder. "We're both adults and entitled to our time. So, Miss Flynn. First, let's go check out what happened to the Edgertons and then if it doesn't demand our expertise—we can play tourist."

****

Samantha sat on the spacious back porch of their rental house—her leg poised on a brightly colored footstool. Its ample cushion helped with the ache from her swollen ankle. A moderate sprain. That was the diagnosis. She exhaled a long thick plume of smoke from her cigarette. She struggled, clumsily pulling the thickly padded chair she sat toward the edge of the porch, so she could get a better look at Misha studying the grounds for evidence—signs that might help him—and them determine who and what had happened the night before.

Sam watched him with fascination. He used thin gloves while he bent; moving and picking at bits of grass, handfuls of mulch, and tiny items—clues she couldn't see. He would put them to his nose, gently inhaling and moving them delicately between his fingers. All with the precision, dexterity, and the finesse of a fine surgeon. Sam stretched as someone cleared their throat purposefully. She turned abruptly, almost tumbling out of her chair when her foot slipped from its resting place. She groaned loudly as it hit the floor.

Shane closed the ten feet separating them quickly, grabbing her by the shoulders and quickly slid her back onto the ample seat's base.

"Oh, God." Sam's groan morphed into a hoarse giggle as she leaned back and put her hand over her mouth. "You're always in the proper place at the proper time, Lieutenant."

"Well, Samantha, it does seem like our paths cross whenever you need someone or something," Shane said breathlessly. "Just not sure whether they're the most opportune or inopportune times," he added, doing his best to hide a smile.

She smiled back broadly, surveying him with subtlety. She was sure he caught her. Sam lowered her eyes as a flush crossed her face. "Sorry."

"For what?" he asked looking genuinely confused.

"Oh. Nothing," she said regaining control of herself. Perhaps because Shane was always there; a vague shadowy presence, lurking dimly on the horizon, never really existing but never really leaving her at peace. Sam couldn't put her finger on why he had such a strong hold on her. But he had. And after his sudden and unexpected visit to the hospital that morning Sam suspected that she wasn't alone in her feelings. "I think I was staring." She shook her head. "We young English ladies are told that staring is…is rude," she stuttered, attempting to turn her preoccupation with this shy handsome man into something humorous.

"It's fine with me, Sam." He paused, looking concerned. "It's all right if I call you Sam, isn't it?"

She raised her eyebrows and put her hand over her mouth again. "All right? You *are* joking, right?"

He shrugged and averted her eyes, studying the outdoor carpeting on the porch floor. "Well, when we met the first time—on the life raft, I mean," he began. "I didn't know you were royalty."

He couldn't be serious, could he? Did her family's status or Poppy's title really intimidate him? "Well Shane, since you mention it, I would prefer it if you referred to me as Miss Samantha or Lady Edgerton. At least when we're with other people." Sam raised one eyebrow, doing her best to put on her most serious expression.

Shane raised his eyes to hers. He looked tentative—unsure whether to grin or genuflect.

Sam showed him her best smile and broke into another loud giggle. "Shane, *come on!*"

His expression softened then morphed into a wide grin. "Well, come on, Sam. I've never been around anyone with the title 'Lord' in their family before." He shrugged. "But then when I joined the Coast Guard, they did tell me I'd meet my share of fascinating people."

"You were the perfect gentleman at the hospital this morning and on the phone when you called this afternoon. And for those four days on the life raft, I might add."

"Thanks." Shane lowered his eyes and grew a thoughtful, almost melancholy look.

"Shane," Sam began, moving so she could put her feet down and touch his hand. "I'm not sure quite how to put this but," she paused. "But well, I'm so sorry that meeting me, helping us survive, cost you your career."

He shrugged again as a slow smile emerged. "Please, Samantha. That wasn't your fault. I made a choice." Shane shook his head slowly. "I was trained to do a job and I did it. I could have stayed in the Coast Guard, but it wasn't the kind of duty I signed up for." He gently moved his hand, taking hers in his. "And helping you and your family, well, I've never regretted that or the time on the life raft. Now, about the whole royalty thing. I guess it didn't really hit me until I met your grandfather and saw this estate and the security people and police and…"

Sam held up her free hand. "Well, Lieutenant, I am neither a Lord nor a Lady so will you please talk to me like—well—like we're back on the life raft again?" she asked softly as the color rose in her cheeks. "Please,

Shane."

He let her hand go and found her eyes. "My pleasure…Sam."

Chapter Twenty-Five

Axe watched the man he knew as Lassiter direct Ivan and Nicolai as they unloaded his SUV and placed the remaining components needed to complete the electronics for the air-tight chamber.

When the boys were done, they resumed their work on the room, putting the final touches on the rough frame. When they finished the interior walls and sealed the small room Nicolai would complete the electrical work by the weekend. His expertise in that area was another reason Axe had agreed to allow Ivan to add him to the team. That gave Lassiter ten days to install his technology and test it thoroughly.

Now both boys lay on the massive deck with a six-pack of beer and their new iPods. Ivan had been in America for two years completing his degree at Boston University, but his friend had never been outside Eastern Europe before, and Axe could see it was a new and heady experience. Axe had his issues with them on occasion, but they were young, eager, and ahead of schedule, so he said nothing when they asked him about taking the evening off.

He pondered what he would do with Nicolai when the task was complete. He had planned everything with painstaking precision but that was the one thing he had no concrete plans to resolve. Axe knew that if he disposed of the young man Ivan would never forgive him. No. He needed to construct a plan—a scenario in which Nicolai met a fatal end without it looking suspicious. But he had yet to come up with any suitable alternative.

Axe breathed easier as the Americans were fond of saying. Relieved after Murphy had called with his report. The situation that could have been a major issue with the Edgertons had been resolved thanks to Murphy's intuitive solution. That was what *he* needed to take care of Nicolai, so he planned to utilize the Brit's knowledge and experience.

Now that the project was close to fruition a part of Axe felt pleased with the way it had come together. Another part of him was troubled. He had worked endlessly to assure that his planning had been cautious and thorough. So that he and Ivan could escape with anonymity. But if something went awry—if their identities were discovered they would be hunted as desperate criminals. And despite his hatred and contempt for James Edgerton, Axe recognized that a man with his bottomless financial resources and political influence would be a terrifying and determined adversary. They would be hunted endlessly. Hounded! They could never stop looking over their shoulder for the rest of their lives. Axe had been willing to accept that fate. Planned well for what the Americans called, the worst-case scenario. It was the price he would be willing to pay for the cruel plan he had put into motion. *But that was the problem. When you rolled a snowball downhill*, he mused staring absently out of the large bay window in his study. *It grew and gained speed. And once it reached critical mass there was no stopping it.*

"Mr. Axelrod." A knock on his office door. It was

Lassiter. "You said you wanted to see me when we were through unloading the equipment."

"Yes. You have all the equipment you'll need to complete your tasks?" Axe asked as he lit a cigarette.

Lassiter entered the room and nodded. "I'm still waiting for one additional component. A small drive for the remote infrared camera system."

"I assume it's something special?"

"Quite," Lassiter answered. "The camera is motion and audio driven. And the technology is more complex."

Axe knotted his brow. "Motion and audio driven?"

"Sorry. Yes. Meaning that when any movement longer than two seconds or a sound above the threshold of twenty-five decibels occurs the camera will follow the action or sound and give the viewer a close-up image. All automatically," Lassiter said with a satisfied expression. "It's quite a fine piece of technology."

Axe extinguished his cigarette and smiled at his employee. "And it will be here when?"

"Friday afternoon. I'll pick it up at a parking lot in Hyannis."

"So then. Bring your bags in. Ivan will show you to your room. It has a wide-screen television, whirlpool tub, and a king-sized bed."

"Thank you. I'll get most of the installation done over the next two days and should be able to complete my installation by the weekend," he said with confidence.

"Thank you. I see and," Axe said, gesturing toward the study door and nodded. "Pardon my ignorance of these technical things."

Lassiter turned.

"Oh," Axe called to him. "You have those throw-away phones I needed? Burners I believe you call them?"

"Of course. I was going to bring them down when I unpack," Lassiter answered. "Six you had asked for?"

"Yes." Axe gave him a smile and nodded.

Axe still had some things to discuss with Murphy. The Brit wanted another vehicle. One with some flash he said. Axe wouldn't question the man. So far, the professionals he'd hired had been excellent. As good as he'd hoped. Better. He allowed himself a small smile while he walked out of his study and headed downstairs to see how Ivan and his friend were enjoying the spectacular early evening on the deck.

Chapter Twenty-Six

"Come on, Sam," Charles said after he flopped into the oversized chair in Sam's bedroom when he returned from the riding stables. "Give me some details about your discussion with your handsome Lieutenant." He sat back and made a smiling face and hugged himself pushing his lips into a teasing pout.

Samantha lay on the bed, popping a pain pill for the throbbing in her ankle. "It's possible I might share a bit of our conversation if you get your stinky breeches and boots off my chair and footstool and *go—take—a—shower!*" she scolded in her best older sibling tone.

Charles shook his head and groaned. He stood twisting his sunburned cheeks into a scowl. "Oh Samantha! Come on. You are becoming quite the poop!"

She sighed deeply.

"But if that's what you require to share your discussion with Shane I will depart!" He made a mock frown and stuck out his tongue when he headed toward the door.

"I swear, Charlie. I think you have a crush on him yourself!" she told him shaking her head.

Stepping into the hall, Charles stopped and turned, putting his hand over his mouth. "Oh, piece of news from Poppy's office." He closed the door slowly and came back and stood next to Sam.

"I can't wait." Sam rolled her eyes comically. "And this had better be good, because every second you stand here you and your riding clothes are putrefying a previously fragrant room!"

"Well," Charles said, stealing a look behind him to make sure the door was properly closed. "When I was coming through the front hall after Jacob left me at the door, I saw Misha head into Poppy's office. Poppy had that angry frown he wears when he's mad. You know. *Really mad!* He slammed the door, so I took a couple of steps and stopped then heard him raising his voice at Misha. I played Sherlock Holmes since no one was around. All I heard was Poppy saying, *'Well as if that business last night wasn't enough now this. Would you like to explain it?'*"

Sam sat up quickly. She knew that her grandfather was angry about what had happened. And being who and what he was, Samantha knew he would want someone to blame. Yes, her mother was still in the hospital, and she was nursing a sprained ankle. Still, no one had suffered any real injury and no damage had been done. But assuming what Charlie told her was true Sam had a frightening feeling that Misha would pay the price—be held to blame for whatever had taken place.

"Oh, God," she whispered more to herself than to her brother. She raised her eyes to Charles'. "He's going to sack Misha!"

****

The Admiral insisted that the sergeant who had driven him and Jeanie from Logan Airport only wait long enough to be sure that they had arrived at the home on Pleasant Street where the Edgerton Family was staying.

"We're here on vacation, Sergeant, so we'll be renting a car after we get settled. But thank you," The Admiral said as the man stood at attention and saluted.

"At ease," he said, holding out his hand.

The sergeant took it, shaking it vigorously and smiling. "It's been an honor meeting you, sir."

The Admiral nodded and stood with Jeanie as the spotless Tahoe with tinted windows pulled away down the endless crushed stone drive. As they turned, his friend emerged from the massive mahogany double doors and rushed down the granite steps to give the Admiral a bear hug. "God, Brian. It's so very good to see you. How long has it been?"

The Admiral took a small step back and shrugged. "Too, long, James," he replied quietly, turning and taking Jeanie's arm, gently pulling her toward his old friend. "This is Jeanie Flynn, James."

"Why yes," Edgerton showed her his magazine cover smile and took her hand lightly.

When Jeanie moved forward tentatively, James opened his arms, surrounding her firmly. "Brian has mentioned you often. May I call you Jeanie?" he asked deferentially.

"Yes. Of course, sir," Jeanie said as they shed their brief embrace. "And I already feel as if I know you, too," she added with a flush.

"Well. It's wonderful that you could both join us. And please, Jeanie. I will not permit you to call me 'sir.'" James smiled. "James will do nicely. Jim if you prefer," he said, positioning himself between them so he could take one of their arms guiding them up the granite pediments and onto the massive wrap-around front porch. "And this handsome young man is my grandson, Charles," he told them when he came out and held the door, beaming a dimpled smile that showed braces.

"My apologies. I just returned from the riding stables and I really need to get cleaned up." He shook his head and blushed "But that aside this is such a pleasure, Admiral Turner and Ms. Flynn," Charles added with his infectious charm.

"Sadly, Millicent, my daughter, is still at the Cape Cod Hospital," James explained as they headed down a long hall with broad hardwood that shone where the oriental runners left a border. "But this…" James gestured toward an overstuffed chaise as they emerged onto a generous screened in porch. "Is my lovely granddaughter, Samantha,"

The young woman's bright smile could have graced the cover of Harper's Bazaar or Vogue. She stood and braced herself as the Admiral gave her a peck and a quick hug. "Yes, it's been too long, Samantha." He stepped back and studied her. "The summer of your fifteenth year. We met at your estate in Cornwall."

Samantha nodded and turned toward Jeanie then sat down. "And you must be Jeanie," she offered holding out her hand. "I'm sorry," she said grinning. "I suffered a rather foolish injury during the excitement last evening." She shook her head. "Tripped over my own feet rather."

Jeanie took her hand.

James motioned to the seats that surrounded a larger glass table. Suddenly he turned toward the hallway again. "If I'm not mistaken that's our tour guides and delightful acquaintances and your dear friends, the Montgomerys."

****

Axe stood at the railing of the massive deck staring into the twilight and the Atlantic beyond, hoping again that if he closed his eyes all this would be a bad dream. A nightmare from which he would awake. Naina would lie next to him in their large warm bed. The one his parents had given them that creaked when either of them moved. They would laugh, waiting until the children were fast asleep before he turned to her, took her lovely heart-shaped face in his hands, and kissed her till both of them were breathless.

"Ilya," Ivan whispered from behind him.

Axe jumped, returning from his reverie.

"I'm sorry, Brother. Did I disturb you?"

"No. I'm the one who should be sorry." Axe pushed his lips together and sighed, staring at the Ocean. "I wonder sometimes," he began unable to complete his thought then sighed and continued. "About dragging you and your friend here with me, employing these…these men who have no honor or sense of decency, of what will happen to you if the authorities discover who we are and what we've done."

Axe turned to his brother.

Ivan looked toward the house. He could see Nicolai playing video games in the large great room and heard the man Lassiter going back and forth between the garage and the cellar. Taking the tools and things he needed to begin his dubious task.

Ivan moved slowly toward Axe's side, putting his hand on Axe's forearm. "You're not going to release him, are you?" he asked quietly. "The boy we take, I mean. You intend to let him die."

Axe took his arm from Ivan's grasp and put both

his hands on the boy's shoulders. He nodded and looked up to the slowly darkening night sky. "Have you known all along?" he asked, showing Ivan a soft smile. "Or did you see or hear something that lead you to that conclusion?"

"A little of both. The way you've been so driven. Like a man possessed. Poe's protagonist in *The Telltale Heart* or Raskolnikov in *Crime and Punishment* perhaps."

"My young brother is no longer a simple peasant, a laborer. He is an educated man." Axe nodded again and showed an ironic smile then pulled his brother close. Holding him tightly he felt the tears slowly overflow and run down his cheeks. "But will this educated man still follow his broken and driven older brother to finish this sad task he has begun?" he asked, backing away and wiping his cheeks with his open hand.

"It is his brother's kindness, love, and generosity that has made him into the educated man he has become," Ivan said returning his brother's look with a sardonic smile. "And though he would rather that they not bring harm to another he always has and always will follow his brother to find their destiny," Ivan added. He pulled Axe close again, repeating the word, "Always!"

****

Shane sat, feet dangling over the edge of the gas dock. He stared absently across the mirror that was the Bass River on this sultry June evening. The lustrous twilight could inspire poetry and romance. But Shane sat conflicted. Terribly conflicted as the sun slipped behind the trees that shielded the large homes from the prying eyes of any boaters returning from Nantucket

Sound as the dusk took hold.

"Hey!" a loud voice called from the edge of the gravel behind the wood bulkhead that protected the parking lot and buildings from the River. "No one is supposed to be here after..." the man stopped and paused. "Shane? Is that you?"

It was Bobby Rodriguez, Shane's uncle and guardian angel of sorts.

"Yeah, Bobby. It's me," he answered. "Just sitting here pondering the mysteries of life, love, and the vagaries of the Universe."

"Jeez, Shane. I thought you graduated from the Coast Guard Academy not Fine Arts at Columbia," Bobby said with a throaty chuckle

Shane sat quietly as his uncle came down the long dock and flopped down next to him. "I did. Just feeling confused tonight."

"Hmmm. Would the cause of that confusion be named Samantha?" Bobby asked, joining his nephew's stare.

"Life is funny isn't it?"

"Yes, it is and that's a question I can understand," Bobby said then shook his head and picked up a small stone from the dock and threw it into the water. "Oh my God. That little lady really likes you, man. There was no mistakin' that."

Shane continued to stare as the lights began to come on along the shore.

"I heard you went over to see her this morning at the hospital after that attack or whatever they're calling it," Bobby said. "I'm not into psychology but I'm guessing that means you like her, too?"

"That I *really* like her?" Shane shook his head.

"So, you don't?"

"After that time in the life raft she tried to find me." Shane found his own pebble on the dock, throwing it into the still water. "And yeah, I wanted to see her again. A lot." Shane continued looking at the river and nodded. "In spite of Emily," he paused. "But once the adventure on the life raft was over and the adrenaline stopped flowing, I couldn't see her again. I mean, how could I?" He shook his head. "I had a life and someone to come home to. But I sure thought about her. There was something about her, Bobby. And sure, she was great looking even after four days in the raft, but it was something else. I know she was frightened and worried about her uncle and the two kids and dying of course. But damn it she showed courage. Real courage. She took care of her uncle like an EMT and made sure the kids ate and drank their rations while she'd leave some of her own, so we'd all have more in case things went really bad. She kept everyone's spirits up and never let anyone even think about anything but what we were going to do to celebrate when we were rescued. I spent four years in the Coast Guard and saw a lot of rescue work, but I swear I never met anyone who was as courageous and unselfish as Sam."

Bobby put his hand on Shane's shoulder. "I think you've answered my question," he said with a gentle smile. "So, am I missing something? I mean why are you sitting here moping?"

"Well, when we met on the raft, I didn't know anything about her or her family. It's not like we were introduced at a cocktail party. Like I said, I knew *nothing* about her," he repeated. "And being the way Sam is she never said anything about it. After we were picked up there was a lot about it and her in the papers and on the news for a few days about "*the lovely heiress and her family survive in the Gulf!*" I was blown away."

"I'm still losin' the thread here, Shane."

"Okay. Bottom line here is yes, I like Samantha. Very much! But she comes from British royalty, Bobby. They have a security force and drivers and live in a twenty-seven-room estate and attended finishing schools and events at Buckingham Palace, for God's sake. I'm a friggin' part-time harbormaster on Cape Cod. Does that sound like a match made in heaven?"

"Oh my God." Bobby looked at Shane taking his arm firmly "Are you kidding me?" He asked as his eyes grew narrow and his jaw rigid. "That girl hung on your every word. She invited you over for high tea this afternoon, didn't she? You just told me that she might be the most courageous and unselfish person you ever met! And let's not forget that she is really not hard to look at."

Shane lifted his arm away forcefully. "Look. I appreciate the positive reinforcement, but I'm sick of sadness and disappointment." He shook his head rapidly. "I'll be polite and play tour guide. *But that's it!*" Shane said, pulled himself up and turned. "Night, Bobby," he threw back and began walking toward the parking lot.

"Je-sus. What the hell's the matter with you, Shane? You are as dumb as a box of rocks," Bobby called back to Shane while he sat shaking his head and watched his nephew leave.

Chapter Twenty-Seven

Lord Edgerton sat in his study smoking a Gurka His Majesty's Reserve Cigar. "Brian," he said, showing his friend a curious smile. "I bought these just to share with you, my old comrade."

"No thanks, James. I think I'll pass tonight," The Admiral nodded toward the great room across the hall where Jeanie and his grandchildren sat. The exclamations and laughter could be heard through the open door. "I think Samantha's giving Jeanie a more difficult match than she expected."

"Yes," Edgerton shook his head and looked toward the great room. "Sam's no amateur on the chess board. She's a damn wiz at everything she tackles." He raised his eyebrows as a proud smile crossed his face. "Graduated from the London School of Economics top of her class, medaled on the European Ski Tour, quit riding events after winning everything in the junior circuit, but she's never really found anything or more correctly anyone that caught her interest. She's a starry-eyed romantic and a dreamer, Brian. But I'm not sure. I have to say that she seems quite taken with that young Coast Guard officer. She moped around for months when she came home after being rescued and found out he was engaged." Edgerton said shaking his head. "But rather than discuss my family tonight, I need to talk to you about something else."

The Admiral nodded.

"The man who's been leading our security team. Misha Ben Canaan. You may remember I sent you his resume and credentials before we hired him after that incident with Charles last spring."

"Yes. He seemed like quite a find. Had him checked out by our expert on private security contractors." He smiled as another robust cheer echoed from across the hall. "I think Sam just bested our Agency's chess master, James."

"Well, you know what happened last night." Edgerton ignored the comment. "At least what we heard and saw. So far everyone seems completely confused. Stymied. Then today—I got this," Edgerton stood and passed a small slip of paper across his desk toward the Admiral.

The Admiral stood, took the crumpled sheet, and studied it. "Yes. I see your concern," he said thoughtfully, and he handed the paper back to his friend. "What can I do to help?" he asked glancing across the hall while Edgerton crossed the study and slowly closed the door.

****

"All right. So now we're ready to execute the most important phase of our plan," Axe said quietly and smiling at the man across the small table from him.

Dylan Murphy nodded while he sipped his espresso. "Yes."

They sat in the Monomoy Coffee Company, a boutique pastry and coffee shop on Main Street in Chatham. Murphy had walked there from the Chatham Bars Inn.

"And you'll want that expensive accessory you

mentioned? Something to attract attention and validate your status as a *gentleman* worthy of interest?"

Murphy smiled and nodded a second time. "Something like that."

"I've secured something I think is perfect. Here," Axe pulled out a photograph and pushed it toward Murphy.

"Oh, yes. That *will* do nicely."

"Ivan will meet you tomorrow. I'll call with the details on a secure line." Axe spoke quietly while studying the other clients.

"All right." He nodded.

"Ivan will meet you here at 6:30 p.m., drive you to the mall, and you can make the exchange with him. Then Ivan's friend will pick him up. Ivan will make the return in Hyannis the next morning. They don't check the person doing the return as long as the property is in good working order," Axe explained taking a large sip of the dark-roast blend he was drinking. "And need I say that the way that pseudo attack you staged on the Edgerton's last evening was handled masterfully."

Murphy nodded and waved away the praise. "I've been at this a long time. Minor theatrics like that are no problem. And from what my contact tells me the note did what is was supposed to."

"I have no doubt it did." Axe shrugged. "So. We're all set then?"

"Yes." Murphy took a final hit of his espresso and nodded at Axe.

They shook hands and left the coffee shop, heading in different directions.

Things were coming together just as Axe had planned. He smiled and headed to the lot to retrieve his vehicle.

****

The Admiral and Jeanie sat with the Edgertons on the large screened-in porch in the back of the house.

"So tell me more about this amazing reunion with that young Coast Guard officer you and Charles seemed so taken with," Jeanie asked as they finished their breakfast tea and coffee.

"Oh, you'll want Sam to give you all the details. She's the one with such a crush," Charles said, batting his eyes comically and made a gesture with his hand that brought smiles to everyone but his sister.

"Oh, *pl...ease*, Charles. You're the one who had those poor young girls waiting in line for a smidge of attention at the beach all week!" Samantha protested flushing crimson. "And..." she began putting her hand over her mouth. "But I think he," Sam nodded toward her brother who sat with an annoyed look. "Has a *secret boyish crush* on Shane as well!" she finished in a whisper loud enough to be heard.

"That's all right, dear," Jeanie chuckled and stole a look at the Admiral.

He held her eyes, staring at her face when she glanced back at him and felt a blush of her own.

"Well, all right. It is a fascinating story. And meeting Shane again almost four years since our time on the life raft is downright precious," Sam began. "For both of us," she added giving Charles a high five while he grinned.

For the next ten minutes she told about their sailboat sinking, how Shane came to be on the life raft with Sam and her family members and their ordeal on the Caribbean. Charles nodded enthusiastically chewing

179

his fingernails while the Admiral sat fascinated. Jeanie had leaned forward in her chair and looked equally engrossed.

Just as Samantha told of the hoist lifting them into the Jayhawk, a soft knock came at the door that lead from the front door to the porch entrance.

"Excuse me," said Misha in a gentle voice. "I wanted to say good-bye."

Charles and Samantha both looked up at his strong slender frame silhouetted in the door. Charles wore a disconsolate look. Sam's face grew hard and angry. She shook her head.

Both stood and approached him, Sam somewhat clumsily.

"Excuse us for a moment," she said nodding at the Admiral and Jeanie.

The three of them walked across the porch and out the back door onto the broad expanse of manicured lawn. Misha assumed the duty of helping Sam.

"This isn't right," Sam said bitterly squaring her jaw. "You're such a good man and none of this was your fault. I've been arguing with…"

"Shhh," Misha whispered. "Life takes us down one path or another for a reason," he added.

"But she's right," Charles said as a tear overflowed while he sniffled. He took Misha's hand and held it tightly. "But…but you've been so kind. So thoughtful." He shook his head angrily.

"You two have been wonderful to me. Perhaps I shouldn't but I almost think of you as friends," he told them, taking out a linen handkerchief he gave it to Charles. "My favorite…clients. So." He took something from the small case he carried. "Take these as tokens of my appreciation." He handed each of them a polished silver cigarette lighter. "If I had the time, I would have had them engraved but. Well. Here"

"Thank you," Sam said feeling her own eyes filling up. "It's like the one you were given by your men."

He nodded.

Charles looked at his curiously.

"I'll explain later," Sam told him.

"Now, if you are ever in trouble press this raised emblem on the front of the lighter." He held it up and pressed the small insignia. "Like this." When he did suddenly a loud buzzing sound could be heard coming from his case. "It's solar powered and linked to a satellite. It sends an alarm and has a GPS tracker. So. You will never be further away from me than this lighter. But...do not lose it and never press the signal unless you are in danger," he looked at Charles and ruffled his thick hair. "I am not attempting to encourage what your sister and I know to be an unpleasant habit," Misha said with a gentle smile, nodding. "But I didn't have the opportunity to get the switch installed into a money clip or something more appropriate."

Both of them approached Misha and hugged him in turn, thanking him as they snuggled close then backed away.

"Good-bye, Samantha, Charles. God Bless you both," he said then shook their hands. "Shalom Aleichem."

"Shalom, Misha. Mazel tov," Samantha said then watched him turn to leave.

As they watched him walk around the house to the front both held the small glistening lighters in their hands.

"A touching remembrance," Charles said when he looked at it.

Sam nodded. "One I hope we never need for anything other than lighting cigarettes," she commented as they headed back to the porch.

Chapter Twenty-Eight

Week of June 21st

"Oh my God, Sam," Charles burst through the front door, his dusty riding boots clattering across the granite entry hall. "You would not believe the man I met at the stables this afternoon. What a cool fellow!"

Samantha stood and made her way to the door that lead to the house from the screened-in porch. "Calm down, Charlie. Calm down!" she offered, holding up her hands in an act of mock surrender.

"Well I was on that long winding trail that leads through the woods to the small pond. Remember the one we were on that first day?"

Samantha nodded. "Yes, dear," she answered evenly then sat down.

"Well, suddenly this fellow came along on a spectacular Arabian. He was so polished and pleasant. Had served in the SAS!" Charles emoted breathlessly. He was consumed—excited by the notion that military service in one of the elite branches was the modern-day equivalent of being King Arthur in Camelot.

Sam sighed and stared at her younger sibling wondering when Charles was going to grow up realizing that she still adored his innocent, endless exuberance, and his delightful if somewhat misdirected naivete. "And just how did you know all this?" she asked sweetly, trying not to burst her brother's bubble.

"He had a ring on. You know, the one they get after they attend Sandhurst," he explained breathlessly. Sandhurst was the British Military Academy. It differed from West Point in that most candidates already had degrees when they attended. And the curriculum at Sandhurst took only forty-four weeks as opposed to the four-year program at West Point.

Samantha nodded and smiled wanly. She was happy her brother had found another hero so far from home, but she had something more pressing on her mind. Shane's sudden and mysterious "disappearance." "Did you and your new hero make a date? Dinner or a movie perhaps?" she teased.

He made one of his faces at her and stood striking a pose, hands on hips. "I'm sorry that your Lieutenant has gone missing, Sam, but you don't have to take out your frustration on me," he said wearing a hurt look.

Sam shrugged. "I...I'm sorry." She took a breath. "You're right."

Charles closed the distance between them and opened his arms. She gave him a big hug thinking how tall and strong he'd become while she'd been away at the London School of Economics and the European Ski Tour.

"I don't know what happened to him, but I know something did. Shane isn't the type to just abandon you," he whispered, giving her a squeeze.

Just then Poppy, the Admiral, and Jeanie approached from the dock with the newest member of the family's security team. His name was Julian and he seemed polite, competent, and respectful. But he was not Misha. No one could replace him in Sam's eyes or heart. Not that she had romantic feelings for him. She simply felt that no one and nothing could harm them when he was with them.

"Well, my goodness. What's all the fuss?" Poppy asked with a grin. "Sounds like something's going on?"

"Charles has met some gallant fellow at the stables who made quite the impression," Sam volunteered with a doubtful smile and raised eyebrows. "I'll let him explain." She shook her head and walked down onto the lawn toward the dock.

Her ankle was much better—perhaps thanks to her long years of athletic training the doctor suggested. But after a week she was able to walk with only a slight limp. Making her way toward the water, she heard someone behind her. Turning, she saw Jeanie. Samantha nodded.

"Thought I'd seek some female companionship. All the testosterone when Brian and your grandfather are together can be a bit overwhelming," she said as looked back toward the porch and sneaked a pack of Marlboros from her shorts and shook the pack offering one to Sam. "Shhh..." she whispered with a conspiratorial smile.

"Thanks. I'm trying to cut back but I'm not making much progress," Sam admitted. "I didn't want to smoke around Shane but well, that doesn't appear to be an issue." She took a long draw on her cigarette and exhaled then pushed her lips into a pout.

"What do you think happened?" Jeanie asked lighting her own cigarette as they walked down the steps from the dock onto the small sandy beach to stay out of view.

Sam shrugged. "I have no idea. He came to visit

me in the hospital the morning after the attack—I think that's what they're calling whatever happened last week—and spent the afternoon with me when I got home. I thought...well it makes no difference what I thought. Obviously, he wasn't offended by the smell of cigarettes on my breath. We never got that close. Except for our time on the raft four years ago." She shook her head as she flushed. "I really liked him. Jeanie. Very much."

They finished smoking their cigarettes in silence.

Sam crushed hers out in the soft sand then stripped the paper and remaining tobacco away throwing it into the gentle breeze.

Jeanie watched her with a curious look "Where did you learn that?" She gestured toward Sam. "Field stripping a cigarette."

Sam shook her head. "Just something I picked up from a long-lost friend."

****

Jeanie took the Admiral's arm as they headed toward the front door. "Do you really need to go?" she asked, twisting her face into a scolding expression as they stood in the Edgerton's entry hall on Wednesday afternoon of the third week of June.

One whole week together, he thought, letting his eyes wash over the perfect symmetry of her face. He still marveled at it. "I'll only be an hour or so. They want me to look at something. Some photos they took of the target they'd told us about." He shrugged then bent and gave her slender arm a squeeze.

"I hope it's important enough to interrupt our vacation," Jeanie said with a frown.

He was thrilled that she referred to this shared

hiatus as 'their' vacation. "I'm sure it is," he assured her. "You're welcome to join me," he told her doing his best to muster a smile.

"Thanks, but I've enjoyed being on a real vacation. First time in longer than I can remember. So," she began, showing him a playful pout. "Go play field agent. I'll go with Charles, Samantha, and Kylie to the stables this afternoon. I haven't been on a horse since I was fifteen and well, I'm kind of looking forward to it. I used to love riding and besides, I'm interested to meet this man Charles met on Monday." She smiled then gave him a gentle push. "Now. Get out of here! See you for dinner."

He looked back when she let go of his arm. He felt the electricity whenever they touched, wondering if she felt it, too. Bending, he gave her cheek a soft kiss and grinned. Turning he headed across the circular driveway to where their rental car was parked. Pressing the remote he opened the driver's door on the glistening black Chrysler 300 sedan.

Merritt and Mendes had asked the Admiral to stop by their hotel telling him they had something important they wanted to share on the surveillance they were conducting on the man called Lassiter, and though he wanted to find something they could pin on this scoundrel he hated to leave Jeanie. Even for a moment.

This trip—their trip—had taken the subtle turn he had hoped it might. To maintain the appearance of professionalism and propriety he and Jeanie had been given separate bedrooms a discreet distance apart. And despite the sudden feelings she had exposed on the day before their trip began the Admiral had done his best to resist the temptation to take advantage of being here with her. But as the days passed Jeanie continued to show him not so subtle hints that left no doubt she shared his affection.

He arrived at the Hyannis Resort and Conference Center about two-fifteen. He'd worn typical vacation attire—sneakers, no socks, plaid shorts, and a white polo shirt, capping the outfit off with a weathered Red Sox hat Eric and Ashley had given him the previous summer.

The Admiral had been here a few times both during and after the frightening adventure of three years ago. The summer he met Ashley, Eric, and Kylie. They'd developed an unbreakable bond. The first time he'd let anyone crack the hard façade he'd surrounded himself with since losing Ellen and the children.

He smiled, nodding toward the clerk at the front desk and headed toward the small restaurant and lounge that bordered the pool. He stopped when he recognized the bartender who leaned over two buxom middle-aged women doing their best to give the man a tempting preview.

The man's face took on a curious expression. He stood and stepped back from the ladies, pointing at the Admiral. "Don't tell me now. Mr....Turnbull, isn't it?" he asked with a lyrical brogue when he spotted the Admiral.

"My God. You're good, Liam," the Admiral responded nodding at the man.

"Here for a cold one?" Liam asked holding up a Corona.

"Heading outside but why not." The Admiral stopped and leaned over the mahogany bar. "Meeting a couple of old golfing buddies by the pool," he explained smiling at the women who had turned their attention to him. "Ladies," he said warmly when he spotted Mendes and Merritt already sitting at a distant table with two Coronas in front of them. He left a ten-dollar bill on the counter and nodded at Liam.

The Admiral walked around the sparse collection of guests scattered at tables and on lounge chairs and sat down between his two agents. The large transient population of tourists hadn't descended on the Cape, but the 4th of July was the unofficial start of the vacation season. So, in ten days a vast sea of humanity—several hundred thousand strong would descend on this spectacular vacation spot for their Independence Day celebrations.

As the waitress saw him, the Admiral held up his beer and shook his head.

The waitress nodded back at him.

When she returned with baskets of kettle cooked chips and mixed nuts the three of them seemed to be studying house and plot plans intently. Merritt did a fine job explaining exactly where the fictitious homes were to be built, using a map of Barnstable County. When his partner leaned back in his chair and took a draw on his Corona, Mario Mendes added color to the pretense by extolling the virtues of the location and amenities of these getaway properties with the energy and enthusiasm of a Tony Robbins.

Hiding between the house plans, elevation sketches, and pictures of the breathtaking views from this faux development were photos of Lassiter and a second man.

"So, you sent these back to the office for facial recognition analysis?" the Admiral asked still pointing at one of the house plans and nodding.

"Yes," Merritt nodded and shot a look at Mendes. "Here's the analysis. Our people double-checked it with FBI, NSA, and the Agency," he added with a shrug. "They all agreed."

"The second man is Derrick Muldoon. Irish national who joined the SAS at twenty and became a legend in the special forces' arena. Fought in the Middle-East, Bosnia, and did some serious black ops things for Queen and country. His favorite alias is the name Murphy. Dylan Murphy."

The Admiral listened intently. "I've heard the name. But word is he's gone private and rogue unless I'm mistaken."

"Yes, sir," Merritt agreed. "At age thirty our man Derrick decided the money and action was more rewarding on the dark side."

They sat staring at the Admiral. He sat trying to think why two highly-paid top-level mercenaries would be on Cape Cod? One an expert at everything electronic, the second a cunning experienced thug. Both were adrenaline junkies who sold themselves to the highest bidder. He didn't want to even think it, but he kept coming back to his friend's presence and the strange incident that took place one week before at his rental house.

"There's nothing tying these two together, right?" The Admiral asked.

The two agents looked at each other and shook their heads.

"Still. Tell the boys back at the capital I want every scrap of intel they can dig up on Muldoon and Lassiter. Without those photos of Muldoon, I could actually imagine that Lassiter might really be here on holiday or between jobs. But I don't believe in coincidences," he said clenching his fist and hitting the tabletop gently. "And tell them to call in every outstanding favor we have." The Admiral set his jaw. "I have a sick feeling this has just become personal."

The two agents looked at each other and nodded slowly.

"Yes...sir," Merritt said quietly as the senior member of the team. "We'll get on it as soon as you leave. Jeanie is with you, sir?" he asked, looking at his partner.

The Admiral nodded. "Yes. We were headed back tomorrow but if there's a chance that what I think may be happening we'll be staying," he told the team.

"I'll take the extra set of photos you have, and send them to my phone, too. I want Jeanie to have a look. There's nothing to prove it but damn it somehow I can't help thinking these slimy bastards are involved with the Edgerton business last week."

"It crossed our minds, too," Mendes said raising his beer toward the waitress to get a refill. "Cape Cod is a pretty place, but I know of nothing and no one else of any import here except for a few local celebrities for the Fourth of July festivities," he added with a shrug.

"Jeanie and I came here because of the Edgerton business but decided to spend a few days taking some vacation time when it looked like it might be some kind of prank," the Admiral said quietly looking back and forth between the two younger men.

Merritt beamed a warm smile at him and then at his partner. "Good for you, sir," he said with what appeared genuine affection. "And her. Maybe this will turn out to be a false lead."

"Maybe," the Admiral said with no confidence.

They discussed a few other cases, none of them of significance, then shook hands as the Admiral took the folder with a glossy photo of Nantucket Sound and the words, *New Seabury, Phase III* stenciled on the cover.

He headed back through the bar that now was more populated. A few raucous customers stood loudly celebrating and joking about a golf match. He gave Liam the bartender a quick wave as he left the lounge. But when he was in his rental car the Admiral opened the folder again, staring at the first photograph underneath the faux house plans and scenic vistas that had covered it.

He tugged at his chin and hit 'send' on his cell phone so that Jeanie could see Merritt's pictures because the Admiral was concerned, almost certain he knew who and what the men in the photos wanted.

****

"What's going on with Shane?" Ashley asked as Bobby Rodriguez poked his head in the office when he stopped to say good night. It was almost six-thirty and he was late for the romantic anniversary dinner that his wife had planned.

"I don't follow you, Ash?" he asked with a shrug but the way he avoided her eyes served as a dead giveaway. He knew exactly what she was asking about.

"Well, last week when he met Samantha again everyone was sure it was a match made in heaven. Two handsome talented kids who'd met four years before in the most bizarre of ways. It was obvious they found each other attractive. Very attractive! He agreed to take her family on a tour of the Sound, and then when an attack sends Sam to the hospital, he rushes over to see her like they were lovers and spends the rest of his day off with her. Then…nada?"

Bobby looked around self-consciously. He tugged at the two-day old stubble on his chin. "I'd rather let him explain 'cause to tell you the truth I don't get it either. Maybe he's gone off the deep end." He shrugged again. "All I know is there's something about his feelings for Samantha that he's not telling anyone. But I really must get goin'. Big doings at the Riverway tonight."

Ashley nodded and let it go. "Okay. Maybe Eric can get to the bottom of it." Ashley knew she and Eric would be seeing Bobby, his wife, and Shane later that evening at a surprise dinner party at the Riverway Restaurant. She could wait till then.

****

The Admiral walked quickly up the Edgerton's front steps and into the hardwood entry hall. Thick Orientals covered most of the wood that spanned the thirty feet from the front porch to the back one.

But he took a sharp right turn and headed up the winding staircase down the long thickly carpeted upstairs hallway and stopped two doors from the end knocking softly on Jeanie's door.

"Come in," she said softly and walked to the door.

When he entered the large well-appointed bedroom, she still wore the riding clothes she'd borrowed from Samantha. She put her arms around him and gave him a robust hug. "Hi."

"Hi back at you. I hope the ride was enjoyable?" he asked.

"Yes, delightful," she agreed. "But my backside

and thighs may be needing that splendid whirlpool tub later this evening," she added with a grin while she stretched and groaned.

"Anything more on the pictures yet?"

"No, nothing. But I've talked to Alan and the team in Washington to give it top priority. Not much they can add, I'm guessing." Jeanie shrugged. "We already know who they are but there's no way to determine why they're here or tie them together. I understand that James and his family would seem to qualify as prime targets but again why and for what?"

He nodded shrugging. "Well, we were supposed to head back tomorrow, but I have to tell you. I have a sixth sense about this." He shook his head. "And as far-fetched as it sounds, I cannot get it out of my mind that those two have something to do with the business that happened here last week."

"No, Brian. I agree. We should stay." She began finding his hand. "There's no intel on anything or anyone else being here outside of a couple of retired pro athletes and some local politicians for the Fourth of July celebrations," she said giving him a quick nod. "I don't like the way this is coming together."

"Neither do I." He sighed. "Thanks. Now I've gotta go back to my room and get cleaned up for dinner and I have to steal James away and talk to him. I have some questions and I'd like you to be there."

She took his arm, pulled him to her, and searched his face for a moment then gave him a gentle kiss on his lips. "I trust your judgment," she said with a grin then walked him to the door. "And thanks, I'd like to be there when you two talk."

****

"Got a minute?" Ashley asked when Samantha answered her cell phone.

"Yes. Hello, Ashley-Jean."

"This may sound rather strange but what are you doing for dinner?"

"Well. It's supposed to be a special dinner for the Admiral and Jeanie but, Poppy just stopped by and told us that they're going to be staying for a while. Something about that incident last week they've turned up. Why?" Sam asked.

"Is there any possibility that you could get away and come to the Riverway Lobster House about eight? It's right at the end of Old Main Street on Route Twenty-Eight." Ashley didn't like playing matchmaker and this idea might blow up in her face, but she was going to give it her best shot.

"I'm not sure," Sam sounded hesitant but curious. "Why? What did you have in mind?"

"Sam, do you like Shane? I mean *really* like him," Ashley asked quietly.

Silence.

"Sam. Please. Just answer me."

"Yes. You know I do. Very much. I never forgot him after the time we spent on the raft. Why?" she repeated raising her voice.

"Well, here's what I'd like you to do…"

Chapter Twenty-Nine

"I don't want to be rude to our guests, Poppy, but Ashley-Jean wants me to come to a party at a nearby restaurant." Sam explained with a combination of excitement and apprehension. If her new friend was correct it could be delightful. Perhaps even life changing? But if she was not it could be painful and heart-breaking. "Besides, you told me that they'll be staying at least till the weekend and I should be home in a couple of hours." She put her hands together in mock prayer. "Please, darling. You know I never ask for anything!"

Her grandfather opened his arms and took her in an embrace. "You know I can never refuse you or your brother anything." He shook his head hugging her tightly. "But. Have Julian drive you and make sure he stays close. Very close so he can keep an eye on you. I know you love to tempt fate, my dear, but we're still not sure what that business last week was all about. So *be careful*!"

Samantha broke their embrace, stood on tiptoes, and gave him a kiss on the cheek. "Thanks. You have made me very happy. And I will, darling. *Very careful*!"

He stood back and studied her. "I'm assuming this has something to do with your Lieutenant. The hero from the life raft," he said raising his eyebrows while he grew a sly smile.

"I hope so," Sam whispered, giggling and heading off to find Julian. "Have a delightful dinner. I'll go make my apologies to our guests."

Sam ran clumsily up the stairs, still favoring her sore ankle and headed into her room to change into something more flattering.

After she'd changed into her white jeans and a turquoise halter, she heard a noise behind her. Charles stood nodding. He smiled. He came close and put his hand on Sam's shoulder. "Hmmm. You know, Sam," he began tugging at his cleft chin. "You look quite fetching in that outfit," he added growing a flush then raised his eyebrows.

"You really think so?"

"Yep," Charles nodded. "And so will he," he said smugly as he started to turn when he stopped, adding, "You know I like him very much, too, Sam, so I hope it works out for you both."

"What? Do you have a secret microphone planted on my person?"

"Nope. Just being a *no-sy* sibling!" He grinned. "Now get that butt of yours downstairs."

Samantha ran clumsily downstairs. Just as Sam and Julian headed out the door, Charles tapped her on her shoulder and whispered, "Don't forget your lighter."

Sam patted the back pocket of her snug stretch jeans and smiled. "Got it covered," She whispered as she hugged her brother and gave him a good-bye wave. "You know, while I was off skiing the alps you've become quite the young man," she winked and followed Julian toward the sparkling black Range Rover.

Chapter Thirty

Shane had pulled out his blue blazer and the
necktie he planned to wear to the surprise party for
Bobby and Stacy's anniversary. It was the couple's first
and Shane and his parents arrived at the Riverway at
six-forty-five p.m. His mother had brought some
decorations and a collection of pictures of her baby
brother and his wife during their engagement and
marriage.

The Riverway Lobster House was in South
Yarmouth directly across from the Bass River. A
popular restaurant with a first-class pub it was located
at the busy intersection of Route 28, Old Main Street,
and Station Avenue. It served as the meeting place for
many of the local service and fraternal organizations.
The restaurant had a tasteful décor that suggested Cape
Cod and its maritime heritage, but Shane and his family
entered by the back door that lead through the pub to
the lobby. It was vintage New England with lustrous
knotty-pine paneling, nautical artifacts and souvenirs
hanging on the walls, and a mammoth brick fireplace at
the far end.

After Shane tacked up some bunting, he spelled his
father, filling balloons with helium. "Here, dad. Let me
do some of those," he said knowing his father was still
recovering from a back injury and bending over the
helium tank could be painful.

His dad nodded and headed out to the bar. "I'll get us a beer."

As Shane gave him thumbs up, he felt his mother's gentle tap him on the shoulder. "When are you going to tell us what's going on?"

He turned and gave her his best *I have no idea what you're talking about* smile. "Nothing, mom. Everything's fine," he assured her, shrugged then finished tying another balloon, and released it to the ceiling.

"You know, since you were a toddler you've never been able to fool me, so I'm not buying it." She sighed and put her hand gently to his cheek. "You've had a rough time. Losing Evan, resigning your commission, Emily's accident." His mother shrugged. "I could see that all that changed you. But you always seem to stay strong. But since the *thing* that happened at the English family's home you haven't been the same."

He stood mute for a minute trying to formulate an answer she'd accept. The real one was so convoluted that he couldn't explain it to anyone. But before he had to come up with something plausible their attention was drawn away by the arrival of more guests, including Eric and Ashley.

****

"James, I want to talk to you more about that business last week," The Admiral said quietly to Lord Edgerton as they finished dinner.

"All right, Brian. When?" he asked.

"The sooner the better," the Admiral told him. He nodded to Jeanie. "Can we go to your office?"

"Of course," Edgerton said and nodded. "Excuse us," he said to Charles and his daughter Millicent.

They stood and headed toward the large pine-paneled office. Edgerton stopped when Jeanie joined them.

"This is about business, James and Jeanie is the best resource I know of," the Admiral explained hiding a smile. Despite his savior-faire, impeccable manors, and worldly exterior his old friend still had more than a little of the old school Brit in him. *Cigars and brandy in the study and ladies to the drawing room!* He mused.

They entered the study and closed the door. When they sat down in the overstuffed leather chairs opposite his desk Edgerton gestured toward them. "Well. I thought we'd put that business to rest. But please. You two are intelligence professionals, so I'm curious and frankly a bit concerned. What do you want to talk about?"

****

Eric and Ashley helped finish with the decorations and arranging the presents on a table set up at the entrance to the generous private function room.

By 7:15 the crowd had grown to almost thirty.

"How many are we expecting?" Eric asked Mrs. Winslow.

"I think we sent out about forty invitations, but you and Bobby have such a big network I wouldn't be surprised if we get upwards of fifty," she said, patting his shoulder.

"I hope you invited our new Police Chief in case things get rowdy," he teased Ashley giving her a push. "Stop it, Eric!" she scolded, hiding a smile and pulling him gently away. "'Scuse, us, Jenny, I need my husband for a minute."

They walked away from the small crowd and

Ashley directed Eric out through the restaurant to the entry hall and into the bar.

"What's going on, Ash?"

"Just got a call from the Admiral. They're not leaving tomorrow afternoon."

"Well that's nice. They deserve some time off…"

She held up her hand. "No. He needs to see us ASAP. Tomorrow morning early."

"What's going on?"

"They've found something. Something important they think may tie in to that episode last week at the Edgerton's."

Eric shrugged. "Sure. He calls, we haul!" he said with a grin.

"Good. Let's talk more later." She nodded. "It's almost time for Stacy and Bobby to get here so let's get back—"

****

Samantha had stopped at one of the nicer shops—an art gallery—not wanting to appear at the function empty handed. Julian accompanied her, plodding along dutifully but every time she was with him it became more obvious that he was no Misha.

Her heart thumped loudly as she dismounted the black Range Rover Sport they rode in. Sam was certain anyone close to her could hear it.

"What would you like me to do, Miss Edgerton?" Julian asked her quietly with a sober expression.

"Come inside and just hang out by the door. Please," she said with a smile. "I…I'm not sure how long I'll be in there," Sam added biting her lip.

Several people stood outside the entrance to the Riverway smoking and laughing. Two young men watched her with interest as one of them opened the door for her and nodded. "Well. *Good evening*," he offered with a grin, nodding when she walked inside.

Samantha took a deep breath, fidgeting with her outfit, squeezing her hands, and second-guessing Ashley-Jean's idea. If Shane really wanted to see her, he'd had ample opportunity. More than ample. Sam was certain he was attracted to her. Everything he had said and done spoke to that. And heaven knows she was attracted to him. Very much. She agreed to come if for no other reason than to find out why he'd paid her so much attention after the incident last week and then abandoned her!

Entering the restaurant, she and Julian followed the neatly printed sign that directed them straight ahead to the private room where the party was being held. Music and laughter drifted through the open door into the half-filled public dining room. As Sam continued flexing her fingers nervously, she looked around, seeing several smaller rooms and the larger ones.

When she turned back toward the door, Ashley-Jean had emerged from the party and headed toward her beaming a smile.

After she greeted Sam and took her hand Sam introduced Julian. They turned and walked back into the room where the party was being held. It was somewhat smaller than the large dining room but decorated with the same popular themes—Cape Cod and nautical memorabilia.

Ashley-Jean directed her to Bobby and a dark pixie of a young woman. She was stunning. Dark eyes, a deep tan, and short black hair surrounded a flawless smile that dazzled.

"Hello, Miss Edgerton. So glad you could drop by. This is my wife, Stacy," Bobby said graciously.

Sam shook his hand and Stacy's. "So glad to meet you, Stacy, and I'm thrilled to be here," she said loudly thanks to the music. "And please, I wish everyone would just call me Samantha." She shook her head and laughed. "No! Correction. Make that Sam."

Chapter Thirty-One

Axe walked into the room. *The* room where they would keep their prisoner. It was small—10 X 12 X 8 feet high. Smaller than he'd imagined. Made even smaller by the color, or lack of it. The walls, cement floor, and ceiling were painted with flat black paint that offered no reflection. There was a small bare light bulb in a fixture overhead. He reached back around the door frame and flipped it on. The tiny twenty-five-watt bulb cast a small gloomy circle of light that illuminated six feet in diameter on the concrete floor.

Yes. In little more than one week all the planning and expense would be over and one of the Edgerton grandchildren would be here.

"Excuse me. I came down here after my walk on the beach. Needed just to get away and collect my thoughts. I want to get a couple of these cameras mounted tonight," Lassiter said as he wheeled a small stainless-steel work cart with two tiny complex looking devices into the claustrophobic space.

"Fine." Axe nodded. "I won't disturb you," he said, closing his eyes. Ivan and Nicolai had installed a small air vent and exhaust fan. Axe had wrestled with the idea, discounting it at first, letting his desire for revenge rule his thinking, but it would prove necessary since it might be difficult for Edgerton to pay the large ransom within a day. Their captive would need more air to survive than the small chamber held.

As Axe stood fantasizing what it would be like to have one of them in the small room Lassiter pushed the small cart against the wall and turned. "May I ask you a question, Mr. Axelrod?"

Axe nodded slowly.

"Your project," he began, studying his employer. "It's more than just a vehicle to get money?" Lassiter tilted his head. "No?"

He stood returning Lassiter's stare. "In your extensive experience with projects like this does that make a difference?" he asked not sure he wanted to share his dark purpose with this man.

"Well. I don't want to pry," Lassiter paused showing Axe a thoughtful look. "Inserting myself into my client's motives is not something I generally do. And in theory it makes no difference, but I gather this isn't something you've done before?" Lassiter asked raising his eyebrows.

"I'm not sure I want to share any of the details."

"I was simply going to offer a comment based on years of experience."

Axe stood, folding his arms while he faced Lassiter. "Feel free," he said with a shrug.

"When you do something for profit you tend to be far more careful. Plan better and execute that plan with precision."

Axe stood silently.

"When you are motivated by hatred, lust, or revenge you're ruled by emotion. Not a good thing when life, death, and mammoth rewards and risks are in the mix." Lassiter smiled slightly, shrugged, and turned back to the cart.

Axe stood immobile for a long minute then turned and left the room, thinking there was wisdom in what this mercenary said. "Thank you for your insights," he offered quietly. Yes. The small fan was the perfect example. But he had no plans of repeating that error and letting strong emotions destroy everything he had worked for.

****

Shane had seen Samantha when she came into the party. He had no idea why she was there, but he would do his best to avoid her. Knowing she had been living only a few streets away had been difficult.

He'd never been the emotional type or classified relationships, but there was no doubt he cared for Sam. Had since their frightening and extraordinary few days on the life raft. Very much. He'd never tried to fool himself. He'd been so excited when he saw Sam at the marina it had been like something out of a fantasy.

But after thinking about her since their brief time together years ago he had to face reality. His parents always told Shane to be a realist. He was. Her family was wealthy beyond reason. And after seeing her situation—a spectacular, immensely talented member of British royalty surrounded by wealth, luxury, and bodyguards he could never imagine them together. But even if that wasn't true there was something else—an even stronger emotion. The reason he'd reluctantly vowed to stay away from Sam despite the strength of his feelings. Guilt!

At first, he'd been frustrated even angry that she'd come to the party. Shane assumed that either Bobby or Ashley were behind her appearance. Both had tried several times to bring them together. They thought they were helping him. They weren't. But he could never explain why.

A tap on the shoulder brought him back to reality. "Earth to Shane Winslow," Stacy said when she sat down next to him at one of the tables. "Is there some reason you're sitting here like a bump on a log?" she asked. "A lot of your friends are here. People are dancing and there are a couple of girls who've been asking about you," she said raising her eyebrows.

"You mean Samantha Edgerton?" he asked.

She looked around. "Actually, no. She's gone outside with Dillon. They seem to be hitting it off. Really well," she added. "Laughing, dancing, joking…"

"Dillon. Dillon Gregson?"

"Yep. They have something in common," she said. "They're both smokers," she added with a grin.

"But Dillon. I mean he's okay, but he's kind of irresponsible."

"So? She'll be here all summer and she seems to love the Cape. So, she may want to meet someone who can show it to her and see it with her. And lots of the local girls think Dillon is what we used to call a hunk!" she said with a push and a laugh. "But anyway, Jenna Meehan and Lauren Cavallo are here and were asking for you, but if you want to sit here contemplating the mysteries of the Universe. Go for it." She patted his arm and stood, waving to one of the other guests.

He stood and walked over to the bar.

Eric came up and patted him on the back. "Great time, huh?" he asked.

"Yeah. It is," Shane nodded and ordered two beers, handing one to Eric after paying the bartender.

"Thanks. Haven't seen much of you lately. How

goes the job?" Eric asked. "You're working the late shift I understand?"

"Going good. And yep, I've been giving the guys with families or girlfriends the earlier shifts and coming in around five, so I guess our paths haven't crossed," Shane explained.

"That's good leadership," Eric said. He nodded as Bobby joined them.

"Another one over here, Jimmy," Shane told the bartender then took out a ten-dollar bill. "This one's on me."

"So, nephew. I see Greg Dillon with the Edgerton girl."

"Yeah. That's great," Shane said, doing his best to smile.

"She's a real class act," Bobby continued shaking his head and grinning broadly. "Gave us a beautiful painting from the Kennedy gallery. Stacy was floored!"

"Yeah. She's a nice girl. Glad she and Greg hit it off." Shane emptied his beer and patted Eric and Bobby on the back. "I'm…going outside for some air," he added stoically then closed his eyes and trudged toward the door.

Chapter Thirty-Two

The Admiral sat with Jeanie and James Edgerton as they huddled around the small table in the corner of his study. Charles was keeping his mother company as they watched the comedy *Central Intelligence* in the home theater in the large home's basement. Jeanie showed James the pictures that the Admiral had received from their team on the Cape.

"Do either of these men look familiar, James?" the Admiral asked glancing at Jeanie when she handed Edgerton her phone.

Lord Edgerton adjusted his glasses, using his fingers to enlarge the faces while flipping through the six photos. "No," he said shaking his head while he placed the phone on the table. "Never seen them. Why is this important?" He glanced back and forth between his guests. "What *aren't* you telling me?"

The Admiral looked at Jeanie again and nodded.

She took the lead. "We think that there may be a connection between what happened here last week and the sighting of these men."

"Who are they and why would they be attacking us?"

Jeanie gave the Admiral an imperceptible nod.

"We have no idea, James. This is pure speculation," he answered showing his old friend a smile. "We have operatives—agents working down here. They were doing routine surveillance and recorded these two men." He stopped and gave Jeanie a look.

"Both of these men are career black ops people, James," she explained. "And they don't waste their time on small projects or unknown people." She touched her host's hand gently. "We remembered you telling Brian about someone attempting to kidnap Charles last spring and," she paused and gestured at their surroundings. "You and your family are celebrities. You're a Lord, a war hero, and a wealthy businessman who's here to lecture at America's most prestigious university. Your grandchildren are beautiful, brilliant, and have achieved academic and sports notoriety of their own. Especially Samantha." She looked at the Admiral. "What better targets to choose? And you still have strong ties high up in the British government and military." She paused. "Please understand, James, we are *not* trying to frighten you."

The Admiral showed his old companion a warm smile. "But we're beginning to think that the attack last week and the subsequent correspondence you received about your security team leader, Misha, was staged. Part of a plan to get him out of the picture to weaken your family's safety."

James sat back and sighed deeply. He shook his head. "That…that business with Charles was just a couple of clumsy idiots! He went into the trailer to change at a riding event and they had hidden there. But they were…"

The Admiral held up his hand. "Please, old friend. Don't get agitated. We have a way we feel can help us determine if there's any real danger or if we've made a mistake."

"Sorry, Brian, Jeanie. I realize you're trying to help. It's just when I think of anyone doing harm to my family because of our position and success it infuriates me!" He patted their hands and nodded. "So. Tell me what you have in mind?"

"Well, we have to speak to a friend. Someone local who happens to be rather talented with electronics and computers. We're going to ask her to search through your files, devices, correspondence, and the like to see if there's evidence of hacking and what she can glean if there is," the Admiral told him.

"So. You think this person can really do that. She's that good?" James asked hesitantly. "I mean I know some people that can..."

"Trust us, James," the Admiral interrupted and grinned at Jeanie. "She's the best I've ever seen."

Chapter Thirty-Three

It had become obvious that Shane was a lost cause. Sam knew he had feelings for her but something— perhaps a ridiculous case of perverse snobbery or something she didn't understand had put a wall around him and it was obvious he wouldn't let her get close enough to break through.

"Is everything all right," Ashley asked as Sam re-entered the function room after her time outside smoking a cigarette with a young man named Greg.

"Sure. Fine," she said forcing a smile.

"Look. I've done my share of schmoozing for a while. Could we take a walk?" Ashley asked.

"That's very kind. But these are your friends and…" Sam offered shrugging.

Ashley held up her hand. "I need some fresh air and," she paused, looking around and showing a conspiratorial smile. "I want to bum a cigarette." She walked over to Eric and whispered something to him then gestured to Sam as they left the Riverway.

Sam spoke to Julian and though he balked she managed to sweet talk him into staying by their car while she and Ashley crossed busy Route 28 then walked to the public dock near the Bass River Bridge.

"So. You asked me about Shane after you two met at the marina last week?" Ashley asked as they sat on one of the redwood benches in front of a small public building that looked over the public dock and boat slips.

Sam nodded and looked around at the twilight as lights sparkled in the homes across the River. "Yes, I did." She shook her head. "I don't understand it. I'm very fond of him, and I'm almost certain he has feelings for me."

Ashley nodded. "I'm sure he does, Sam. But for some reason none of us can fathom he's determined not to give in to them." She sighed and studied the River. "When he came home after your time on the raft, he was different." She shook her head. "Completely different. Shane had never been a bubbly personality, but he was strong and friendly and genuine. A young man everyone looked up to and liked."

"And he wasn't that way when he came home?"

"No. Not in the way he always had been. He seemed to go inside himself. He got a medal from the Coast Guard for helping to rescue your family." She leaned forward and sighed. "But he never talked about it. After all the press about it people would joke with him. You know. Being on a life raft with a beautiful heiress. That's the only time anyone ever saw Shane almost hit someone. People quickly learned it was a taboo subject."

"Maybe it was because he had to resign his commission. That must have changed his life," Sam said with a shrug. "I've always felt so guilty about that. Helping us stay alive cost him the career he trained so hard for and wanted so desperately."

"Sounds good but I never bought that. He didn't resign from the Coast Guard for eighteen months after your rescue. No. Shane changed long before that. He was engaged to a sweet girl named Emily. But when he came back that first time after the rescue it was different when he was with her. Everyone noticed it." Ashley smiled putting out her hand. "Now. How about that cigarette?"

"Here you go." Sam took the pack from her purse and gave her one and the lighter that Misha had given her. She looked at it and smiled as Sam took it.

"Sam. This is going to sound kind of crazy. But now that I've met you and seen the way Shane is around you, I have an idea."

Sam lit her own cigarette, taking a drag and turning toward Ashley. "And…"

"I have no idea what happened on that raft…"

"Nothing, Ashley. Oh my God. I…*I give you my word*," Sam said holding up her hand to interrupt.

Ashley laughed softly and shook her head. "I'm not suggesting anything like that. No. I'm saying that you two bonded in some very deep and personal way." Ashley fixed Sam with her eyes. "I think he fell in love with you."

Sam sat dumbfounded. "What?" she asked in a whisper. "You…you think he loves me?"

Ashley nodded and put out her cigarette, setting her jaw. "If you think about it. It answers all the question marks about his odd behavior. He fell in love with you and when he came home, he didn't know what to do about it. And by the way he's acting now I'm betting he still doesn't."

"So. If that's true why is he ignoring me now?" Sam asked, trying to comprehend this revelation.

"I'm not sure. I have an idea but that's something you'll have to ask him about."

****

214

A giant sigh emerged as Shane left the Riverway. He had no specific destination in mind just a need to escape the endless praise directed at Samantha by everyone he knew. Not that she wasn't worthy. He needed no reminder of her virtues.

His jeep sat twenty feet away in the bank parking lot next door, so he headed that way. Hearing muffled laughter, he stopped and turned. Seeing cigarette smoke coming from around the corner on the restaurant's north side Shane assumed that Sam and Greg were back there, but when he surveyed the area, he saw no security person. If Sam was around someone should be looking out for her. He stood wondering when the reason became obvious. Coming around the corner he saw Greg emerge, but his partner was Liz Coleman, a girl they'd gone to high school with. No Sam?

Greg saw him and gave him a wave and a salute then headed back inside with Liz.

Shane stopped. Standing there he gave Greg a weak smile and a wave. He took a few steps and searched looking behind the Riverway scanning the parking lot. He spotted a man in a sport jacket standing near what he thought was one of the Range Rovers the Edgertons were using. The man stood smoking a cigarette while he swept the surrounding area with his eyes.

If the bodyguard was there Shane wondered where Sam was. He shouldn't care. But he did. No matter how much he tried to stop thinking about her—it wasn't working! Not anymore. Shane had come close to finally forgetting the sweet, courageous, and lovely girl he'd known for four endless days a lifetime ago, but since he'd seen her again Samantha Edgerton had returned to his mind with a vengeance. Her smile, her face, her intoxicating accent...

He shook his head and approached the man at the spotless Range Rover. "Where's Miss Edgerton?"

The man immediately went to Defcon three, moving away from Shane while assuming a balanced stance with knees slightly bent. His hand went to the belt inside his lightweight jacket. Shane spotted the large automatic. "And you are?" he asked narrowing his eyes.

"Oh, I'm sorry. I'm an...an old friend. Name's Shane Winslow," Shane explained lifting his hands slowly in a gesture of surrender. "You may remember I visited her at the hospital last week?"

"I wasn't there, sir. But I recall hearing your name," the man said. He stood erect, removing his hand from his weapon. "She went for a walk. With Ms. Montgomery."

"Oh," was all Shane could manage.

"They insisted I stay here," the man volunteered, which made no sense to Shane, but if Sam was with someone she trusted he felt relieved if still conflicted about the depth of his feelings. "Matter of fact. Here they come now," he added as Shane turned and saw Sam and Ashley across Route 28 waiting at the stoplight.

"Thanks," he whispered and turned heading back inside.

Chapter Thirty-Four

Axe sat at the large colonial style kitchen table. He studied the four men surrounding him. "All right. You all know that one week from today we will carry out the plan." He spent a moment fixing each of the men with a hard stare. "Mister Lassiter, you have completed your installations? Everything is ready?"

"Almost," he nodded, showing Axe a neutral expression. "I have several final tests to perform over the next two days. The most critical is the one on the oxygen sensor and of course I need to seal the room and have a surrogate inside for that."

"Yes. Nicolai. You will be our...guinea pig for that test."

Nicolai moved nervously in his chair, flexing his hands. Axe showed an even smile to the youngest team member. "Pardon that expression," he said deferentially. "Are you all right with that?"

Nicolai nodded and showed a weak smile while he studied the others.

"You'll be fine," Ivan said confidently. "I promise I will not let them leave you in there," he said to his friend smiling and giving Nicolai a rough push.

"When we've completed testing the oxygen seal, you and Nicolai will finish the insulation and padding on the exterior walls. We need the room to be completely soundproofed." Axe directed this instruction at Ivan. "With the sophistication today, the slightest background noise can be detected by any high-level technology professional." He looked at Lassiter who nodded. "Even though they will be unable to triangulate our video or audio signals, these people are very wealthy and powerful, and it is understood that regardless of our warnings and threats they will employ the best security and electronics people. We cannot allow them to use their expertise and technology to find us."

"And you, Mr. Murphy, have laid out a brilliant plan for the abduction. No one will suspect it or be able to stop it."

Murphy showed a confident smile. "That's correct."

"And once you have performed that service and delivered the boy the next installment of your compensation will be deposited in your offshore account."

Murphy nodded. "That's also correct," he said with a patient expression.

They all stood making casual conversation with each other amiably. Axe watched. Lassiter and Murphy went to the great room where a chess board served as a diversion. Ivan and Nicolai each took two cold Sam Adams Summer Blends from the ample Sub-Zero refrigerator and headed out to the large deck where a large can of insect repellent sat on the umbrella table.

"Do you want to join us, brother?" Ivan asked holding up one of his beers.

Axe stood tugging at his chin, shaking his head. "No. I think I'll go up to bed."

Ivan nodded and opened the slider as they headed

out onto the deck.

Axe stood; eyes fixed laser-like on Nicolai as the young man walked outside. He smiled to himself. *Yes, my young friend, you will make a fine guinea pig...*

****

Samantha had caught a glimpse of Shane heading back into the Riverway when she and Ashley hustled across Route 28. When they reached the door, Ashley held it open and nodded inside.

"No. Thanks," Sam said hesitating, looking inside.

Ashley shrugged.

"I have to think about what you said." Sam explained. Her new friend's suggestion had amazed her. *Shane in love with her? It made no sense.* She shook her head and took out another cigarette and lit it as Julian stood watching her. No. It made no sense. *And yet—somehow it made perfect sense.*

She stood smoking her cigarette as Julian approached. Sam decided. She narrowed her eyes and put the cigarette into the sand tray next to the entrance. Taking two tic-tacs from her purse she nodded toward the door.

Julian nodded and stood next to the entrance.

Sam took a deep breath and pulled the double doors open, heading inside with a purpose.

****

Eric saw Ashley coming toward him. She held her phone in her hand and turned it toward him. The signal someone needed them. After their earlier discussion he was sure it was the Admiral.

Though no one in their local circle of friends would know it they both did their part to keep the country safe. But in distinctly different ways. Eric had come home from his three tours as a Green Beret Team Leader in the Middle East trying to escape the horrors he'd witnessed. Too soon he discovered that in the millennium world you cannot. You have to fight against the frightening evil that surrounds you. Ashley had been a brilliant young technology protégé. One of the best. But what she thought was a harmless hacking sortie had killed her mentor and sent a psychotic domestic terrorist hunting her and Kylie. She had found Eric at the insistence of his brother Ralph—a Chief Petty Officer who was in fact a high-level undercover operative working for the Admiral. Both had been instrumental in saving Ashley, Kylie, and Eric when his single-handed rescue attempt failed.

Ever since their terrifying adventure Eric and Ashley had helped the Admiral when a specialist was needed. Eric when a top-level, highly trained operative was required for an "off the books" job his usual teams could not handle. Ashley when a hacker of unequaled talent was essential.

Neither resented their friend's requests since both enjoyed the adrenaline rush these adventures offered. They especially enjoyed the times when both were needed, and they had the chance to work together. On more than one occasion Eric had even recruited his best friend Bobby Rodriguez and wife Stacy to help. Bobby had been a top-level Ranger NCO with plenty of combat experience and Stacy was a crack investigator at the State Police Fire-Marshal's Office. She'd also been a Warrant Officer and decorated Investigator in the Air Force. Together they made a daunting foursome.

"Hey, babe. Where'd you disappear to?"

"I took a walk with Samantha." She nodded toward the street outside. "Had a soul-searching discussion."

"You're determined, aren't you, dear?" Eric grinned at her attempts to play matchmaker. "Still trying to light that fire, eh?"

"Yep," she said nodding toward the door to the lounge. "I know Shane really cares for Sam." She made a face. "I told her I think he loves her. Has since their time on the raft."

"You *what*?" Eric stopped short and stared. "You told her Shane loves her. Je-sus, Ash!" He took her arm as they went through the door. Eric waved to the bartender who pointed to a booth at the end that offered some privacy. "Have you become a psychic?" he said in disbelief. "What were you thinking?"

"I'm thinking that's the truth. Trust me," she said with a conviction he had no interest in challenging as they sat down in the booth deep in the far corner of the lounge.

"Okay," he shrugged. "Now. I assume it's the Admiral who called?" he asked, letting the other thing fade away.

Ashley nodded then took his forearm in a tight grip. "Yep." She nodded.

He showed agreement. "Right. I'm guessing this has something to do with the Edgertons," he asked.

"Yep," she repeated.

"When and where?" Eric asked as Ashley's attention was suddenly focused on the door that lead into the back-parking lot.

Eric turned and saw Shane facing Samantha.

Sam held his arm tightly, talking in an animated way and shaking her head.

Eric turned back to Ashley. "Dear Abby. I think your chickens just came home to roost…"

****

Shane stood at the bar trying to avoid looking in Sam's direction. She looked so…what? Lovely? Spectacular? How about hot? Yes, as tacky a description as that was it fit. But Samantha was so much more to him than a great-looking girl.

He turned and stole a look at her talking to Stacy. Her short auburn hair, curly and fragrant pushed behind one ear, those enormous dark brown eyes he had never been able to put out of his mind and of course, the perfect athletic figure that glided gracefully while he watched.

But he thought again every time his mind turned to Sam and it had endlessly, especially since her remarkable reappearance in his life that Samantha's beauty while captivating was only a small part of what made her so special…

"A penny for your thoughts," she said suddenly when he emerged from the pleasant fantasy he'd been fighting since she reappeared.

"Huh," he stammered finding her hypnotic eyes with his, and managing a weak, "Pardon?"

"I'm beginning to wonder, Lieutenant," she began softly in the sexy accent he loved. "Was it simply because we were stuck floating around in that life raft that I was able to attract your attention?"

"I'm not sure I understand," Shane said doing his best to sound casual.

Sam tilted her head and narrowed her eyes. "Graduated number one in his class from the Coast Guard Academy, first in his class to be promoted to full

Lieutenant, given plum duty as a Junior Military Attaché to the Court of St. James, and one of a select few to ever receive the Coast Guard Medal." She gave him a sad look. "And yet you can't understand my question about why you're avoiding me?"

Doing his best to unlock his eyes from hers Shane managed, "Really, Samantha. I'm not dodging you." He showed her a plastic smile he knew was weak at best. "It's just well, this is the busiest time of year at my job so I'm trying to help the older men with families." He paused. "And how did you know all that about me?" he asked with amazement.

"I was there that day, you know?" she said avoiding his question.

"What day?" he asked confused.

"When you received your medal, Lieutenant," she said calmly. She found his eyes again. "Quite an honor." Sam shrugged. "And then I just played detective. I do that when I find someone I really care about."

He stood not sure what to say. "I…I didn't know," was all he could come up with. "You should have told me."

"The medal ceremony? I felt I owed it to you. We all did." She let her gaze fall momentarily. "You were busy. We were just visiting, and I assumed your plate was full."

"Really. All of you came?"

She nodded, finding his eyes again. "Yes, Mortimer, Charles, Holly and me," Sam whispered then averted her eyes quickly. He thought they were moist. "It was a lovely ceremony. Your fiancé must have been so proud." She took a deep breath and smiled gently, touching his arm as she turned. "Good-bye…Lieutenant. I won't bother you again. Ever," she said softly adding a gentle, "Promise," she added, crossing her heart.

Shane stood staring after her. He closed his eyes and took a deep breath then pushed his beer back at the bartender. "Keep this cold for me, Kenny," he said trotting after her.

****

Samantha walked through the door that lead to the pine-paneled lounge brushing her cheeks. She stopped and exhaled deeply. Enough. She'd been thinking about him. Hoping that he'd come to his senses and follow her lead. She was sure he had feelings for her. After Ashley's revelation Sam had thought—hoped that perhaps she could break through that wall her Lieutenant had built around himself. It was not to be.

Spotting Ashley and Eric talking quietly in a corner booth Sam was about to head over and say goodnight. Before she had the chance, someone took her arm tightly. "Hello," she said turning quickly.

Shane stood staring at her with a determined face. "I need to talk to you," he whispered nudging her toward the parking lot door.

"I don't like to be bullied and God knows you've had every chance to talk to me." She shook her head. "No more excuses or dodging and weaving. I'm going home," she told him doing her best to pull away.

Shane turned her gently toward him, pulling her close. His expression softened. He smiled gently then pulled her lips to his.

Sam closed her eyes and pressed her lips to his gently at first.

He pulled her closer, opening his lips.

Samantha surrendered, as their bodies became one.

After an endless moment she had only dreamt about Sam giggled breathlessly as they parted. She found his eyes. They showed warmth, kindness, and desire. The things she'd seen years before as they bobbed up and down in the Gulf of Mexico. "I've been dreaming about that for four years," she said, standing on tiptoes and gently brushed his cheek with her lips.

He returned her soft peck then nodded showing her a shy smile. "So have I," he whispered as his face flushed.

Samantha pushed back and returned his smile, looking beyond him and freeing her arm to wave. "I think we have an audience," Sam said, giggling again.

Ashley beamed a smile toward them then toward Eric returning the wave.

Chapter Thirty-Five

The Admiral and Jeanie sat on the generous screened-in back porch making casual conversation with Millicent. She was lovely but seemed a shy fragile woman. Millicent suddenly came to life when she and Jeanie spoke about competing on the equestrian circuit as teens. Jeanie related her days as a competitive show jumper at events around her hometown of Middleburgh, Virginia and Millicent shared her youthful adventures in Gloucestershire when she competed in dressage.

"Oh, my goodness," Jeanie said with admiration. "I always admired you dressage riders so much. So much finesse, discipline, and patience." She shook her head. "I never had that dedication or ability."

Millicent laughed quietly and nodded. "Funny, isn't it? I was always so jealous of you show jumpers. Going right at those gates and obstacles with a sense of reckless abandon." She made a funny face. "I was always begging daddy to let me have a go at it."

"Well, ladies," the Admiral chimed in. "Just to keep up my end on the conversation, I was raised on a working cattle ranch, so I always thought you spoiled little princesses in your expensive riding habits were a bit too *cheeky* for me," he ended with a flourish, making a comic face.

They all laughed, and the two ladies continued their spirited conversation as they re-lived their days on their respective equestrian circuits.

Just as Charles joined them, they heard laughter. Julian appeared in the hallway and Samantha and Shane giggled their way into the backyard and headed for the dock. "Hello," Sam said still laughing. She took Shane's hand and pulled him along while he waved back at the group on the porch.

Jeanie and Charles looked at each other with amazement as they laughed out loud.

"*Oh—my—God!*" Charles whispered, watching through the screens and shaking his head. "My God," he repeated then laughed loudly and turned. "Looks like Sam finally got her man."

"Julian," Millicent said looking curiously at him. "What happened?" she asked pointedly while she turned to watch Sam and Shane run onto the dock just as James joined them.

Julian shrugged. He seemed frustrated. "Hard to say, Ma'am," he began. "The young man—Shane— seemed to be sort of watching Miss Samantha but not really speaking to her." He looked as confused as the people on the porch. "Then suddenly she took a walk with Ms. Montgomery and went back to the party. Next thing I knew they came out the back door, kissing with their arms around each other."

"Way to go Sam," Millicent whispered beaming at the couple as they sat on the dock's edge.

"Should I go? You know. Follow them to the dock?" Julian asked.

"No," James answered as he patted the man on the back. "Why don't you go out and spell one of the others on watch," he added with a smile as Julian nodded, opened the porch door, and padded around toward the garage. James sighed and looked at the Admiral and Jeanie. "He's no Misha."

****

"So, Lieutenant. What guarantee do I have that you won't simply disappear or go into a funk like you've done before?" Sam asked doing her best to sound concerned. She caressed his hand lightly while Shane held her around the waist as they dangled their bare feet over the edge of the dock a foot above the tranquil high tide.

Shane shrugged and sighed, giving her a gentle tickle. "What if I said scout's honor?" he asked holding up three fingers then crossing his heart.

Shaking her head, Sam tightened her grip on his hand. "Seriously." She turned her face toward his. She loved the strong chin, thick curly light brown mop of hair, and his eyes. Them most of all. Golden brown and large—they filled with excitement and twinkled when he smiled or laughed. "I was so thrilled when we walked into the marina office and saw you standing there. It was like a fantasy. My dream come true. You were so kind, so caring when I was in the hospital then my fantasy became a nightmare because you were gone. *Again!*"

Shane turned and released her waist then brought his feet up and sat legs crossed facing her. He grew a thoughtful expression when he raised his eyes to hers. "I know. And I'm sorry. So very sorry," he whispered with a nod. After taking a deep breath he continued. "Something happened to me on that raft, Sam. Something I never saw coming but something I could never forget."

Sam still held his hand, smiling but nervous. She

wondered where this was going. There was no need for worry.

When he spoke again Shane took her other hand in his. "That something was you."

Her nervous smile broadened when he raised her hand to his lips, kissing it gently.

"I had a great life; a loving family, an exciting career, and a wonderful girl back home I was engaged to. But those four days changed my life. You changed it." He took another deep breath. "I knew it on the raft, I knew it in the hospital, and I knew it the minute I got off the plane that flew me home, and saw Emily standing there. I had never met *anyone* like you. So selfless and courageous and so caring. Samantha. I was in love with you from that first day and wanted to see you again so desperately but…I didn't know what to do."

"You must have known I felt the same way." She ran her hand up his strong forearm.

"I thought you did."

"I know you had a life here, but you could have found…" He put his fingers to her lips and nodded.

"Yes. I could have. I thought about it while I was recovering at Walter Reed. But when I arrived home, my sister's husband had deserted her, my mother and dad were still numb from losing my brother in the Middle East and Emily, my fiancé, had lost her mother after a long agonizing battle with cancer." Shane explained as a tear ran down his cheek. "And I…I guess I was afraid that when I never heard from you that I'd been wrong about how you felt so…"

"Oh my God. What a litany of mistakes," Sam said, shaking her head with regret. "I wanted to find you and see you and tell you how I felt so desperately, but the Base Commander told me you might lose your Commission because of your injury and that you were engaged. What could I do? Chase after someone whose courage and dedication in saving us may have cost him his career and who was going to be married?"

His laugh had the hollow sound of irony. "No. Of course not. But Emily knew that things weren't the same. Right away. That my feelings had changed so," he paused. "When she died in a car crash, I was consumed by guilt. Guilt because I didn't love her anymore and because she could see I regretted our engagement. She knew I'd met someone else. Someone I could never forget and wanted to be with." He leaned forward, took her face in his hands, and pulled her to him. The kiss was tender but evoked feelings that Samantha had only dreamt of. Shane smiled shyly. He backed away and leaned against her forehead. "Your picture was plastered all over the news after we were rescued. She only had to look at your photo and then see the change in my attitude. Emily was bright and sensitive. She knew," he told her then bent and found her lips again.

The kiss began gently but grew more passionate as they played over and around each other's mouths in a breathless celebration of long overdue desire.

"Oh…oh, Shane. *My darling,*" Sam panted clutching his shirt as if her life depended on it.

"Oh…Sam…yes, *yes,*" Shane whispered as he kissed her damp hair then brought his lips down to her ears and neck.

Sam pushed him away with a breathless giggle, grabbing his hand. "I think it might be polite if we went up and said hello to my family since I know they're all sitting on the porch, probably with binoculars straining to see what's going on," Sam said putting her hand over her mouth.

Shane nodded then sighed deeply doing his best to hide a smile. "Well okay. You're the boss, Miss Edgerton! But do not think you're getting away that easily."

"Thank you, Lieutenant." She giggled. "Oh, darling," Sam said standing on tiptoes giving him a quick kiss. "I'm so very, *very* happy!" she told him, doubling over and laughing giddily.

She pulled him by the hand, and they laughed, waved at the crowd on the porch, and trotted up the long lush expanse of lawn...

Chapter Thirty-Six

Eric and Ashley rang the doorbell at the Edgerton house at 8:15 a.m. the next morning.

"I'm not sure I need to be here," Eric said, looking up casually at the home's impressive façade. "From what the Admiral told us last night they need someone with *your* skill set."

"Well, I only know what the Admiral and Jeanie told me. Lord Edgerton thinks he made a mistake when he let Misha go, and they may want your advice on what to do now?"

He shrugged. "All right," he agreed as the Edgerton's housekeeper opened the door.

They were ushered into Lord Edgerton's well-appointed study. It held the competing odor of expensive furniture polish and cigar smoke.

"Good morning," he greeted them, beaming a broad smile then entered looking bronzed, fit, and focused. "Brian, or should I say, the Admiral, and Jeanie will be right in. We were up quite late last evening having a splendid time getting better acquainted with Samantha's new beau," he said looking pleased.

"Yes, we saw them at the function we attended and were so happy to see that they'd connected with each other," Ashley told him as James seemed to glow with pleasure and pride. "It took a while, but I suspected for a long time that Shane had deep feelings for someone. I'm very happy it turned out to be Samantha," she finished with a nod.

"Quite an amazing coincidence," James said as he raised his eyebrows. "Finding each other like this after that experience on the raft. And yes, it was never any secret that Sam was very much smitten with Shane. Rather more than smitten I'd venture to say," he added as the Admiral and Jeanie joined them.

"Would you be wanting anything, sir?" the housekeeper asked entering the room.

"Yes, Alice. Be a dear and bring us coffee and some of your delightful scones and butter if that would be quite satisfactory," he said surveying his guests pleasantly.

"Sounds great," Eric volunteered. "We were up pretty late ourselves."

Alice curtsied and bounded off toward the kitchen as the Admiral shut the door. When he and Jeanie sat down she placed a thick envelope on a large side table after finding a chair. "These are photos of two men well known to us as international criminals. They were taken over the last two weeks," she explained.

"Cape Cod in the Summer. The perfect place to hide in plain sight," Eric offered, looking at Ashley then at the others.

Jeanie nodded. "Yes. We just picked them up on routine surveillance. The British CCTV system is amazing. One was spotted at Logan Airport and then two of our agents down here got these pictures three days ago." She pushed her lips together then continued. "Then suddenly they disappeared." Jeanie shrugged showing a look of frustration.

"And that disturbs you?" Ashley asked.

"Well, the obvious thing that comes to mind is the presence of the Edgerton family here on Cape Cod," the Admiral said, shooting a look at James. "But that brings up why we've asked you two here," he added looking back and forth between Ashley and Eric. "Ashley, we'd like you to check their emails, Internet, phones, and everything electronic to see if there's any evidence of hacking. If you're all right with that?" he asked.

"Of course. Since when could I ever refuse you, darlin'?" Ashley said with a bashful grin batting her eyes comically. "Sure," she added adopting a more serious expression. "I assume that because of what happened with that business here last week you want me to get on this right away."

"I feel guilty, my dear," James began showing an ingratiating look. "You've spent so much time entertaining us I hate to ask you to do anything more…"

Ashley tried to hide a smile. She failed and raised her hand. "I'm not a tour guide. This is what I *really* do," she said quietly with a blush.

****

"Why would that couple—the Montgomerys—be visiting the Edgertons so early in the morning?" Axe questioned while he studied the live video that streamed from the hidden camera Lassiter had mounted high on a telephone pole a week before the Edgerton family had arrived.

"Breakfast perhaps," Ivan shrugged. "They have been the Edgertons tour guides and chaperones. They've become very close."

"Perhaps. But let's ask our friend Mr. Murphy.

There may be more to this apparently friendly little gathering than it appears."

Ivan stood. "You know, Ilya. Every closet doesn't hide a skeleton."

Axe stood next to him, placing his hand on Nicolai's neck giving it a gentle squeeze. "Of course, you're right, but until we're counting the ransom money in Brazil let's assume that it may."

Smiling gently, Ivan patted his brother's strong forearm then started up the stairs from the basement room.

"And, Ivan. Until that day please. Refer to me as Mr. Axelrod. Да?"

"Да," Ivan agreed in Russian and hustled up the stairs to find Murphy.

****

Then you will know the truth and the truth will set you free! Mark, Matthew? Shane thought. No John. Somewhere in John. He'd research it later. All he knew when he awoke that morning was that he had—finally told Sam the truth that is—and like that biblical miracle it had set him free. The regrets, the guilt, how much he cared for her. All of it!

He grabbed his phone and went to recent calls. Her number was there. He'd called her last night at 2:45 a.m. and she giggled deliciously when she answered. Of course, scolding him for waking her up only to admit that like him she hadn't slept a wink. That lasted for about eight seconds! Maybe ten.

"You...you promise, my dearest, dearest Lieutenant. You completely absolutely cross your heart and hope to die. You will never go back to that sad dark place you were living in," Sam whispered in that accent he could never hear enough of.

"Scout's honor, Milady," he answered with a gentle laugh of his own. "I can't explain how our conversation tonight has changed my life, Samantha." He lay in bed shrugging. "But it has. Forever and always."

"I believe you copied that from a song, but I'll let it go this once," she said, sighing and laughing softly…

Their conversation continued till 3:30 a.m. when both were yawning more than talking. "Can I see you tomorrow, Sam?" Shane asked, adding. "And how about every day for the rest of my life?"

"Oh, my goodness, Lieutenant. Beneath that gruff standoffish exterior, you really are a true romantic," she whispered then paused, "Now that you've borne your secrets to me."

He lay, eyes closed as he shrugged again. "Actually, I never have been," he said followed by a muffled yawn. "I…I guess it's the company I'm keeping."

"Shane?"

"Yes?"

"If you could see me, you'd know that my face feels so flushed I may have turned purple by now. You, sir, are quite the provocateur." She sighed again. Each time she did Shane closed his eyes, imagining her face as it was when she snuggled close to him and he sheltered her from the wind and spray four years ago.

"And of course, we can see each other tomorrow. I will send Poppy's security people out after you if we don't. What's your schedule?"

"Hmmm. I may have to make some changes because I've been working the late shift but well if you want to go out somewhere…"

"No. Don't change anything for me. Ever. That's an order," she whispered and giggled softly. "Maybe you could come to the beach with us tomorrow. It's supposed to be a spanking grand day!" she enthused.

"Spanking, eh?" he teased in a faux British accent. "It's a date. What time," he asked followed by another yawn.

"About oneish. Meet us at the house. If it's convenient."

"Sure. Hey. We can put down the top in the jeep and go—in—style." He paused. "Unless you have to bring along one of the security people."

"I will sweet talk Poppy and we will—be—alone. Maybe one of your delicious Cape Cod ice creams afterwards."

"Got just the place. Called Krista K's. Great local people and the best frappes—that's the Bostonian word for milk shakes—on the Cape."

"Ummm. Delicious!" She sounded like he was losing her to fatigue. "Sounds scrumptious. And Shane. I know what and who I'll be dreaming of tonight."

"Me, too," he whispered then gave the phone a soft kiss.

Sam returned the gesture and Shane lay back, falling asleep in less than three minutes with a huge smile on his face.

Chapter Thirty-Seven

Ashley stood and stretched. She'd been intent on searching James' technology, spending the morning scrutinizing his laptop and cell phones. When her cell phone rang, she jumped, looking at the screen Ashley smiled.

"Anything?" It was Eric.

"Yes. Definitely something. And they did it on a regular basis. But whoever did it was no amateur. It was a classic Man in the Middle attack."

"So they somehow got access to their computers and electronics?" It had taken Eric years of eavesdropping, asking questions, and reading, but he now understood a lot of the tricks and dialect that hi-tech experts like Ashley used describing what was becoming known as the Dark Web.

"Yep. At first, I thought it might have been a computer technician James hired but he said that they used a retired officer he'd worked with in the Royal Navy, so I doubt it. This is a high-level infiltration. And after seeing how smooth and transparent the coding was, I'm betting they did it surreptitiously. This was no paparazzi trying to steal a few photos for the British tabloids." She raised her arms over her head and stretched at the waist. "This guy—or girl—was a pro."

He smiled to himself. There weren't many people in the world who could see the actual code that an expert hacker used to infiltrate a secure network. His wife was one of the few.

"Lu's gonna pick up Kylie and drop her at Lola's for the afternoon. I have a couple of ideas I want to pursue on my own," he told her. "I think Misha was on the right track when he did a search of their property. I'm gonna check out the area around the entrance. And I've got Shane checking out the water side this afternoon."

"Don't you want to ask James about that? I mean he is paying those people for security," she asked sitting at the oversize laptop again. "And you're enlisting Shane?" she asked sounding incredulous.

"Misha was the only real pro in the bunch. I talked to the Admiral and he agrees. The five he has doing his security now aren't much better than rent-a-cops." She heard him sigh. "And I suppose I'm not a security person by definition," Eric said with some irritation. "But come on, Ash, you *do* remember I spent five years with my team in Iraq and Afghanistan staying alive by finding and debugging tripwires, hidden electronics, IEDs, and every other deadly device you could imagine. That was our unit's specialty. And why the Admiral asks me to be a part of some of his more difficult cases." He paused. "And you may not know it, but Shane had some serious training in intel and surveillance when he went back on active duty after his injury."

"Yes, darlin'. I was not suggestin' that you would not be a great person to check the Edgerton's out. Just wondering why you think that there may be more to this than hacking?"

"We went out on the porch while James showed

you their electronics. The Admiral told me that he and Jeanie think they may be the target of the bad guys their people saw in those photos."

"Well, I have no idea who of importance is visiting the Cape this summer, but they'd be prime targets for a whole host of things—kidnapping's the one that comes to mind first but maybe extortion or even somethin' more sinister. I'm assumin' that James has a load of information from his time in the Navy and there was…" She paused then stopped. Her words trailed off.

"Something else?" Eric asked.

"Well, remember what I told you. About that night a couple of weeks ago after Kylie went to the riding stable with Sam and Charles?"

"Yep." He smiled remembering he'd fallen asleep after a passionate interlude while Kylie was out getting an ice cream with their neighbor.

"When I felt guilty I hadn't spent more time studying about them."

"Oh yeah. I remember what you told me," Eric said.

"Yep. Those links on Google I found about some things that happened to one of his ferry operations that served the Baltic—and three accidents they had," Ashley reminded him of her discoveries.

"Got it. I remember you thought that someone might have a serious grudge. Maybe have it in for James?" Eric asked.

"Yep. Especially since the investigation found some serious negligence in their safety procedures and inspections. Even bribery of some safety inspectors."

"Huh. I know people can fool you. Put on a front but does that sound like the James we've gotten to know?" Eric asked thoughtfully.

"No. And I wondered about that, too so I couldn't resist...digging a little deeper a few days ago."

Eric laughed softly knowing what 'digging' meant when Ashley used the word. "And your digging discovered?"

"Well. Not anything you could use in a court of law but," she whispered into the phone. "There were several discharges—firings—of key personnel at James' ferry operation after the lawsuits were settled."

"He was making scapegoats of some poor bas..."

"No darlin'. Just the opposite. He did exactly what we'd expect a special friend of the Admirals to do. The firin's were hush-hush. Never made the papers or the news. All done quietly. Very quietly. James stepped up and took the blame completely in public." She breathed deeply. "Rather than blame the bastards that seemed to deserve it he accepted it all. Even paid the settlements against his company out—of—his—own pocket."

"Je-sus! How much did that come to?"

"It's not a matter of public record. But the estimates are well into the millions."

"So, he is a first-class guy," Eric shook his head. "But he's such a first-class guy that no one knows it. Maybe someone who lost a loved one could logically blame our Lord James for it. He paused as the import of what Ashley'd said sank in. That opens a whole new cast of characters. We have to tell the Admiral and Jeanie."

"Agreed. But give me till about three o'clock to see if I can get anything more on who's been doing the hacking."

"Will do. I'm gonna do some more checking

241

around the grounds and points of entrance and exit," he told her. "Nothing to show for it yet, but if this really is a vendetta that could be a hell of a lot more dangerous. Revenge could be a much greater motivator than money…"

****

"Ever been riding?" Sam asked, taking off her dark glasses as she turned. She lay with Shane, basking in the spectacular sunshine at the West Dennis Public Beach.

"Riding. You mean like on a horse?" Shane made a frown. "Up on one of those big smelly things that could throw you and break your neck?" He gave her a push and grinned. "Yes, I went with…with one of my old friends. A lot."

"Please stop that," Sam whispered looking frustrated.

"That what?" Shane asked looking confused.

"That," she said quietly holding his eyes. "Stumbling over that 'with one of my old friends,' line every time you did something with Emily."

He pushed his lips together.

"I know you had a serious relationship, Shane. You were engaged for God's sake." She shook her head and smiled gently. "I never expected you to arrive in my life solitary and celibate."

"But my dear, Miss Edgerton. I have and I am," he said in a high-pitched voice.

She reached over and gave his slender waist a pinch.

"Ow!" Shane shook his head and rolled over. "Jesus, *come on, Sam!*" he yelled then rolled back and began tickling her. "Vengeance can be a…"

"I hate that word," she said laughing loudly as they wrestled with each other then lay side by side as their hands found each other's. "So. Does that mean you'll go riding with me sometime?"

"That's a definite yes!" He handed her his phone. "My schedule is on there. Just hit the calendar icon." Shane told her looking innocent.

"Wait a minute. Who is Sue Ellen?"

"Oops. Oh. I...I'm sorry. You shouldn't have seen that..."

"Who is Sue Ellen?" Sam asked with a scowl.

Shane laughed and gave her another gentle push. "My sister. I'm going to lunch with her and her kids." He shrugged. "Sorry. Couldn't resist!"

"All right, Very clever...*Lieutenant!*"

"Want to come?" he asked showing a conciliatory smile.

"Yes. Just to make sure you're not pulling a fast one!" She said narrowing her eyes.

"Oh my God!" Charles approached and showed them a comic expression. "Can you two *pl-ease* stop it!"

"Why? Are you jealous, brother dear? I see you're not shy around your collection of young groupies?"

"No. I'm not. But we're not rolling around on the beach groping each other!"

"Ignore him," Sam told Shane and rolled closer to him. They both laughed loudly and stood, smiling as they ran into the gentle surf.

****

"Well how was it in the room, Nicolai?" Axe asked thoughtfully as the younger man exited the airtight room, taking several deep breaths. Ivan's friend had served the role of guinea pig, spending most of the day in the airtight prison they had finished. His rather dubious task was to make sure it would do what they planned.

"Frightening at the end of the time. The air became foul and thin." He shook his head and shuddered. "It was very…what's the word in American? Claus…claustro…" He stumbled with his vocabulary.

"Claustrophobic," Ivan grinned at his friend's thought then asked, "You felt frightened because of the conditions."

"Oh yes," Nicolai said playing up his moment of glory and value to the project. "Very *claus—tro—pho—bic*!" he finished with a proud smile.

"Yes, my friend. Just think how much more frightening it would be if you were an innocent young boy who didn't know if you'd ever see the outside world again," Ivan said and glanced at Axe. "Eh, Ilya?" he added with a coy expression.

Axe turned and studied his younger brother. "Yes, Ivan. I'm certain it would have," he said with a nod. "I have to go upstairs and hear the good news that our friend Lassiter wants to tell me. This *test* was very important. Thank you, Nicolai. Now there is *nothing* that can keep us from success!"

****

Ashley asked for a summit meeting after her endless day searching through the Edgerton's laptops, phones, and tablets. Eric told her he'd found some disturbing things on the property and nearby and she wanted him to share as well.

So, at 4:30 James Edgerton, the Admiral, Jeanie, Eric, and Ashley met in James' study for the second time that day.

Ashley sat at James' nineteen-inch laptop which showed a split screen display. Her own laptop sat on the small table next to her covered with an endless parade of scrambled code.

"Well," she began glancing at the others. "I've found that your electronic presence," she faced James, "has been compromised for some time. For exactly how long I can't tell but certainly as long as you've been here in the States."

"I assume you'd need access to our home network back in Britain to determine if that had been compromised?" James asked then leaned forward looking curious. "Could you tell anything from what you found?"

"Actually, yes. But I've gone back and accessed that, too," she said sitting back in her chair. "And from what I've seen I was able to determine that whoever is doing this is interested in your grandchildren."

James look changed from curious to concern. "Interested. Interested in what way?"

"Hard to tell. As I said, this person is no amateur. And getting anything substantive would be almost impossible." Ashley frowned. "All I can tell you is I could see their names and also mention of the 4th of July and fireworks events." She shrugged. "They used proxy servers and Tor software, but it wasn't foolproof. So I got some text but couldn't see who or where they were."

"I believe the name proxy server explains itself, but did you say Thor?" James asked. "Like the Norse god?"

"No." Ashley replied. "I said Tor. T-O-R." She paused. "It originally stood for The Onion Router. It was supposed to shield users from the constant unwanted solicitations we all get. Think of peeling an onion and you get the picture. It makes it difficult to find out who you are electronically." She shook her head. "Sounded good when it was developed more than ten years ago, but as you can imagine it has some rather dubious uses by those on the Dark Web who want to remain anonymous."

The Admiral nodded. "I told you she was the best." He smiled and cleared his throat quietly.

"Yes, Brian. Feel free," James said, making a gesture in his friend's direction. "You and Jeanie are the intel and security brain trust here."

"Eric found some other...troubling things, James." The Admiral nodded at his young friend.

"Well, for one thing there were two remote cameras hidden across the street from the entrance.
" He paused. "And I'm no forensics expert but when I looked at the things that Misha discovered when he searched the property the day after that incident last week, the shell casings were blanks. And when I spoke with my friend at the Dennis Police, he told me he was asked by someone well above his pay grade to forget the whole event. He argued and fought back. Said he thought his detectives and forensic people should investigate more but the head of the FBI Field Office in Boston called and said to drop it. In no uncertain terms!"

The Admiral and James looked at each other.

"What the hell is going on here. Brian, Jeanie, do you know anything about this?"

They looked at each other and shook their heads in unison. "Of course not," the Admiral said emphatically.

"And I'm betting when I call my friends at the FBI, they'll know nothing about it either."

They spent a few more minutes exchanging ideas then broke for dinner.

"Need I ask that no one share any of this with the family. Especially after the attempted kidnapping last year. I recognize that there may be some real danger here," James tugged at his cleft chin and did his best to show a smile. "I wanted Sam and Charlie to see the beauty and splendor of the States not feel like prisoners. And," he continued after giving a gracious look to the Admiral and Eric, "I intend to find Misha, apologize, and re-hire him if he's willing," he finished with a nod.

As they headed to the back porch for cocktails and less serious conversation Eric took the Admiral's arm. "Ash and I would like to talk to you guys," he nodded in Jeanie's direction. "Perhaps later this evening. Some things we need to share."

****

"So, are you satisfied?" Eric asked Ashley as they walked from the paneled bar at the Riverway Lobster House again.

They'd spent the last hour engaged in an animated discussion with the Admiral and Jeanie about James and Ashley's suspicions that the danger she discovered may have been because of the mismanagement of ferry operation and the resulting tragic accident.

Ashley looked up, studying the sky as the quarter moon sank on the horizon. "Yes and no," she offered with a tentative shrug. Not a gesture Eric often saw in his brilliant headstrong mate. "They confirmed that James is a stand-up guy but had no idea about the accident and fall-out."

Eric nodded, twisting his mouth into a frown

"So he really did take the wrap for those problems and that terrible accident?"

"Apparently so." Eric surrounded her with his arm.

"Yep. That's a noble gesture and says a lot for his character, but like I keep saying the problem is that whoever is behind those hacks and potential attacks may not know James is such a noble character," Ashley posed while she leaned into Eric.

"I know. I only hope they can find Misha because the crew they have on security now are next to useless if there was real trouble," Eric repeated, agreeing with Ashley.

She nodded. "I'll head over there tomorrow and work with Jeanie to see if we can chase anything more out of their electronics, but I'm scared."

He stopped. "Scared?"

"When he asked us to be tour guides for James and his family, I agreed but well, I thought of it as an inconvenience. But I don't think of it like that anymore. I really like them. And I'm especially fond of the kids. I know this sounds kind of funny, but I think of Sam like the younger sister I never had."

Eric put his arm around Ashley again and hugged her tightly. "Not funny at all. They *have* sort of grown on us, haven't they? Sam and Shane and Charlie?" He laughed.

"So if there's someone out there who wants to hurt them," she said putting her head on his shoulder. "I want to find those bastards before they can get to Sam or Charlie…"

"I wouldn't expect anything else, darling," he whispered and pulled her close.

"He didn't say it, but you know he's gonna need our help with this," she said as they reached Eric's Jeep.

Eric nodded. "I'll call Bobby as soon as we get home. James gave me the last contact number he had for Misha. I think it's important we get him back on board. But not in the open. It's obvious that whoever planned that charade last week was targeting him," he told her as they hopped inside the Jeep. "Question is why?" he showed her his best smile then started the Jeep and pulled out of the half-empty Riverway parking lot. "Keep a casual eye on your mirror," he told Ashley as they drove slowly along Route 28 toward home. "Let me know if you see anything."

Chapter Thirty-Eight

"We're having a cookout for Brian and Jeanie before they head back to Washington." James told the family that Friday at breakfast. "They have to get back to saving the world," he joked then gave the Admiral's forearm an affectionate pat.

As they left the generous breakfast room Sam hung back. She'd heard the Admiral and Poppy talking quietly about finding Misha.

Clearing her throat, she came up behind them. The mood around the compound had taken on a somewhat cautious tone since Eric and Ashley-Jean had visited earlier that week. They'd been sequestered with Poppy and his friends from Washington.

"Excuse me," she said quietly then took her grandfather's arm lightly.

He and his friend stopped. Turning, Sam stood next to them. "Yes, darling. What can I do for you?" he asked pleasantly.

"I apologize for being so…so presumptuous, but I believe I heard some conversation regarding how to contact Misha." She shrugged. "You tried his phone and had no luck?"

They looked at each other, showing surprise. "Why yes. We did. But how did you know?" Poppy asked as he looked at the Admiral again.

"I…I was walking by your study and wanted to ask

you something. The door was supposed to be shut." Sam showed them an apologetic smile. "Well, you know I was fond of Misha and the door was slightly ajar. So. When I heard his name, I admit I eavesdropped," she added with a crimson blush.

"All right," Poppy began evenly then took her hand.

"I know how to get hold of him." She whispered then slowly opening her hand she gave them the lighter.

****

"You're as good as I suspected," Eric said. He and Misha stood in the front hall of the Edgerton's house. "Damn clever idea that. The lighter I mean."

His companion stopped. Growing a distant look Misha turned. When he faced Eric again his face was inscrutable, but his eyes were dark. He wore a distant look. "I...I lost someone once," he said in a brittle tone then rubbed his nose and took several of the tiny microphones from the case that he and Eric had brought with them. "I'll put these in the staff quarters. In good locations," he said nodding taking a handful of heavy-duty plastic clips then stopped on the stairway. "I promised myself it would never happen again," he said without looking back then mounted the long stairway. "Pretty clever yourself," he said nodding to Eric.

Eric stopped and grew a curious expression.

Misha turned. "The cookout," he said smiling. "Getting everyone off site."

Chapter Thirty-Nine

As predicted, when the Admiral had talked to the Special Agent in Charge at the FBI Boston Field Office, he had never contacted the Dennis Police. The Admiral gave him the particulars and agreed to meet with him and Jeanie when he headed to Logan Airport on his return to Washington. Evidence was mounting that something related to his old friend's family might be in the works. The problem now was determining what, where, and when!

He had asked that Jeanie stay and oversee what they both thought could be a serious situation. A brainstorming session took place at the Montgomery's which included Misha, Ashley, Eric, Jeanie, and the Admiral. James was not included since they wanted complete transparency and the predominant feeling was that any threats against his family might be the result of something from his past.

However, to get every shred of information he could, the Admiral had spent some private time grilling his old friend and ally about any reasons he thought his family might be the target of criminal or terrorist activity. He broached the subject of the ferry tragedy that Ashley had discovered even though the Admiral doubted it was relevant. James said he'd never been threatened or received any hate mail as a result. On the contrary. He said he'd even received praise for how he handled the situation. And while James had been known to inflate his accomplishments or accolades the Admiral believed him.

"So, we've come up with the following," Jeanie said in summary after the long brainstorming session. "Best possibilities are kidnapping one or both of the grandkids for money or to get James to use his influence."

Eric and Misha shot skeptical looks at each other.

"No on kidnapping, gentlemen?" the Admiral asked showing a curious expression. .

"Yes. But for money," Eric said quietly. "With all due respect. Does James have enough influence now to make that risk worthwhile?"

"You might be surprised." The Admiral shrugged and looked at Jeanie.

"Remember that for half a dozen years he was the equivalent of our Under Secretary of the Navy. He worked as a special assistant to the First Lord of the Admiralty," Jeanie volunteered. "And don't forget he'd been a Fleet Officer for British NATO Command. His area of expertise was the North Atlantic and the North Sea. That was just prior to his retirement four years ago."

That brought a long period of silence as the five of them sat back to collect their thoughts.

"Well, everyone agrees that kidnapping is the most likely scenario whether we agree on the motive or not. I'm not sure that it's vital we know it." Ashley verbalized their thoughts. "So, our goal should be first, to shield the kids from any potential danger and second, to find out who these people are and round them up." She sighed deeply and leaned back in her chair at their dining room table then got up and poured herself another black coffee.

"Agreed," the Admiral said, nodding as he surveyed the others. "I've asked Jeanie to stay to add her talents and experience and manage our team here," he continued, showing her a smile. "I'm long overdue, so I'll be heading back tomorrow morning."

Jeanie nodded giving him a reluctant smile.

"I should be going back with you, Brian," Jeanie said as the meeting broke up.

"I'm asking you to stay here to help keep my oldest friend and his family safe," he answered taking her hand and squeezing it tightly.

"But that's not our job, Brian." She paused. "And all this is based on supposition. One unexplained attack that appeared staged and some emails that spoke about the Edgerton kids." Jeanie shrugged and shook her head looking skeptical.

"I've spent my life serving my country." The Admiral grew a look combining anger and sadness. "And I've never asked anything in return," he continued. "And it cost me…" the Admiral stopped in mid-sentence shaking his head. "I'm asking you to make sure that doesn't happen to James. I know I'm out on a limb here, but I need your help, Jeanie," he finished, holding her eyes.

Jeanie nodded. "You know I can never refuse you." She laughed quietly. "Just remember to take these." She reached into her bag and handed him the vial that contained his Tramadol.

He winked at her and kissed her cheek.

Chapter Forty

Week of June 28th—Monday, 10 a.m.

"Oh, Lieutenant, you are such a *poop!*" Sam chided him. "You promised."

"Yes, I know," Shane said in a voice filled with disappointment. "But honest to God, Sam, I can't help it if one of my people is sick with the stomach flu. Trust me I was looking forward to this."

She believed him, and Sam was not about to take her frustration out on Shane. No need. Ever since they'd connected the night of the party the two of them had been inseparable, spending every free minute together. Yes, her Lieutenant had been everything she could have wanted in a beau, so she'd give him a pass. *At least for today*, she thought, feeling a broad grin cross her face.

"All right, but remember we're chaperoning the dance at the Yacht Club tonight," she reminded him doing her best to sound angry. The West Dennis Yacht Club held a dance for teens every Monday night. Sam had found out about it and volunteered them for chaperone duty. "And tomorrow we're meeting your sister and her children for lunch at one."

"Yes, Miss Edgerton. And how much am I paying you to be my social secretary?" he asked. Sam could hear the amusement in his voice.

"Oh, stop it!" she demanded with a giggle. "But you're not getting off the hook that easily. Remember, I have your schedule on my phone so the next free morning I expect you to put that delightful bottom of yours in the saddle."

"Deal. Now I have to run!" he said, kissing his cell phone loudly. "Pick you up at seven." He paused and added a soft. "Dear."

Sam kissed *her* phone, smiled broadly then hit off and went into the bathroom to brush her teeth. She and Charles would have a nice ride with Jeanie and Julian then come home to take a quick swim in the river before lunch. She felt her smile broaden wondering if life could get any better…

****

11:00 a.m.

In a large house twelve miles toward the east two tall young men closed the doors to a nondescript panel truck. In the driveway a tall man in riding clothes nodded and gave them thumbs up while he slid into his spotless British racing green Jaguar XK convertible.

"You think all the false Internet chatter has convinced them?" Axe asked Lassiter as they stood in his study and watched their companions leave.

"I can never be certain but yes, I'm reasonably sure that it has. At the very least what I've done by sending the traffic through hubs all over the East Coast and into Canada will make it impossible for them to find out where our location is."

"Well, we drilled all weekend like a military unit to make sure we get this done as we planned it." Axe shrugged. "In about two hours we'll know if we're successful," Axe said sighing and praying that they had.

But it occurred to him that prayer might be inappropriate for a mission such as theirs. "We must be ready in case something goes wrong."

Lassiter nodded and put his hand on his employer's shoulder. "The detonators are set and can be set off remotely if we need to…" he hesitated. "To escape."

Both men walked onto the back porch, sitting down heavily. Axe lit a cigarette as they looked at the thick morning haze trying to break through over the Atlantic. Somewhere in the distance they heard Chatham Light announce the fog with two long and one short blast.

11:30 a.m.

"Be careful," the Admiral said into the secure line he'd established with Jeanie. "We don't know what these people have planned or when they may carry it off. Everything you and Ashley heard could be a smoke screen. False info to mislead us."

"Yes, sir," she said evenly, not sure it was appropriate to refer to him by his given name. When they'd spoken on an open line since he'd returned to Washington she'd returned to the use of 'sir' in their conversations. "I understand. Julian and I will be with Charles today when he goes riding. Samantha was coming but changed her mind at the last minute when Shane had an emergency at work and couldn't come. And her ankle is still a little tender so she's heading to the beach around ten and meeting him for lunch at one. Misha will be with her."

"All right but please. Be careful."

"I will," she promised. "And oh yes, *Admiral,*" Jeanie whispered in her best southern accent

"Yes."

"I miss you," she added and gave her cell a secret

kiss.

Admiral Brian Turner sat in his office, clearing his throat self-consciously and scanning the four twenty-seven-inch screens. He stood as a warm smile and a bright flush emerged and grew as it crossed his face.

11:45 a.m.

Ashley kept staring at the screen in her office. Something kept gnawing at her. It had since the morning she and Jeanie had discovered the hacking on James' laptop and phone. But it had taken some time for the concerns to coalesce. It had all been easy. Too easy!

Suddenly she felt a pair of strong hands on her shoulders, working their way toward her throat.

"Oh!" she cried out.

"Oh my God, Ash! What's the matter?" Eric said. He dropped his hands and backed away.

"Oh," she said with a sigh. "Sorry. I've just been staring at this stuff too long. It's got me spooked."

He closed in and bent over her shoulder. "You mean the stuff you and Jeanie found?"

She nodded. "I was so proud of myself for discovering this with the Admiral, Jeanie, and James that I may have let myself be fooled."

"Fooled how, honey?"

"I was so caught up, full of myself with my success when I found Sam and Charles' names and those dates I didn't even question how easy it was." She shrugged. "I think that…that maybe I was snookered, darlin'."

Eric stood and put his hands back onto her shoulders, caressing them gently. "No. I'm sure you got it right." He kissed the back of her neck. "I mean Jeanie agreed, didn't she?"

Yes, Ashley thought, *Jeanie had. But Jeanie didn't have her expertise. Not with this kind of material.* "I only hope you're right," she managed with a deep sigh. But at times like this Ashley remembered one of her mother's favorite Bible verses: *Pride goeth before a fall*

****

12:30 p.m.

Charles looked over at his new friend and smiled broadly. He liked this fellow. Very much. The man had the calm, confident bearing of someone who'd seen a lot and had the wisdom and courage to deal with whatever came along. That's what Charles aspired to achieve: wisdom and courage.

Eric Montgomery, Misha, and Poppy exuded that same quiet confident assurance. And of course, Sam's Lieutenant, he thought with a grin. He had those same qualities. Charles Liked Shane. Very much. Had since that first night on the life—

Suddenly he heard something. Behind them. Looking around Charles couldn't see his new friend Geoffrey. Odd since he'd suggested this rather out of the way trail.

Julian and Jeanie had stopped suddenly and wore looks of concern as they scanned the woods beyond the trail. In a split-second Julian had dismounted and drew his automatic weapon as Jeanie leaned over and kept straining to see beyond him, "Get down, Charles, and get behind me. *Now!*" she added in an urgent whisper.

Charles turned in the saddle and felt his throat go dry when he saw hooded figures. They approached through the woods from opposite sides.

Julian yelled, raised his weapon. He fired.

Charles jumped as the loud report echoed in the

thick growth that surrounded them.

Two men returned Julian's shot as Jeanie's mount rose up. She tried to balance while she drew her weapon and fell backward off her mount, landing on a log with a groan. Then silence.

Julian fell. Charles swallowed deeply. He wanted to dismount and run but felt paralysis numb him as the men approached.

"Get down, Charles," the lead man said evenly.

They knew his name. Who he was. Charles slumped and raised his hands, knowing he was in desperate trouble...

****

12:50 p.m.

Sam sat slightly separated from Poppy, her mother, Misha, and Jasmine, the newest member added to their security detail. They lounged on their towels or beach chairs in what she had come to think of as their spot. Samantha smiled, sitting about twenty feet from the group. Luxuriating in the warmth she felt the bright midday sun deepen her tan. Closing her eyes she pictured her Lieutenant.

While she drifted into a pleasant doze, Sam dreamt she and Shane were on the life raft again. She snuggled next to him while he pulled her close to keep her warm. A dream she found herself enjoying often when she closed her eyes. In the past it held a bittersweet flavor. Since their delicious reunion two weeks ago it had taken on a whole different texture. She thought about meeting for a delightful calorie filled decadent lunch with him at a popular local tourist spot...

She turned, smiling toward Shane in her delightful daydream when Sam heard a disturbance. Shouting! It was Poppy and Jasmine. Then Misha. His voice was never raised or excitable. Until now!

Her mother shrieked crying out, "No! *Not again!*"

"Miss Samantha!" Misha called loudly. "Please. Come on. We must go. Now!"

Sam sat up sleepily, reluctantly leaving her pleasant fantasy. "What…what's happening?" She rubbed her eyes as the sunscreen irritated and stung them. "I wanted to wave at Shane when he goes by," she explained.

"Come on, Sam, something has happened," Poppy said through clenched teeth. "Something bad."

She nodded. "All…all right," she agreed. "What is it?" Sam asked. Standing, she gathered her beach throw and assorted lotions stuffing them into her shoulder bag.

"It's Charles," Misha said quietly taking her arm and moving her toward their SUV as Jasmine ran ahead to start it. "I'm not sure," he added. "I received no signal from him." He held up his lighter. "And he's not answering his phone. Neither are Jeanie or Julian."

"Oh," was all she could manage. She felt a sudden wave of guilt surge through her. *Oh God*, Sam thought with dread. She should have been there to watch her little brother!

Chapter Forty-One

2:00 p.m.

"Your grandson is safe," the mechanical voice said calmly over James' cell phone, adding, "At least for the time being." It had been sent through a scrambling device to prevent voice-printing or recognition. Misha put it on speaker. "Turn on your laptop and go to the video feed we've sent," the voice instructed. "We know you've discovered our intrusion into your electronics."

A haunting image with a greenish tint appeared.

James sat in his office.

Misha and Jasmine sat facing him.

James turned the seventeen-inch laptop and showed them the picture on the screen.

A tall person dressed in black stood next to Charles. He or she wore a hood.

The boy stood crying softly and visibly shaking. He'd been gagged and blindfolded. His hands appeared to be bound behind him. The picture filled the 17" screen. It had excellent quality. The sound of his grandson's whimpering both terrified and angered James.

"You're an intelligent and successful man, James," he began. "May I call you James?" the voice asked in a patronizing tone.

"Shut up, you *son of a bitch!*" James yelled into

the phone. "Don't pretend to..."

Misha held up his hands and shook his head and stood, fingers to his lips. He raised his hands over his shoulder's then brought them down slowly, mouthing the words, *Calm down.*

James closed his eyes and nodded closing them and breathing deeply. "Yes. You can call me James," he said quietly.

Good. Misha mouthed, nodding while he held up his hands.

"That's better...James." The garbled voice said pleasantly. "This is purely a business transaction. We want no trouble."

James closed his eyes. "Then you shouldn't have hurt that woman so badly. And you killed our man Julian."

"That was unfortunate about the woman, but I sincerely hope she'll recover." The Voice paused for a moment. "Your security person drew his weapon and shot wildly at us. No one wanted any deaths or injuries. I assure you." The Voice sounded sincere. Almost apologetic.

But James didn't care about this man's equivocations. He wanted to tell these people that one of the most powerful men in the American security establishment was headed their way with a vengeance, but he looked at Misha again and held his tongue. "All right, what do you want?"

"Charles is frightened but he has not been harmed. As long as you follow our instructions he will not be. He's being put in a small room in a remote location you will never find. The room is air-tight, but we have a small circulating fan. If we turn it off the air will only last eighteen hours." The voice paused as another person appeared, also in black clothes and wearing a hood. The second person took Charles by the arm and turned him. A small door appeared. The person opened the door. When Charles turned, they could see his hands were cuffed behind him.

When he was pushed toward the open door he staggered and cried through the tight ball gag he wore, shaking his head and resisting his captor.

"Just do what he says, son!" James yelled at the screen, adding, "Please. Don't hurt him!"

"Sorry, James. But he can't hear you," the Voice told them and turned toward their terrified captive. "Your grandfather suggested you do what we tell you, Charles," he added.

He slumped and entered the room through a second inner door. The inside looked completely dark.

Just then Ashley opened the door. "Nothing yet," she whispered to Misha, holding her tablet up with a shrug.

He nodded and stood motioning for Jasmine to join him.

"We'll let Charles get used to his new home," the Voice said almost casually. "It's now five minutes past two. Our next call to you will be at six p.m. with our requests. Demands sound so offensive. Don't you agree?" the Voice asked as they paused. "Need I warn you that if you contact or involve law enforcement or make any attempt to find us, we'll simply walk away. You don't want your beautiful young grandson to die of slow suffocation, do you, James?"

"No," James said doing his best to control his anger. "I understand." He nodded at Misha as the feed was ended. He stared at the darkened laptop. "We have to find out where those bastards are. I'm going to find out how Jeanie is and then contact Brian. He should be on the ground in two hours."

Misha nodded. "Eric wants to help," he told James while he stood in the doorway. "So does Shane." He shrugged.

"Eric would be a great asset." James nodded. "And Shane." He raised his eyebrows. "I'll leave that up to you. But if he wants to help, he's more than welcome but I'm afraid he might be in the way or get hurt."

"Eric and Sam both say he's got a cool head under pressure and Eric added that he had quite a bit of training in security work with the Coast Guard after he was injured," Misha added with a shrug. "And if we get a lead on where these people are, he could scout the location and draw far less attention than any of us. They have no idea who he is."

"All right," James said quietly staring out his study window. "That's your call. I have to go talk to Millicent," he said with a weak smile as he headed out and down the hallway. "She's been sedated but I want to see her…"

Chapter Forty-Two

2:20 p.m.

Charles sat on the hard cement floor trying to control his fear. He was losing the battle. *Control your breathing*, he kept telling himself. That's what Sam would do. After all he'd survived for days on a life raft in the Caribbean. But they'd been together. He and Sam and Shane and Holly. Helped and supported each other. Charles was alone now. And he was terrified.

At least his kidnappers had removed the gag, the blindfold, and the handcuffs. They had actually been quite polite. Charles wasn't fooled. He was certain that any deviation from their plans or demands and he'd be left in this tiny room to die. He'd only been there for a little while, but it was already very hot and completely dark. He'd heard them say it was air-tight, but they had also said that there was a small circulating fan. Charles heard a soft background hum. He prayed that meant it was running!

He huddled, holding himself tightly. He tried to think positive thoughts while he sat next to what they said would be his toilet—a small plastic bucket with a box of Kleenex on top.

Oh, please Poppy, do whatever they say. I'm begging you. Don't leave me here! he begged silently tightening his grip on his arms. Closing his eyes tightly

Charles trembled then curled into the fetal position on the hard floor.

****

The Admiral sat in his car as it sped toward Joint Base Andrews. "All right. Tell me what happened?" he asked in a rigid tone.

Mario Mendes breathed deeply on his end of the phone. "Jeanie and Julian, the man from the Edgerton security team, were riding with Charles. According to the stable owner and her staff they were accompanied by a fourth person. He was well dressed, friendly, and drove a hundred-thousand-dollar sports car. He'd gone riding with Charles before. Seemed to have liked and befriended him. There's no sign of him and during the confusion after the kidnapping his expensive sports car disappeared from the parking lot. It's possible he may have been part of the kidnapping plot." Mendes paused. "An important part."

"I'm guessing that we've just found out what Derrick Muldoon was doing on Cape Cod," the Admiral observed with a heavy sigh.

"The detectives on the scene say that two additional individuals appear to have intercepted them when they were on an out of the way trail that bordered an old side road," Mendes continued. "We know that Charles failed to activate the emergency signal on a small lighter he'd been given by the head of their security team, a man named Misha. He became suspicious when Julian, their security person with Charles, failed to check in on the half-hour—a procedure Misha initiated when he returned to the Edgerton's. He then attempted to reach Julian, Jeanie, and Charles on their phones. When none of them answered the local police were called and after a search with the stable owner and her staff, they found the scene where the kidnapping apparently took place. They found the horses, Jeanie unconscious, and Julian's body. No evidence of a struggle or shell casings."

"All right," The Admiral said then added impatiently, "Thank you, Mario. Excellent report. But please. How is Jeanie?"

"Jeanie was on the ground apparently having been thrown by her mount. She was rushed to the Cape Cod Hospital. It appears she hit her head on a log and may have a fractured skull, sir. She's still unconscious and being evaluated," he said in a whisper. "I...I'm sorry, sir. The security man Julian was found dead on the trail. Two nine-millimeter slugs to his chest and one to the back of his skull. Execution style. Misha suspects he may have been working with the kidnappers. But no confirmation of that. No one reported hearing shots, but they were deep in the woods and there was no one else around during the time the kidnapping occurred. It's possible the thick growth could have kept the shots from being heard."

"Thank you, Mario," the Admiral said. A quiet anger continued to grow as he dismounted from the Tahoe and headed for the Gulfstream G650 that awaited him at Joint Base Andrews.

The Admiral heard Mendes. He was concerned for Charles. Very much. Assuming this was what they'd all expected there was a good chance that this might not end well. But he was also terrified for Jeanie. The Admiral was silent for a long moment.

"Sir," Mendes said sounding tentative.

"Yes, Mario."

"I…I'm not sure, sir." He hesitated. "I need clarification. Do we have jurisdiction here?"

"Yes, son. We're unique. This is not our normal type of case, but we have a presidential charter to engage in any issues that violate National or International law or threaten the security of the United States."

"Thank you, sir. I hope you…"

"Not a problem, Mario." The Admiral sighed deeply. "I'll see you in about ninety minutes. I'm heading directly to the Edgerton's."

"Yes, sir. Let me know when you want to meet," Mendes said. "Safe flight."

****

2:30 p.m.

Suddenly, as Charles huddled on the hard floor, he felt something—a bump—something sticking into his left side—the lighter. His emergency signal! They had patted him down. The way he'd seen in detective stories. But he'd put the lighter in a small pocket inside his riding jeans. A place they wouldn't have seen or felt since his jeans weren't as snug as his breeches.

Charles slowly turned and sat up, searching the darkness he looked for a tiny light or shine—any telltale signs of cameras. None could be seen through the warm inky black that surrounded him. The sound of the small fan had stopped—only temporarily he hoped. Charles moved from the bucket—toward the corner of his small prison listening to detect a slight sound that might indicate movement. He slid across the hard floor then stopped suddenly. There it was. The faint sound of something electrical or mechanical in both corners of the room high up on the opposite wall.

He subtly reached for the inside pocket of his riding jeans and depressed the small button on its face, closing his eyes and silently praying that the signal would get through to Misha and Poppy. Despite his frightening circumstances Charles managed a small smile.

****

2:40 p.m.

Ivan entered the kitchen. The room that was the nerve center for the Project.

Axe stood staring at the greenish image on the seventeen-inch laptop screen. A smile worked its way across his chiseled face.

"Something amuses you, Ilya?" Ivan asked continuing to use his given name.

"This young man. Charles." He nodded at the screen. "He's not the timid little rabbit we thought he'd be."

"How so?"

"He's clever. Figured out that we have cameras and where they are," Axe said, shaking his head in admiration.

"So?" Ivan asked while studying the ghostly greenish image of the boy on the screen.

"I admire his courage and intellect. Most young people, especially one brought up in such privilege, would be whimpering and begging for help or release." He pointed to the refrigerator. "Sad that he may come to an early end. Why don't you bring him a water?"

"I thought we weren't going to give him any sustenance or comforts?" Ivan searched his brother's face. "And you qualified your comments. You said he 'may' come to an early end. Could it be that you are

270

having second thoughts about letting the boy die?"

"I have learned in life that wanting and having are seldom the same, brother." Axe shrugged and walked toward the refrigerator. "Never mind. I'll bring it to him myself."

Chapter Forty-Three

2:55 p.m.

Ashley sat in the Edgerton's great room, hovering over her laptop while her tablet went through several data iterations. When she glanced at the smaller screen, she banged the finely finished mahogany table.

"*Shit! Shit! Shit!*" Ashley exclaimed then pushed away from the table.

Eric, Sam, and Shane ran into the room and stopped. Ashley paced and set her jaw in an angry pose.

"No luck," Eric said quietly as Misha joined them. "Damn it, Ash. You're doing your best," he added putting his hand on her shoulders and rubbing them gently.

She sighed deeply and felt tears of frustration fill her eyes. "No. Nothing," she told them shaking her head.

Misha had detected a weak intermittent signal from Charles emergency lighter. When he gave her his phone with the code to access it, she could find nothing.

Samantha looked around. "Please. We need *to do something!*"

Shane put his arm around her and pulled her close. "Our best chance to find something is when they contact us at six, Sam," he said glancing to Eric and Misha.

"He's probably correct, Miss Samantha, but…" he looked toward Eric. "When you were in the Middle East, Eric. Did you always count on technology— electronics to find the enemy and complete your mission?"

Eric sighed but stopped then gave Misha a thoughtful look. He was silent for a long moment then walked to the large dining room table. "No. We didn't always have great connectivity and perfect equipment. Sometimes we had to rely on our creativity and imaginations. What did you have in mind?"

****

3:10 p.m.

James entered the dining room. When he did conversation stopped abruptly.

"I just got off the phone with Brian." He wore a grave expression. "He's been on with the hospital about Jeanie." He sighed and sat down heavily. "It doesn't look promising. She has a skull fracture in two places. They've done some emergency surgery to reduce the swelling, but it will be some time before they know if she'll recover completely. This will be especially difficult for him…" his words trailed off.

"I'm so sorry," Eric said as the group glanced at each other, nodded, and murmured their sympathies. He looked at Ashley who nodded imperceptibly. "Did he lose someone before, sir?"

James nodded slowly. "Yes." He paused. "Of course. None of you would know." James stood and surveyed the small group. "Lockerbie. Scotland. December twenty-first, nineteen eighty-eight …"

"Oh my God," Eric said falling into a chair. "His family. They were on that 747." He shot a look at

273

Ashley. "We—we'd always wondered."

James nodded. He looked shaken. "His beautiful wife Ellen and two precious children, Ian, six, and Natalie, four." He stopped and seemed to compose himself. "Brian had been at a high-level conference. Of course, at the time he was only a Commander. Just been promoted and we teased him about wearing scrambled eggs—the gold braid—on his service cap." He smiled and looked away for a moment then continued. "His family had headed home for Christmas in New Hampshire, but he stayed on." He shook his head. "For a reunion with some old shipmates. I'd been seconded—temporarily attached—to the cruiser he was the exec officer of. I was one of those shipmates."

Silence hung over the group for a long moment. "We think we have something that will help us find Charles," Misha said, clearing his throat. He nodded at Eric.

"Yes, James. The kidnappers have warned us about the local police and FBI, but they don't know about the NIRA agents on the Cape and they don't know Shane," he explained. He looked around and they all smiled. "So. Here's what we've come up with…"

Chapter Forty-Four

3:50 p.m.

"You landed sooner than expected. Didn't you, Brian?" James asked the Admiral.

"Yes. We just left the Barnstable Airport in Hyannis. I asked the pilot to modify his flight plan and land on Cape Cod instead of at Logan. It saved us about thirty minutes. I'm calling you on the number that Ashley texted me at Andrews. I'm using a secure satellite phone," the Admiral explained to his old friend. "I need to check on Jeanie," he said, setting his jaw.

"Don't worry, old friend. We sent Sam there and she's back here now. Wanted to give her something important to do. The poor child blames herself for Charles situation." James snorted angrily. "As if her being there would have changed what these bastards did."

"If she'd been there, they would have made her their prisoner, too," The Admiral agreed.

"Don't you worry. We'll get them," James said evenly. "And our young friends have come up with a fine plan. They'll need some assistance but…"

"It's all set. I've spoken with Eric. Twice. Our team is at their disposal. They have access to a small state-of-the-art drone they can use once they narrow down the search area." The Admiral cut him off. "Sorry," he added by way of apology. "I'm just in the zone. And I'll make sure these bastards will be sorry they ever drew a breath!"

"I understand, Brian." His friend's tone and words caused him concern. "Please. Go check on Jeanie then call me."

"Thanks. I will and I'm in touch with our team on the Cape constantly. When they hook up with Eric, Misha, Shane, and Sam I'll get you updated on a secure landline."

"All right. Thank you, Brian. For your friendship and loyalty."

James hit end and reviewed the plan that Eric and company had come up with. Brian told him the FBI Field Office in Boston was sending down their best team, assuring him that they knew how to maintain a low profile. Since the kidnappers obviously had world-class technology skills it was doubtful that even Ashley could get a fix on their location based on the signal, they were sending...

"...We've looked at some recent maps and Ashley is using Google Earth to scope out the area around where they took Charles," Eric had explained only a few minutes before. "The fact that they used such a remote trail is to our advantage."

"How so?" James asked, not certain he understood the significance.

"Because that area has only one access road close by." Eric explained as Ashley pulled up the Google Earth view and enlarged it. "And you can see that there's only one cross road that it feeds into." Ashley pointed to the screen. "There are several houses along that road. Shane knows a couple of people who live there. He used to be friends with a boy whose family lives near that intersection." Eric took a deep breath and continued. "He's going there as we speak and ask the family and their neighbors if any of them saw a truck, van, or SUV within a few minutes of the kidnapping. They wouldn't take a chance driving through a busy area at this time of year and at a time when folks are coming back from the beach or heading to the mall, so we're betting that they turned east and headed toward the ocean. And they also wouldn't drive for more than twenty minutes since they must have assumed that someone may have come across the kidnapping site within a few minutes." He shrugged and took the map of the Chatham-Brewster area. It showed a circle.

James nodded and felt a surge of confidence. "So you're assuming that Charles is somewhere in this area." He felt a weak smile emerge. "That's a damn clever plan!"

****

4:05 p.m.

Charles heard a noise and sat up, fidgeting. His hands shook as the inner door opened. The small pitch-black prison had two entry doors. They had opened the first when he was gently pushed into a small anteroom. Then one of the kidnappers unlocked a narrow second door.

He immediately understood the terrifying reason. The design meant that the inner door did not open to the outside, so no fresh air would enter the small chamber where he was kept. His hands now shook more violently but he leaned forward and stood up clumsily.

He saw movement near the entrance and heard a

click. The room was bathed in a soft yellow light.

"Please. Keep your seat, Charles," a quiet baritone voice said as a well-built figure with a black robe and hood walked across the small distance that separated them. The voice had a distinctive foreign accent. "Please…" the voice repeated then motioned with his hands to indicate he wanted Charles to sit.

The man stood over him.

Charles squatted on the hard floor then plopped down awkwardly. "Here," the smooth-talking man said holding a small bottle of water. "I'm sorry that it's warm in here, but this is cold." Though Charles could not see the man's face somehow, he imagined him smiling. His words had that intonation. In a different situation Charles would have even thought his words sounded kind.

"Th…Thank you," Charles managed in a stutter then slowly reached up with a shaking hand and took the bottle from the man.

The man deposited a second bottle on the floor next to the bucket. "I'll leave that one here for…later." He heard the robed figure sigh. "You haven't eaten. We'll bring you a sandwich for supper. Is peanut butter and jelly all right?"

Charles hesitated, doing his best to maintain control of himself. "Yes…yes, sir. That would be fine." He exhaled a deep breath unsteadily. "Thank you," he repeated.

The figure nodded. "Please, Charles. I know this must be frightening for you, but we are doing this for a…a reason. I *do not* want you to worry." The figure knelt and touched his hair gently. "I'm sure your grandfather will deliver what we ask for and you will be home again in no time."

The man stood and walked to the entry door.

Charles followed him with his eyes.

The man lifted his hand toward the switch then let it fall away then exited leaving the light on.

****

4:20 p.m.

The Admiral stared into the post-surgical suite where Jeanie now rested after her first surgery. The neurologists had performed a procedure to relieve pressure on her fractured skull.

Two Hyannis Police officers stood watch immediately outside her room. Several others had been on duty throughout the intensive care ward though the Admiral thought it was overkill. He doubted Jeanie was under any threat from the kidnappers.

Turning, he saw two men in surgical scrubs approach.

"You're Brian Turner? The Admiral." the one who was obviously in charge held out his hand when the Admiral nodded. "I'm Doctor Alison. And this is Doctor Alvarez," he added nodding at the younger man. "We performed the surgery on your colleague."

"Yes, Doctor," the Admiral said taking the man's hand. "How is she?"

"Stable for the time being."

"What's the prognosis?" the Admiral asked with a hollow feeling in the pit of his stomach.

Doctor Allison turned and looked at his colleague. "She'll need several more surgeries, but we have confidence she'll recover. At this point we can't be certain if they'll be any long-term issues. Short-term amnesia is always a distinct possibility," he added with a non-committal smile as he glanced at the younger man who nodded. "But she's strong and in good shape."

"Never met anyone stronger," the Admiral agreed. "May I go in for a moment?"

The doctors looked at each other.

"I'd rather you didn't, sir, but go ahead." He put his hand on the Admiral's sleeve then shrugged. "But please. No more than five minutes."

****

4:40

Shane had found the area where the kidnapping had taken place. He'd driven by without stopping in case the kidnappers had some method of surveillance. He doubted they did, but no one wanted to take a chance with Charles' life hanging in the balance.

He looked at Samantha. She wore dark glasses and a Red Sox baseball hat pulled down around her ears…

…*Charles is my baby brother. I adore him!* she had told the group assembled at the Edgerton house. *If I can't go with Shane, I'll take my bicycle!* she insisted when the team had discussed their plan to narrow down his whereabouts…

So she now sat beside him, biting her fingernails and staring straight ahead.

They stopped at the place where the small back road that bordered the riding trails met a larger one. Shane knew this place well. His best friend from his high school had lived less than a mile from the intersection. His friend Nolan had enlisted in the Marines after high school when Shane had gone to the Coast Guard Academy. They hadn't kept in touch and Shane thought he was still away on active duty. But

Shane hoped he could use their friendship and stop at his friend's house to get information.

Traffic was scarce on this back road and it was just possible that his friend's family or a neighbor may have seen a vehicle drive by. It was a very slim chance, but it was still a chance. Shane turned the Jeep right—east toward the Atlantic. Everything seemed to be moving too quickly. He stole a quick look at the dashboard clock: 4:45. The kidnappers would be calling in just over an hour.

As they approached their destination Sam closed her eyes and squeezed Shane's hand while she mouthed a silent prayer. *Please God...don't let my sweet beautiful brother die!*

Chapter Forty-Five

5:05 p.m.

"Nothing from Shane?" James asked in a trembling voice while he paced the large dining room that now looked like mission control. Ashley's laptops sat next to three more from the Dennis Police and the Boston Field Office of the FBI.

Two teams had arrived in clandestine fashion disguised as house cleaners. Whether their costumes had fooled the kidnappers no one knew. But everyone hoped that Eric and Misha's discovery and removal of the two hidden surveillance cameras had eliminated their ability to see what was happening at 109 Pleasant Street.

"No. You'd be the first to know," Eric threw over his shoulder while he stopped and watched Ashley entering code and text into her HP Pavilion. A moment later she pounded the table when her efforts ended in frustration again!

"Damn! These people are good," she muttered through clenched teeth. She'd been doing her best to reconstruct a location from their earlier communication. It was a small percentage play at best. She and Eric both knew it. But it was an alternative to their doing nothing. "I may be able to get something when they call at six," she said trying to offer some hope. Ashley had never come across her equal when it came to technology, but she'd finally met her match and then some! Yes, this person was not only her equal but the best she'd ever seen.

****

5:15 p.m.

Axe sat in the kitchen, his eyes fixed on the twenty-seven-inch monitor that showed Charles sitting with his legs pulled up in a corner of his stuffy prison.

"You keep staring at the boy," Ivan said when he entered the large kitchen putting a fresh cup of coffee next to his brother. "Your words to him were very kind. Reassuring."

He turned and nodded. "After speaking with Edgerton, it seems likely that the people we're dealing with will be more inclined to give us what we want if we treat the boy with kindness." He shrugged. "Or as much kindness as you can when you hold someone prisoner in an air-tight chamber," he added as the trace of a frown crossed his face.

"I wondered if you might have changed your mind about the boy after seeing him," he repeated from their earlier conversation.

"No. Not really" Axe shook his head. But Ivan could hear some doubt in his brother's voice. He paused and drew a deep breath.

****

5:19 p.m.

Sam stood on the broad front porch of the sprawling expanded Cape tapping her foot and peering through the foggy windows that bordered the front door. The house showed signs of neglect which lead them to fear that the occupants—Shane's friend and his parents—no longer lived there.

He knocked forcefully on the front door after ringing the doorbell twice failed to produce a response.

Sam shot him a look that showed a combination of frustration and anguish. "What…do you think?" she asked in a nervous stammer.

He shook his head. "I'll check out the garage," he said. "See if there's a car or truck in there." He turned and headed for the equally neglected outbuilding forty feet away.

Sam followed him with her eyes when suddenly the front door creaked open.

"Yes," the narrow six-inch opening showed a withered old woman who peered out. "Can I help you?" she asked in a gravelly voice.

Shane glanced at Samantha and turned back toward the door.

She nodded imperceptibly at him.

"Yes. Hello. My name is Shane. Shane Winslow," he said amicably showing the woman a bright smile. "I've been away, but I used to be good friends with Nolan Hennessey. Does he still live here?"

The woman stood looking back and forth between him and Sam suspiciously. "No," she said continuing to lean against the door to prevent them from forcing it open. "He's gone," she added after a long moment of surveying them.

"Is he still in the Marines?" Shane asked doing his best to add more charm to his voice and smile.

The woman suddenly stood up straight and let the door open a bit more. "You and Nolan were friends?"

"Yes. We played ball together in high school." He took a step closer to the door. "I was the shortstop.

Nolan played second base," Shane said proudly.

The information seemed to satisfy the old woman. She stepped back and came out onto the porch. "I'm Hattie. Nolie's great-aunt," she explained. "Moved here when his parents moved to the North Shore. They live in Gloucester now. And yes, he's still in the Marines."

"Oh," Shane said stealing a look at Samantha. "Well then. We won't bother you anymore Ms. Hennessey."

Sam stepped forward and offered her hand. "Nice to meet you...Hattie. I'm Samantha."

They shook, and Samantha touched the woman's frail shoulder.

"By the way," she began casually. "On the way here, we were almost cutoff by an SUV. We wondered if you might have seen it."

Hattie pushed her lips together thoughtfully. "Not one of those S—U—Vs," she offered deliberately. "But I did hear a noise a couple of hours ago. It woke me from my nap."

"Oh," Sam nodded then shrugged. "And...?"

"Oh, nothing important. It was a van. Black but there was one of those fancy sports cars behind it. Dark green. Don't really know what it was but it was loud." She shook her head showing annoyance. "That one woke me up."

Shane and Sam looked at each other.

Bingo! Shane thought. "And it headed east. Toward the ocean?" he asked pointing toward the water.

Hattie nodded.

They all shook hands and Sam and Shane rushed off the porch and into his Jeep.

Sam hit re-dial, calling Eric. She put the phone on speaker. His phone had a secure line thanks to Ashley.

"Hi," she said breathlessly when he answered. "We found them. A van and a sports car—must have been the Jag—headed east."

"Good job," Eric said with excitement. "We'll wait for the six o'clock call. It's still possible Ash can get something from that but if not, we can get the drone up in the air and see if we can find anything. You two should head home," he said. "The Admiral said his team can take over if we locate them."

They all agreed on that strategy, but after they ended the call Shane sat staring straight ahead.

Sam saw him sitting immobile and shook him "Shane. What is it?"

He sat, eyes fixed on some invisible target.

Showing Sam a curious smile he jumped to action, started the Jeep, and put it into gear, pushing the accelerator down as the large off-road tires squealed on the dusty back road. "I've got an idea," he told her. "Just remembered something…"

For the first time that afternoon she felt a tiny sliver of hope.

****

5:22 p.m.

Charles continued to sit on the hard cement floor, swallowing deeply while listening for the sound that told him the circulating fan was running. Perhaps it was his imagination, but he thought the room was getting warmer and the air had taken on a distinctly unpleasant odor. He hadn't heard the whir or felt the slight movement of air that indicated the device was working.

He had stood and walked the perimeter of his tiny

cell several times, counting the steps. Fourteen. Yes. That was the number. He'd done it a dozen times. Then he paced back and forth. Seven steps. Anything to keep his mind from the terrifying possibility that this small sterile space might become his...his coffin.

Doing his best to appear casual, he turned from where the small cameras were poised—high up on the wall that faced him. Every time he moved, he heard the faint noise and watched them subtly move to follow him. He slid his hand inside his snug riding jeans and found the lighter again, depressing the small emblem on the front which served as a trigger to send a signal then rapidly removing his hand and turned again to face the cameras.

Closing his eyes, he felt a hopeful smile emerge. He imagined the great room at the house on Pleasant Street. Poppy, Sam, Eric, Misha, and Mother all surrounded a large laptop staring at the screen as they saw the signal from his lighter.

Yes. They would see it and they would find him. He was certain of it. He had to believe they would. They would not, could not leave him here to die in this small stuffy tomb...

****

5:26 p.m.

"How is she?" James asked the Admiral when he had returned to the Tahoe that he was riding in.

He sighed. "Not good." He paused. "They've done a procedure to reduce the pressure on her brain, but they won't know for a couple of days. They're keeping her heavily sedated. What's happening there?" he asked not wanting to dwell on Jeanie's condition.

"Well. Nothing from Ashley on the electronic

front. She says whoever is managing the technology for these people is world class."

"It has to be Lassiter. He's a slimy son of a bitch who sells himself to the highest bidder but he's one of the best. We've run into him before."

"We just got a call from Shane and Sam. They're sure they've narrowed down the area where the kidnappers may be," James explained. "They said they should be back here in a little while."

"That's good to hear. Now we can use the drone," the Admiral said feeling his adrenaline surge. "I'll be there in ten minutes. I'll tell our team and have them get it ready." He pressed 'end' and sat back. The familiar sights of Cape Cod's hectic Route 28 flew by as the Tahoe sped toward the Edgerton estate. He glanced, paying little attention. Lassiter and his friends were filth. Detritus. Parasites gaining wealth by feeding off the good, the kind, and the privileged. He'd been fighting their kind his whole life. He would take no prisoners. Give them no quarter. They would pay in full for what they'd done!

Chapter Forty-Six

5:28 p.m.

Ashley sat staring into the screens of the laptops that surrounded her. Suddenly she saw it. "*Eric! Misha! Come in here!*" she commanded.

Both men rushed into the large dining room.

She pointed to the smaller laptop that sat on her right. "*A signal!*" she said pointing at the screen. "It's been flashing for a few minutes," she explained. "At first I thought it was just a rogue transmission I'd stumbled across by accident. But I took a chance and did a quick system's reset. When I did the signal grew stronger," she said smiling for the first time in hours. "This is definitely from Charles!" Ashley pointed at the smaller of her laptops showing her first smile of the afternoon.

They all stared at it.

"Great work!" Misha said with admiration.

"You had the foresight to give them those lighters," she said shrugging off the praise. "All I did was set the laptop to the preset signal frequency."

Ashley had set the smaller machine on Google Earth. A satellite picture of a ten square mile circle surrounding the scene where the kidnapping took place. She turned and typed some instructions and suddenly the Google Earth view was overlaid with a map of the

Brewster-Chatham area. "Let me try to magnify it," she said swallowing deeply.

She was about to strike the keyboard, when the signal disappeared.

"Damn!" Ashley swore, shooting a glance at Eric. She immediately rebooted the system. They all held their breath. Eric crossed his fingers and exhaled loudly. When Google Earth and the analog map appeared again the signal had disappeared.

****

5:36 p.m.

Shane and Samantha knelt in the thick woods overlooking a large sprawling colonial on Nickerson Path. When they'd driven down the small out of the way road in West Chatham, they'd spotted them—a non-descript van and a Jaguar convertible in British racing green in the driveway.

She looked at Shane and leaned over giving him a quick kiss on the cheek.

"What was that for?" he asked shifting his glance toward her.

"For being the Edgerton's hero once again," she whispered with a flush.

Shane continued to look at her. Despite the tension he couldn't control the urge to smile.

"Call them, Sam," Shane said gesturing toward the house. "Tell them what we found."

Sam nodded and pulled out her cell phone hitting redial when she found Ashley's number. "Hi," she whispered when Ashley answered.

"Where are you?" Ashley asked sounding concerned. "Are you all right? You should be back here soon! And why are you whispering?"

"Shane had an idea, so we followed his hunch," she explained. "I'll tell you all about it when we see you, but we've found them!"

"Them?"

"Yes, we found a large house on an isolated road in Chatham. Shane can tell you exactly where it is. There are two vehicles in the driveway. A large van without any markings on it and dark green Jaguar convertible."

"I'm putting you on speaker, Sam," Ashley said sounding animated. "Can you repeat that?"

She did, hearing excited voices in the background. She repeated what she'd told Ashley. Sam recognized Eric, Misha, and Poppy's voices in the background.

Shane nodded toward her. "Can I speak to Eric?"

She handed him the phone.

"We're on a side road—Nickerson Path—off Red Fawn Road next to Nickerson State Park in Brewster," he paused momentarily. "Didn't one of you say that you had access to a drone?" he whispered while he continued to study the house and grounds. "What capabilities does it have? Night vision? Thermal imaging?"

"Not sure, but both from what I understand," Eric answered. "But please. Do not do anything stupid! *Please. Stay put and keep hidden,*" he ordered.

Shane looked at Sam and nodded. "All right. Yes. We'll stay here." He stopped and listened, then mouthed the word, *'Okay?'*

"Of course," Sam whispered.

"All right," he said into her cell. "My Jeep is parked on a small overgrown trail. Pulled off to the side." He nodded and touched her hand.

Sam took his and squeezed it tightly.

Shane handed her the phone. "We're going to get closer," she said into the cell phone. "If we call you on my cell when we get closer you can ping my phone?"

"Great idea." Shane nodded.

She was about to end the call when Poppy came on her cell. "Please, Samantha. We'll get Charles back. I promise you. But I don't want you to risk yourself or Shane!" he said, his voice cracking with emotion. "Come back here at once!" he ordered.

"Don't worry, Darling. We'll be careful. Very careful," she promised, adding, "But we are staying here!"

When Sam hit 'End' they both stood and studied the thick woods. She pointed toward an opening that lead to a small level spot that gave them a good view of the house and grounds.

Shane nodded and lead the way to their new vantage point.

****

5:40 p.m.

After they disconnected with Sam and Shane, Eric, Misha, and Ashley studied the map that was overlaid on the Google Earth graphic.

"This is…just plain amazing!" Eric said. "I should have known Shane would figure this out." He shook his head and showed a curious smile. "There's no one knows the back roads and woods of the Cape like that boy does."

Ashley left Google Earth then recalled the area map, blowing it up to a four-hundred percent view.

Eric leaned close over it, studied it for a few seconds then pointed to a spot on it. "About here," he said.

"When Sam calls us back, we'll ping her phone and get a fix. Then the Admiral's team can do a fly over with the drone." She suggested playing with her lip. "I wonder if these people would have any way to detect a drone?"

Ashley, Misha, and the others looked at it.

"We can coordinate with Brewster and State Police," Lieutenant Angela Pagliarulo from the Dennis P.D. Detective Division said. Eric had called them despite James protestations. They assured him they would be incognito. And she'd arrived an hour before in a shiny SUV wearing a beach outfit covered by a bright robe. "I know the area they're talking about very well. Back in my day it was a lover's lane," she explained hiding a shy smile.

That was probably how Shane knew about it, Eric thought. His fiancé had lived on the Brewster—Dennis line not far from it.

****

5:50 p.m.

Charles immediately stuffed the lighter back into his pocket when the man who entered his small cell opened the inner door. He wasn't certain whether the small raised emblem on its front sent a continuous signal after the tension was released. He also had no idea whether the room's ceiling and walls were too thick to allow the signal to penetrate and call for help.

He closed his eyes and said another silent prayer. He clenched his fists and stood when his captor motioned for him to do so. When he opened his eyes, he groaned inwardly seeing that this man—different from the one who had visited him earlier—held handcuffs and the hideous gag they had used on him earlier. The man was silent but turned him roughly.

"Hands behind your back, boy," he ordered Charles in a guttural baritone with a thick accent.

Charles turned and pushed them behind him. Despite his fear he determined he would not show it to these devils…

Chapter Forty-Seven

5:55 p.m.

James kept glancing at the Grandfather Clock while pacing back and forth between his study and the dining room. Yesterday it had been a beautiful antique. Today the loud ticks served as a reminder that each minute might bring his kind, beautiful, fun loving grandson closer to a terrifying death. He massaged the back of his neck trying to rub away the annoying ache that had grown into a sharp pain.

The dining room held the technology team. Ashley, the top tech from the Dennis P.D., and assorted others who had arrived surreptitiously. The recent call from Samantha and Shane had spun new hope.

And the search team—Eric, Misha, Jasmine, and two others who had recently joined them while he'd been comforting Millicent—stood in James's study intently surveying his large laptop. The Google Earth image with the enlarged map that overlaid it was displayed.

He sighed and glanced at the laptop. "I don't like Samantha and Shane being so close to these devils," he said, clenching his fists, and shaking his head.

Misha looked up "I understand, sir. Neither do I," he agreed. "But from what little I've heard about Shane from Samantha and Eric I think they'll be fine." He smiled warmly and patted James gently on the shoulder. "We're lucky to have someone so knowledgeable about the local area," he added. Ashley came into the study and held up her watch. "Should be any minute," she said doing her best to sound upbeat.

Everyone paused and looked up.

James nodded.

"Please, remember, sir," Misha said finding James' eyes. "Stay calm, but don't let them think they're in control." He paused. "That only gives them confidence."

As he spoke the Admiral rushed through the front door. "Any more word from the kidnappers?" he asked breathlessly.

"No," James shook his head. "They're due to call any minute."

Everyone moved quickly to the large dining room, glancing at each other, then at Ashley's laptop. The Admiral stood next to James and put his arm around his friend's shoulder. "How's Millicent?"

"Not well. The doctor's given her a sedative, so she's resting now." He offered showing a weak smile. "Thanks for asking. And Jeanie?"

The Admiral nodded and checked his watch. "Still no definitive word. They say it may take a few days before we really know anything," his old friend added trying to look positive. But James knew him too well.

"So sorry," James said looking at the time. 6:03 p.m. As the seconds ticked off, he did his best to stay calm. James clenched his fists as Charles' face came to mind. He had lived through air attacks, vessels sinking, and clandestine undercover work—all of which put his life in serious jeopardy. *This was different. Very different*, he thought when he turned, looking at the grandfather clock behind him: 6:06 p.m....

****

6:08 p.m.

"All right," Axe said looking at his watch. "Get the feed from the room up and send it to them." He nodded to Lassiter. "They should be in a frenzy by now."

When Lassiter had followed instructions, he looked at Axe. "All set," he said. The screen came to life with an image of Charles standing handcuffed and gagged. He looked up at the opposite wall. . .

"Good evening, James," Axe said evenly.

"You're *late!*" Edgerton said loudly. "How's Charles!" he demanded.

"You can see for yourself," Axe answered. "He's fine and will be if you comply with our demands."

"Why is he still tied up and gagged?"

"It's for his own safety," Axe lied. He had done it to intimidate Edgerton. The boy looked so vulnerable and helpless. Just the way he'd planned it.

"All right," James said, his voice softened but trembled when he spoke. "We just want him safe and home with us again."

"All right," Axe began. "You will need to take down these instructions. Any mistake, error, or oversight and we walk away."

"Of...of course. We're recording what you tell us. If that's permissible?" Edgerton said with a voice filled with emotion.

Axe shot a look at Ivan. "That is permissible. Our voiceprints are not in any data base and once this is complete you will never hear from us again. You have my word on that, James," he said to instill some

297

confidence in Edgerton. A perfect strategy. Frighten them dramatically then show them a dose of sympathy and reassurance.

"Please, go ahead," Edgerton said impatiently. "What do we have to do to get Charles home safely?"

"You are a man of the world and a man of substance, James, so I assume you are familiar with Bit Coin?" He waited for a moment. "The most fluid type of Crypto-currency."

There was a short pause. Axe assumed that the large crowd of people with Edgerton were staring at each other trying to ascertain what this might mean for them. "Ye...yes. I'm familiar with it. With Bit Coin," James answered nervously. "But I've never used it or done business with it before."

"That's fine, James. I must disconnect for now, but I will call again at 8:00 p.m. giving you our specific instructions with the amount and where it should be deposited. I suggest you contact your financial people so there is no delay." Axe looked at Ivan and nodded. "One of my associates is going to appear on the screen with Charles. He will chain him to the wall. We will leave this screen on so you can watch him. If we do not receive our compensation by noon tomorrow, we will simply leave him in the room, and you can watch him die slowly of suffocation..."

"No...*please...wait!*" They heard Edgerton's voice as the connection was broken.

****

6:15 p.m.

"James, why don't you talk to your investment people or bankers to make arrangements for the transfer of the Bit Coin," the Admiral said nodding toward his friend's study.

His friend nodded thoughtfully. "Yes, Brian."

"I don't want to usurp authority here," the Admiral said apologetically.

"No, Brian. I appreciate you doing it." James shook his head. "I've never been through this before, thank God. So your leadership is welcome." He turned then stopped. "I want to head upstairs to keep Millicent's spirits up. The doctor gave her a sedative—oh, I had told you that. Sorry. So hopefully she'll sleep through all this till…" He paused and took a deep breath. "…till we get Charles home again."

The Admiral went back into the dining room and motioned for Eric and Misha who stood awaiting him.

"Nothing…" Ashley said in a hollow voice. "Four minutes isn't enough time for someone whose using so many proxy servers," she explained.

Eric crossed the large room to where she had stood and stretched, rotating her neck while flexing her long slender fingers.

"You said Shane and Samantha were certain they were watching the house?"

"Yep," Eric said. "A plain van and a green Jag convertible in the same driveway. What are the odds of that in the back woods of Cape Cod?"

Both Misha and the Admiral nodded. "Yeah. It must be them. But just to make sure," he turned toward Ashley. "Ashley, if you took some of your portable technology could you hook up with them and check for the signal they're broadcasting?"

"I think so," she said. "The video signal is being constantly scrambled. Sent through a series of servers based on a preset program that the tech has fed into a laptop. It never stops on a tower for more than a few seconds. But if I'm only a couple of hundred feet away I can definitely tell you if they're broadcasting from the house."

"All right, how about this," the Admiral began. "You and Eric find them and Eric, bring some firepower. Is Shane okay around weapons?"

"Absolutely," Eric explained. "He went through the Coast Guard Academy, served on a cutter patrolling for drug traffickers, and he spent six months in security training after the rescue."

"And Samantha's no stranger to them either. Lord Edgerton took her and Charles hunting all the time. And she came to the range with me several times," Misha added.

They all nodded.

"I know where they are," Eric said nodding. "We brought a few…things with us figuring we might be needed beyond Ash's technology skills. The Admiral can explain who they are and what they bring to the table."

"Okay. I'm going to scout around the property just to make sure they didn't plant any more surveillance. Jasmine has the watch with the others. She's a pros pro."

They shook hands and nodded as the Admiral gave them all thumbs up. It all sounded good. Almost too good. *Those were the missions that had a habit of blowing up in your face, he thought,* heading outside to call the hospital for an update.

Chapter Forty-Eight

6:27 p.m.

The Admiral closed the front door to the Edgerton's quietly, sitting down he let his anger and fatigue wash over him. Since his return to NIRA the day before he'd buried himself in his work trying to ignore the situation. Their situation. His and Jeanie's. What was the cliché? No fool like an old fool? He wondered how he would live with the sadness if she…

"Brian?"

"Oh, yes. James." He put on his best strong face. "How did you do with your finance people?"

"All right," he said. "I'm sorry. Did I interrupt your thoughts?" James asked when he sat down next to his friend.

"Ah. No, James." He took a deep breath. "Not at all."

"Well, here's what my banker told me…"

****

6:35 p.m.

Samantha and Shane lay propped up behind a thick pine log staring down at the house they thought Charles was being held in.

"Eric and Ashley should be here in about fifteen minutes," he said quietly handing her the small high-powered binoculars he'd had in his Jeep. "Nothing moving down there."

"No," Sam said while she adjusted the focus. "Looks like the shades or curtains are all closed," she added putting them down. "Another sign that something's going on in there."

"Yeah," Shane agreed scanning the area surrounding the house. "It's a great night out. Sun setting. Cool. Nice breeze coming from this direction." He shook his head. "Anything's possible but it doesn't figure."

Sam looked away, sniffling and trying to collect herself.

"Hey," he whispered, reaching for her hand. "We're gonna bring him home again. I'm betting before the night is over. I need the strong girl I found on that raft."

"I'm sorry. I know. Whenever you're around nothing bad can happen to the Edgerton family." She wiped the touch of dampness from her cheeks. "*Nothing*," she said giving his hand a squeeze.

"Sam, I want to take a look at the ocean side of the house but here." He removed the 9 mm automatic from the back of his waistband.

"No, darling. You keep it," she told him pushing it away with a gentle smile. "Why don't we wait till they get here. I'll go back down the hill and wait for Eric and Ashley but please. Stay here till they arrive," she asked holding his hand tightly. "I'm not letting you go." Samantha insisted, whispering, "Ever again!" and pulling him to her.

Shane took a deep breath and looked as though he was about to argue.

Sam shook her head. "No. Please. For me,

Lieutenant," she maintained.

****

6:42 p.m.

"Well, brother. Are you satisfied?"

"Yes, Ilya. Apparently, you're still determined to go ahead with the original plan," Ivan answered.

"Mr. Lassiter." Axe gestured for the technology professional who had done such a fine job with their communications. "You are absolutely positive that we can keep broadcasting the boy's picture with no risk of having one of their people determine where we are located?" Axe asked.

"I have the signal travelling to proxy servers— across the US and Canada. These devices accept the signals and pass them along giving the illusion that they were initiated at that server. I've programmed them to be sent at random intervals. Unless one of their experts is a psychic or clairvoyant, I'm promising they won't find you or us." He smiled in a patronizing way. "Mr. Axelrod, we're not broadcasting a live feed. We're using a static image of the room. I send a small pulse through every few seconds, so we create the impression that they are watching the boy." He held up his hands. "Understand?"

Axe looked at Lassiter again. The man seemed to anticipate the question. "Yes, soon as you give me the signal, I'll send them the location we've agreed upon. Correct?"

"Yes. Thank you. And after we have sent them the instructions for the transfer of Bit Coin, we will stay on line until we have confirmation of its receipt then we will send them the location and disappear for the rest of our lives." Axe smiled and patted Lassiter on the back.

The man nodded at him and Ivan then waited indulgently. When Lassiter had headed up to his room on the second floor, he patted his brother on the shoulder. "By this time tomorrow we will be twenty million dollars richer." He smiled and excused himself. "Have to go up and pack."

Ivan stood and walked to the window, pulling the shade up so he could see the evening. He stood thinking about what his brother had just said. The boy had done nothing to them. He did not deserve to die, Ivan thought again.

Suddenly he felt a hand gently placed on his shoulder. Startled, he turned to see Lassiter again at his side. Ivan jumped.

"You seem troubled," Lassiter said.

"No. Not at all," Ivan said letting the shade fall back into place. "This is not my decision," he added trying not to sound defensive. "And I think the die is cast," he turned and gave the other man a shrug. "Not my decision at all," he repeated with a deep sigh and walked away.

****

Charles stood and walked around the room. "One, two, three…" he counted again. After they'd performed their charade. At least he assumed that was what it was since after only a few minutes two of them returned and removed the bindings. He could no longer see the small lights or hear the small electrical sound from the cameras mounted on the opposite wall.

He did hear a light whirring sound from the ceiling and now that the light was on, he could spot the small air vent overhead. That was reassuring.

The two men had been very courteous. Much more

than he expected. The large one assured him that they had had discussions with his family and that they hoped he would be freed in the morning…whenever that was. They had taken his watch and phone away.

"Twelve, thirteen, fourteen…" he said sitting down and taking a small drink from the second bottle of water they'd left and sighed, trying to convince himself that soon he'd be back in his bed with Sam, Poppy, and Mum.

****

6:54 p.m.

James sat at his desk and hit end as the Admiral entered the room. His face must have shown concern since his old friend stopped and held up his hands.

"Is everything all right, James?"

James stood and began rubbing his forehead feverishly. "I can't be sure, Brian." He shrugged. "I have no idea how much these devils will ask for Charles' return. No matter how well off one is it's difficult to lay your hands on millions of pounds at the drop of a hat." He paused. "Do you have any experience in things like this? I mean…how much do you think they could demand?"

The Admiral shook his head. "I'm sorry, but I haven't." He closed the distance between them and put his hand on James shoulder. "They obviously know your family is an old and affluent one. I do know of some cases we've discussed with other agencies where the kidnappers demanded ten million dollars or more. How much could you get with short notice if necessary?"

"Well if we sold off a good portion of our liquid investments, we could come up with about twelve million pounds. That's almost sixteen million dollars, I think." James shook his head. "Perhaps a million or two more if they gave us another day."

"I'm thinking they want to get this over with quickly, James. After all, if I'm the kidnappers I'm assuming you have the FBI, police, and your security team scouring the area for them—no matter how much they warned you not to. And no matter how good they are at their electronics they must worry that we'll be able to home in on their signal. I don't know how many of them are involved but that's a tidy sum and they have to know that you can't simply snap your fingers and get millions," the Admiral said, doing his best to reassure his friend.

"Perhaps I could offer myself in exchange in addition to the money. Yes…I'll volunteer to take Charles' place and pay them, then we could raise more…"

"James, don't. Please. Let them give you their terms. Once you've heard them, we can discuss options," the Admiral said evenly. "Eric and Ashley have just arrived. And if Ashley can definitely determine that there's a signal coming from the house, we can surround them and then we'll be in a strong bargaining position."

"All…all right," James agreed. "I just hope you're right. Any word on Jeanie?" he added.

"Nothing new. Still in a medically induced coma till the swelling goes down."

"Then we both have a lot to pray for, eh?"

The Admiral nodded. *Yes, a lot to pray for…*

Chapter Forty-Nine

7:02 p.m.

Samantha sat huddled on the side of the steep hill that overlooked the large rambling house below. She and Shane were certain it held her brother and his captors. She bit her lip, staying low but straining to hear the sound that told her Ashley and Eric had arrived.

She couldn't see Shane, but she hoped that he had stayed prone behind the log that had hidden them from view. There was no way to tell what the people inside the house were watching. And even though the blinds appeared closed it was possible that one of them had peered around the shades and was watching the hillside. The cover was not that thick between where they had lain, the open lawn, and house only a hundred feet away.

She closed her eyes but opened them suddenly when she heard Eric's powerful Jeep pull in to the secluded side trail she and Shane had parked on.

"Hello. Up here," she whispered loudly, waving to get their attention.

Both nodded and they headed up toward her. Ashley had a small carry case and Eric wore a backpack.

"Hi, Sam," Ashley said, giving Samantha a quick hug.

Eric smiled and gave her thumbs up. "I think you guys have found the spot. Let me get in touch with the Admiral so he can get that drone in the air…"

"Nooo," Shane insisted when he appeared over the crest of the small hill. He shook his head violently. "I just took a look down below. Went around the back to the water side to scout it and there were two guys on the back-porch smoking. They might be outside again and might spot the drone."

Eric looked skeptical and shook his head slowly. "I don't know, buddy. That baby flies at a thousand feet, is virtually silent, and has thermal imaging."

"Got it, Eric." Shane looked wary. "But what do we need it for? If Ashley tells us they're sending out a signal we've got them. It's ninety-nine percent sure that Charles is in the basement. Right?"

"Yes," Eric said thoughtfully, and the others nodded in agreement. He pulled off the backpack and opened it, removing a Glock, and handing it to Shane.

Shane shook his head, removing an automatic of his own from the back of his waistband. "Thanks. This is my service weapon. I fired expert every year," he said quietly studying the carpet of pine needles and leaves.

"I know," Eric said. He smiled and gave Shane a slap on the back. "Stop being so darn modest. We're only *here* because of you."

Shane shrugged as Sam put her arm around him.

"Okay. I'll call the Admiral and tell him we don't need the high-ticket technology. Ash," Eric said, turning toward her. "Can you get setup and see what you're picking up from the house?"

"I'm on it," she agreed and took out her Lenovo

mini and brought up her search and analysis programs.

****

7:12 p.m.

"That sounds great," the Admiral said feeling a slight uptick in his mood for the first time that day. "Let me put you on speaker." He called out to the small crowd that had gathered in the dining room explaining that they were sure that they'd found Charles' location.

After hearing the good news, the Admiral, Misha, and the team leaders from the Dennis PD and the FBI Field Office sat down to plan what came next. James insisted he be included.

"Of course." The Admiral agreed. "I wouldn't have it any other way."

After thirty minutes they all stood.

"So local police, the FBI, and my men will form a tight perimeter in the cover about fifty yards from the house. John," he nodded to the FBI Agent-in-Charge. "You'll coordinate with the Coast Guard in Chatham and the local Harbor Patrol and Police to have them stationed off shore for two miles in either direction from the house." He paused. "My team has talked to State Police. They'll have a helicopter stationed over the house at exactly eight-ten." He shifted his attention to James. "Now, old friend." He touched his shoulder. "You have the most important role to play. Don't do anything to give away your excitement or the strength of our position. Please. Continue to sound like the terrified grandfather."

James nodded and patted his friend's shoulder. "Yes," he said nodding. He wore a faint smile for the first time all day. "But until Charles walks back through that door I still am!"

****

7:55 p.m.

Last phone call, Axe thought. *By tomorrow evening at this time they would all be on their way. And their captive would be...*He paused, admitting to himself that he was not glad about the outcome he had planned. The boy Charles was courageous, intelligent, and beautiful. He wondered what his son would have been like. And Charles' death would not bring them back. But shouldn't he make those who quietly controlled the world with their power and influence pay? Strike a blow for the common man? And who better to do it than someone who had suffered at the hands of the thoughtless, powerful, and rich ones who had no idea what their callous indifference meant to their innocent victims.

"Ilya," Ivan called out. "Almost time," he said coolly.

Axe knew that Ivan was bothered by his brother's unwillingness to change their plan. Could he be right? Wouldn't he learn that life belonged to those who were hard and refused to weaken when faced with adversity?

He sighed and nodded as he studied his beautiful brother. "We'll let them wait again," he answered evenly then took a seat in front of the giant laptop and smiled at Lassiter.

****

8:02 p.m.

"Everyone agreed that there was no need for the drone," Eric said to Shane while they lay prone behind the thick pine log that had become their temporary station. "Only thing is it would have been nice to assess the number of bad guys we're facing." The pristine

310

early summer evening belied the tense situation they faced. Even though Ashley had confirmed that the kidnappers were inside they still had a giant trump card: Charles was their prisoner—chained in an air-tight room! Eric touched his young friend's forearm. "I think that young lady is in love," he said with a grin nodding back down the hill toward where Samantha and Ashley waited behind the Jeeps for the FBI, Police, and NIRA agents who would cordon off the area surrounding the large farmhouse. The Chatham Police had closed the small side road that the large rambling farmhouse sat on.

"She's not the only one," Shane answered quietly while he stared through the compact binoculars at the windows. He handed them to Eric. "I...I loved Emmy. You know that." It was a statement not a question. He looked back toward where Sam waited.

"Of course." Eric sighed. "No one ever questioned that."

"But Sam was like something out of a novel." Shane shrugged. "The most special girl I'd ever met. She was only nineteen when we were in the raft, but she looked after everyone like a mother hen. Including me. Never thought about herself. Hardly slept. Nursed her uncle like an RN. I practically had to spoon feed her and make sure she drank her water ration. She was so worried about the rest of us..."

"I get it," Eric said. "And I can see it in her. Ashley adores her. Says she's like the younger sister she never had and she's only known her for a few weeks."

"Funny. It's like in their genes, Eric. Charles and his little cousin Holly. They were all the same. Never complained. Never asked for more." He shook his head.

"I keep thinking about him. That poor kid. Frightened out of his wits. Locked up down there. Chained up like an animal. Not knowing if he'll live or die in a slow terrifying way."

"I know," Eric said in a hard voice. "Me, too."

"When we get those guys," Shane continued.

"Yeah?"

"I'd like to spend a few minutes alone with the mastermind."

Eric nodded. "I understand. But a couple of them are real bad dudes from what the Admiral says. SAS and that kind of shit. So, let's let the law take over." Eric patted his young friend's arm.

Shane looked back. "Well, we'll see." His jaw was set, repeating, "We'll see."

***

8:07 p.m.

The Admiral sat in the study with James, a Dennis Police Detective, and two FBI Agents. He nodded his agreement.

"A classic tactic. You're so worried about when they'll call you can't concentrate on anything else," one of the FBI Agents agreed.

"How many things like this have you…" James question was interrupted by the buzz of the phone terminal they were using.

James looked at those surrounding him. The atmosphere was tense even though they now knew where the cruel devils were holding Charles.

"Good evening, James. And the rest of you there with him," the mechanical voice greeted the small group. "It's my fervent hope that this will conclude our dealings. By now, James, you have ascertained what your ability to raise significant funds in the short term is so we can send you directions to find Charles."

The screen that had been blank suddenly came to life, glowing with the now familiar green tint and view of the small room and Charles. He now sat on the floor, drinking from a bottle of water, and eating a sandwich. He suddenly turned and raised his eyes toward the camera nodding and showing a weak smile.

"You can see," the Voice continued. "That we have done our best to make him comfortable. Now, rather than make unreasonable demands please tell us what you can raise and transfer within the next twenty-four hours."

Everyone in the room looked at James.

He raised ten fingers followed by another five. Mouthing the words: *Fifteen million pounds.*

Since they were sure that the money would never have to be sent, they had agreed on that amount reasonably sure the kidnappers would agree.

"I can transfer fifteen million pounds in Bit Coin by midnight," James said evenly. "To anywhere you specify."

Silence.

James wondered if they were surprised by his large offer. "Please. Did you hear me?" he asked again evenly.

"That sounds like a...a reasonable amount. Now I will give you the special instructions and when and how we will send you Charles location."

The group in the study looked at each other with knowing smiles. For the first time it sounded as if they'd called the kidnappers bluff. The Voice sounded nervous.

"All right. Please proceed," James told the Voice.

The kidnapper gave him specific instructions about how and where the bit coin was to be deposited. He told James that once they had received acknowledgement of its receipt, they would send him a message on a special channel with his location and a map overlaid on Google Earth. And they would bring up the screen with Charles live image on it to show that he was alive and in good health.

"At this point in our negotiations do I need to suggest that any indication of outside interference will result in a sad conclusion to our brief and up to this point very business-like relationship?" the Voice asked, sounding self-assured and in command again.

"No. You need not," James assured them.

"Thank you for keeping your head and letting us bring this to a fruitful conclusion."

James hesitated and was about to say something when the lead FBI Agent shook his head vigorously, mouthing the word, *No!*

"Yes," he said quietly and sighed deeply as the connection was terminated.

"We now have the upper hand. Please, sir, you didn't want to say something to let them think we feel we have any control."

James put his hand on the young man's shoulder and patted it gently. "Understood."

"All right," the Admiral said with a hard expression. "Let's get a sitrep from Eric and get that drone in the air." He held up his hands. "I know there was talk that it might attract attention but in ten minutes we'll be cordoning off that dwelling and we need to know what we're dealing with inside." He paused and breathed deeply. "I'm betting there are three, maybe four of them in there but if they have six or eight in there then we may have our hands full. And Charles' life hangs in the balance."

James nodded. "All right." He knew the latest news on Jeanie had been encouraging. He'd seldom seen his old friend this angry. Too many years dealing with things that were dark, tragic, and evil perhaps. It had been obvious from their arrival that he and Jeanie cared for each other. Very much. And for years Brian had kept himself above the world of emotional involvement. Or at least had masked it well.

"I'll call Eric and give them a heads-up on that. And get my team to get the drone into the air. They have it in a van." He paused. "Agreed?" the Admiral asked evenly.

Everyone in the room nodded their approval.

Chapter Fifty

8:14 p.m.

"The drone is in place, Admiral," Mario Mendez told his superior. "We're getting a good signal from it here in the van," he added. "The operator is activating the thermal imaging sensors, so we should know in two to three minutes what we're facing."

"Excellent, Mario. And your partner is with the team surrounding the house?"

"Yes, sir, Merritt is with the FBI AIC. He should be online, so I'll let him give you a sitrep," the young agent told the Admiral.

"Fine. Thanks."

Two minutes later Jim Merritt had given him their situation report. The property was completely surrounded, even on the water side. Two forty-seven-foot patrol boats from USCG Chatham and two smaller thirty-four-foot Boston Whalers from the Chatham Harbor patrol—the waterside version of the Chatham Police Department—stood guard one-hundred yards off the beach in front of the house.

"What's the drone's thermal imaging picking up?" the Admiral asked Merritt.

"We've got six thermal signatures inside, Admiral," his agent began. "But this unit isn't that sophisticated. We're not getting any elevations."

The Admiral understood. That could be an issue. They had no way to discern on what level the images, e.g. the bodies were located. The more sophisticated units would indicate by color or shading which images had higher elevations. But the fact that there were only six of them and at least one of them was Charles, gave him some relief.

"Well, five of them being hostiles is better than I expected. I'm also going out on a limb here and adding that the tech guru, the one we call Lassiter, is not a heavyweight combatant. I can never recollect any cases that involved him in a shootout."

"Yes, sir." Merritt sounded skeptical. "But I assume that he usually isn't involved in the final takedown. He may not be former SAS like Muldoon, but I don't think he's been on the dark side for years and has no idea how to handle an AR-15 or a MAC-10."

"You're right." The Admiral closed his eyes. He wanted to be there for this takedown. More than anything he'd wanted in a long time but these men—his agents, Eric, Misha, and all the others were pros. He sighed and continued. "And we don't know whether the others are high-level operatives or the brains—the planners. Usually they don't employ a high roller like Derrick Muldoon unless they are."

"The calls up to you? But I understand the FBI has tactical command, sir."

"Hold tight for another ten. I want to talk to the boy's family." He paused. "They have a major stake in this."

"You got it, Admiral," Merritt said. "I'll pass that along to the AIC."

****

"Well, that sounds reasonable," Axe said with a deep sigh. "I had researched their assets but was not able to ascertain how much Edgerton could get in a twenty-four-hour period. Fifteen million pounds is about twenty million U.S. Dollars." He showed a satisfied smile to Ivan who sat across the desk from him. "Where's Nicolai?'

"Upstairs." He answered his brother. "You asked him to pack everything that we brought that would indicate who we were?"

"Yes, I did. To keep him out of the way while we were negotiating."

Ivan nodded. "Besides, you've told me on many occasions, they have no fingerprints, voice recordings, pictures, or anything else to give away who we are."

Axe ran his hand through his thick hair and nodded. "Yes. Nothing I can think of. And I checked with Lassiter and Murphy, our resident professionals. They agreed."

"What about them? Heaven knows I'm guessing they're well known to Interpol, British Intelligence, FBI, and a variety of other police organizations."

"Of course, but they don't seem worried. They don't exactly have a home in the country with a wife and children. They're constantly using assumed names and identities. And there's no reason to assume we won't make a clean getaway."

"Not much of a life," Ivan said shaking his head.

"No, It's not. But they don't care. I think they enjoy the adrenaline rush, the thrills, and the money." He shrugged. "Here. This is the address I want Lassiter to send to Edgerton when we get confirmation that the

Bit Coin is deposited. Can you give it to him?"

Ivan sighed and nodded then stole a look at the address. Suddenly he stopped and turned to see Axe wearing a faint smile.

"But this…this is the address here."

Axe nodded. "You see, Brother. I do listen to your advice."

Ivan stepped closer and patted his brother on the arm. "Thank you," he said adding, "Spasiba," repeating his thanks in Russian while he headed to find Lassiter.

****

8:20 p.m.

It was agreed upon that Allen Callahan, the FBI Boston Field Office top specialist in hostage negotiation would talk to the kidnappers. Callahan was a fortyish agent who had a fine resume in negotiating with everyone from irate druggie boyfriends to Muslim terrorists.

He was located behind a fifteen-foot long wall assembled from portable Kevlar panels and located one hundred yards from the farmhouse's oversize front door. The Agents and officers all wore their Kevlar vests bearing the name of the specific organization they represented.

Eric and Shane wore vests supplied by the NIRA agents. However, since they had no official position, the FBI AIC had insisted they stay behind the first line.

The three of them slowly moved forward, refusing to be left out of the action when Eric heard a whistle behind them and turned. Misha was crawling up to join them on all fours with a more sophisticated vest that bore the initials IDF, for Israeli Defense Force.

Eric smiled and motioned him to join them.

"Nice party. Thought I'd stop by since I had nothing else on the calendar for the evening," he said amiably.

Eric was growing to like this young man. He was a warrior and he definitely knew his business.

Misha and Shane clasped hands.

"How's Sam doing?" Shane asked. "I know she didn't like being left below to tend the horses," he added with a grin.

"Your lady is anxious but fine, Shane," Misha told him. "She's very nervous. Pacing around and to continue the equestrian imagery she's chomping at the bit you might say."

They caught the FBI Agent in charge of the perimeter flash the signal. He pointed at his watch and flashed eight fingers, followed by three and then held up both fists with none showing, telling them the negotiator would begin hailing the house at eight-thirty p.m. He wanted to wait until the sun had dropped below the horizon. They also had good position since the light would be behind them and in the face of anyone in the front of the house when the sky darkened.

Eric showed him thumbs-up and nodded then showed his companions a confident expression. Now they simply had to wait. Eric picked up the binoculars to catch a look at the house again one more time he froze. There was no mistaking the two loud reports from inside. They were gunshots!

Chapter Fifty-One

8:26 p.m.

"What the hell are you doing?" Axe screamed at
Murphy who held the smoking automatic weapon in his
right hand.

Nicolai lay on the kitchen floor, crying and
writhing in pain. He grabbed his left bicep and groaned,
"Je-sus!"

Ivan leaned against the counter holding his right
arm. Blood was soaking through his gray jersey while
he stared angrily and cursed the man who stood four
feet from him. "You fucking son of a…"

"Shut up. All of you," Murphy said evenly
motioning for Ivan and Axe to move near to Nicolai as
Lassiter ran down the stairs.

"What the hell…" Lassiter began when he entered
the kitchen and saw the situation. He took a deep breath
then collected himself. "What's going on?" he asked.

Murphy motioned for Lassiter to join the others
with his large automatic.

Axe fixed the former SAS operative with a
withering look. "Can I assume that this is a coup, Mr.
Murphy," he asked through clenched teeth.

"Sadly yes, Mr. Axelrod." He paused and showed
the four others a sardonic smile. "Though not entirely.
Please…you and Mr. Lassiter get some towels and take

321

these bandages," he told them, backed into the hallway, and retrieved a small knapsack, throwing it toward the two men. "I regret doing this, but you see I find myself in a precarious situation and I need to take some of that rather large ransom that you'll be collecting from…"

"Hello. Inside the house." The amplified voice came through the windows and doors. "This is the FBI. We have you surrounded." There was a brief pause followed by, "The Coast Guard and the Harbor Patrol have four vessels off shore."

Murphy turned toward the voice but quickly returned his gaze and the automatic toward the four men in the kitchen.

"We want to talk about releasing your hostage, Charles Edgerton."

Axe showed the Brit a wry smirk. "Even more precarious than you supposed."

"Yes. And it sounds like you're all in the shit with me," Murphy said in a mocking tone.

****

8:33 p.m.

Suddenly someone grabbed Shane's arm while he and the others on the hillside sat eyes fixed on the house—terrified what those shots might mean.

"Oh, God," Sam cried. "What… what was that?" she asked as Ashley joined her and the others.

Shane pulled her up and put his arm around her tightly. "They wouldn't…do anything to Charles. They want him in good shape." He played with his lip, silently praying he was right.

"Shane's correct, Miss Samantha. Master Charles is the last one they'd want to harm. But it's not a good sign," Misha said looking at Eric for agreement.

Eric nodded. "Yeah, I agree with Shane and Misha. Something's gone very wrong with the kidnappers."

"We just heard two gunshots. Is Charles Edgerton all right?" The FBI negotiator called out to the house. "Please respond!

Shane, Sam, and the others stared intently at the house while they exchanged the binoculars.

"I see a shade being raised on the front of the house next to the door," Sam announced handing them to Shane.

"Yes...and they're opening a window!" Shane whispered with excitement passing the binoculars to Eric while he pointed.

Eric nodded and shared them with the others.

"Charles has not been harmed," a strong voice with a British accent shouted from inside the house. "And he will not be unless you make an attempt to close in."

****

8:38 p.m.

"Well, Mr. Murphy, what do you suggest?" Axe asked. "Can you see any way out of this situation?"

Lassiter had used the towels and bandages to patch up Ivan and Nicolai. Their wounds were superficial. They had obviously been intended to threaten and partially disable the two younger men.

Murphy wore a bitter expression. He shook his head. "You heard them. But let's delay them for a while to see if we can see any way to get out of this. In the US kidnapping is a Federal crime. It could be a life sentence."

Axe stood and crossed the large room. "I've accomplished what I wanted to. I've made Edgerton aware that all his money and advantages are mere window-dressing." He shook his head. "If they would let the boys go, I will give myself up."

Murphy stood and joined him, bending to sneak a look out the window. "It's getting dark. In thirty minutes, we can…"

"In thirty minutes they will illuminate this whole area. And you heard them. They've even got the shoreline closed off." Axe smiled ruefully. "And you've seen to it that Ivan and Nicolai aren't in any shape to be scurrying around in the woods after dark."

"I can't be taken by these people," Murphy shook his head. "I'm wanted across the UK, Europe, and the Middle East. If they get me, I'll be extradited and either disappear or be summarily executed. *I cannot surrender*!" he said with a tightly clenched jaw.

"Isn't it the Bible that says…what you sow so shall you reap," Axe asked shaking his head while he headed back to check on the boys.

****

8:43 p.m.

"I had an idea," Shane said crawling over toward Eric and Misha. "Charles is still in the air-tight room, right?"

"That's what we heard." Eric nodded. "We're not in control of this op but yeah, I haven't heard anything different."

"Do the police still use tear-gas?"

Eric turned toward him nodding. Misha smiled.

"Yeah, I…I think they do. Use it more for riot control and things like that. Let me check with the FBI Agent in Charge and the guys from the Dennis PD."

"That's a hell of an idea, son," Misha said.

"I…I don't get it," Samantha said wrinkling her

brows.

"Here's what I was thinking…" Shane began slipping over next to her. He explained that if Charles was held in an airtight room, they could use tear gas to disable the kidnappers without doing him any harm.

Eric got off the phone with the FBI Agent. "He says that Dennis PD have some in one of their SUVs. He's sending two of their officers to bring the weapons and the cartridges. One of their Sergeants is trained to use it, so he'll set up a plan with their assault team. His compliments." Eric gave Shane high five then slid back over to Misha "I guess it's a little outdated with all today's technology, but he says it's a perfect strategy."

Sam moved closer to Shane, sneaking her arm over his back. They lay side by side. *My Hero*, she grinned, mouthing the words and giving him a quick squeeze.

****

8:45 p.m.

"I told you. I'm willing to give myself up," Axe said evenly. He and Murphy stood peering out the living room window. The dark was closing in. "Perhaps you can all escape under the cover of nightfall?" He shrugged.

Murphy shook his head. "No, we both know they'll be lighting this place up like a sports stadium in a few minutes." When he spoke, he turned and let his grip on the automatic relax.

In a swift motion Axe lifted his elbow and brought the full weight of his body into the back of the Brit's skull. Murphy groaned then collapsed to the floor. Axe bent swiftly and picked up the large weapon.

"Ivan, come in here, *at once!*" he commanded.

His brother appeared with a makeshift bandage

325

wrapped tightly around his right bicep.

"You and Nicolai get something to tie this bastard up with. Right now and send Mr. Lassiter in here."

Ivan nodded agreement and hurried back to the kitchen.

Lassiter came into the living room and stopped when he saw Murphy lying unconscious on the rug. "Yes...wh...what do you want," he asked turning his focus to Axe.

"You have behaved in a professional and compassionate manner throughout our dealings. In each of two suitcases in the front hall closet there is a quarter of a million US dollars." Axe said while he opened the door and retrieved the bags pulling them out and putting them in front of Lassiter.

Ivan and Nicolai appeared with some clothesline and proceeded to bind Murphy at the ankles and the wrists.

"Good, now," Axe said pointing. "Tie his wrists to his ankles very tightly," he said smiling softly. "These suitcases contain a large amount in US dollars. Ivan, you and Nicolai will take one and Mr. Lassiter will take the other," he paused. "My friend here and I will await the authorities. I will tell them we need thirty minutes and you three will escape using the hidden door that only Ivan and I know about. It is an old tunnel used by bootleggers—whiskey smugglers—during what the Americans called prohibition." He smiled raising his eyebrows. "It was one of the main reasons I rented this house."

Ivan nodded. "But you can come with us, brother," he said shaking his head violently. Closing the distance and grabbing him by the arm. "There's no need to sacrifice yourself for…"

Axe put up his hand. "Stop! You are my family." He shook his head. "I talked you into taking part in this sad adventure." He put his hand behind Ivan's head and pulled him close. "You will go on. You have an education, intelligence. Go! You can live your life." He whispered gently. "Now grab your getaway bags quickly and get down to the basement. I will get the boy and bring him up once you three have escaped."

Ivan wiped his eyes and gave his brother a stoic look. "As you wish, Ilya."

Axe watched them go upstairs where they each retrieved a small suitcase they had packed in case their situation grew desperate which it now had. "I'll give you five minutes to get downstairs and out the door. Ivan will explain. It is almost a mile long and exits on a small side road where we have hidden a small SUV. You can take it to somewhere off Cape Cod and make reservations for a flight wherever you choose." He took Ivan's arm and smiled then raised his eyebrows. "We always knew this might happen. Please…put flowers on their headstones," he added hugging his younger brother. "Be safe. All of you."

The three men hurried to the stairway and down.

Axe checked his watch then approached the window and opened it. "Please," he yelled to the outside. *"We will surrender in thirty minutes. I give you my word. I will bring Charles out with me. He is unharmed."*

****

8:55 p.m.

"The head FBI agent says they're going to give them the thirty minutes. The drone is hovering

327

overhead and has night vision capabilities so they are not getting away and his negotiator says that in ninety-five percent of these cases the hostages are released unharmed," Eric told the group on the crest of the hill.

"But what about Charles?" Samantha said shaking her head. "How can we be sure they won't use him for a shield or kill him?" Her words were angry. Frightened. Shaking.

Shane slid over next to her and put his arm around her. Tears blossomed and worked their way down her flushed cheeks. "Nothing that we've seen or heard would suggest that these people are stupid or seeking revenge, Sam." He caressed her back softly. "These people," he nodded toward the cordon of police and FBI concealed in the woods below. "Are experts. And they're close to Eric and the Admiral. They wouldn't agree to anything that would put Charles at risk." He showed her a gentle smile. "Promise," he added crossing his heart.

"O…Okay," Sam whispered, nodding.

"Charles is gonna be fine, Honey," Ashley said sneaking over and plunking down next to Sam.

Sam looked at Shane who held the binoculars and put out her hand.

He handed them over as Samantha laughed self-consciously.

Chapter Fifty-Two

9:05 p.m.

Charles lay on the floor. The last person who had come into the small room had told him that he might be released early tomorrow morning. He wondered if they might even do it later that evening.

He had tried not to think about the other thing. The terrifying possibility that they had placated him simply to keep him quiet. But since they had kept him tied and gagged for some of the time that made no sense. All they would have to do is leave him bound up, lock the door, and never turn on the circulating fan. Right?

He stood and walked to the door putting his ear against it. Suddenly, Charles heard the outer door being unlocked. He scurried back and sat down flexing his fingers and closing his eyes. The sound of the inner door opening sent a sharp stabbing pain through his stomach.

The tall hooded figure entered. "Good evening, Charles," the deep accented baritone said quietly.

Immediately Charles noted that he had left the doors open. Both of them. He could see outside of his small prison for the first time. Sitting up Charles clenched his fists nervously peering beyond the large figure. He averted his eyes quickly when the man approached.

"It's all right, son," the man said sighing deeply. "You're going home."

"Wh…when, sir?" Charles asked in a trembling voice.

The man gestured. "You may get up. You're going home right now."

Charles could barely stand. Partly nerves that he couldn't control. Partly relief. "Thank you, sir." Charles offered in his strongest voice and waited.

The man turned and motioned with his right hand. "After you," he said.

Charles nodded and hurried to the door and outside. Once there he waited, not sure where to go or what to do.

"I'll show you the way out, Charles." The man paused. "Men are outside. The FBI, police and perhaps your grandfather or sister."

The man passed Charles and then stopped and turned.

Suddenly Charles was terrified. Has this been some cruel tease? A ploy? He need not have been concerned.

"You've behaved in a mature and courageous way," the man told his captive. "More so than we had expected." The man turned, adding, "Your family should be proud that you acted in that manner."

And with that the hooded figure opened another door and headed up a stairway. Charles followed. When they reached the first floor, the man ushered him around a large figure that lay groaning and tied up tightly on the floor. He recognized the man he thought was his friend from the riding stable. Charles stared for a long moment then looked away.

"Please wait at the door, Charles."

He wanted to pull it open and run, but nodded, even managing a weak smile.

The man who had escorted him upstairs went to a large shaded window. He pulled the shade up and stayed in the shelter of the wall and window frame. "Hello," the man yelled. "I am sending Charles out. He is safe and has not been harmed. I ask you to get him and bring him a safe distance from this house. I warn you. I will blow it up when Charles and the rest of you are a safe distance away." The man looked at Charles. "Tell them this is not a ruse or a ploy to gain time. Just get out, up, and over the embankment quickly…"

****

Shane, Sam, and the rest of them sat looking at the house and then at each other.

"Jesus," Eric said breathlessly. "These people really *are* crazy!"

"*Here he comes!*" the man yelled from inside. Suddenly the oversize front door opened, and Charles appeared.

Shane was up and over the crest of the hill before anyone could speak, calling the boy's name. At the same time two men broke from the cordon of FBI and police below.

"Shane!" Charles ran crying out, then stumbled.

"Got him," Shane called out. He reached Charles first and yanked him to his feet and half pulling, half carrying him up the hill. Samantha and Eric met them when they ran clumsily up and over the small incline.

Shane released the breathless boy into his sister's arms. Sam hugged him and kissed his face, hair, and neck continually whispering his name.

"Thank you for releasing the boy unharmed," the

FBI negotiator announced to the kidnappers once Charles was safe. "There is no need for you to…"

As the man tried to get those in the house to surrender it exploded in a giant fireball. Scraps of wood, siding, shards of glass, and debris flew across the lawn. But the kidnappers had somehow managed to direct most of the damage toward the ocean. The cordon on that side was father back and sheltered by thick trees and underbrush.

When the debris and fiery residue had settled none of the men and women in the net surrounding the large house had been injured.

Several pieces of fire equipment had been waiting on the small street the house fronted on. More arrived in a matter of minutes. The problem was that no one could be certain that the kidnappers, having failed to get the enormous ransom they demanded had not left another device somewhere on the property for payback.

The fire department continued spraying water then insulating foam on the smoldering remains for several hours. This not only prevented further explosions it also served to summarily destroy any substantive way to perform any forensic or DNA tests on the scant scattered remains of whoever and whatever was in the house…

****

9:52 p.m.

Ivan and his two companions heard the loud noise and felt the vibration while they made their way along the narrow passage that had not been used in decades. He stopped and closed his eyes knowing that his brother had sacrificed himself in the hopes that they could escape.

The plan was a good one. Not only would the explosion and fire erase all traces of their presence but, the noise and attention it drew would almost guarantee that all law enforcement attention would be focused on the remains of the house. Of course, when his brother had explained it Ivan had thought the boy Charles would be in the house—a casualty of their sad project.

Exactly what had changed his brother's mind and why he decided to release the boy Ivan would never know. He only knew he was very glad that Ilya had. And though he loved and respected his older brother there was no way he could ever continue to look him in the eye if he had let the boy die.

"Up ahead," Ivan pointed with his flashlight. "There's a door that leads to a small shed. We have a car we can use to get off Cape Cod. If we need to get treatment for our injuries, we should wait till we're far away. Perhaps at one of the Boston hospitals."

"I just want to get on a plane. The wound is trivial. I will get treated when I return home if I need it," Nicolai said.

Ivan nodded. A former resident of Boston, he knew several clinics, but felt nauseated and exhausted after what they had all gone through. "I agree. There is a large parking area where we can find a bus to the airport and with the cash we have we can buy tickets and be home or anywhere in the world in a matter of hours."

Lassiter agreed. "I have a flexible return ticket I can use whenever I choose. So when I get to the airport, I'll bid you all good-bye."

They arrived at the shed and opened the door. A late model Chevrolet Traverse sat in waiting.

Ivan opened the driver's door.

"You're all right to drive?" Lassiter asked.

"I'm fine. This is just an annoyance," he said and found the keys hidden in a jar when he opened the trunk. They left what they called their escape bags inside.

They drove at a leisurely pace to the large parking lot across the Sagamore Bridge, parked the Chevy SUV, and took their bags, heading inside to purchase bus tickets.

In less than two hours they would be arriving at Logan Airport, where they had all arrived weeks before. There were no overseas flights at that hour of the evening, but they all found rooms at the Hyatt Hotel in the airport and would secure their passage to their chosen destinations the next morning.

Ivan lay unable to sleep, staring at the reflection of lights on the ceiling. Sometime in the night he arose, walked to the bathroom, and stared at his hollow visage in the sterile light. He closed his eyes, put his head in his hands, and sobbed like a baby…

Chapter Fifty-Three

The remainder of the night was a sweeping panorama of confusion, reaction, and relief. The FBI wanted any tidbit of information they could get from Charles but thanks to some heavy politicking from the Admiral and the fact that the kidnap house was nothing but an empty smoking hulk they agreed to debrief the boy at the Edgerton's compound on Pleasant Street.

"Thank you," Sam whispered to the agents. She continued to watch her brother, perhaps fearing that another band of villains might swoop down from overhead and tear him away.

Charles had wanted to ride back to their house with Shane and Sam, but the authorities drew the line at that breach of policy. Shane drove his Jeep while Samantha rode in one of the Agency's spotless Tahoe's next to her brother, pulling him close while beaming a continual smile of relief and happiness his way.

****

"Now that Charles is free and headed home unharmed I…" the Admiral hesitated not wanting to dessert his old friend but wanting to be with Jeanie.

James held up his hand. "Of course, Brian. Please go to her and call me with updates." He nodded. "You've been the best friend I could have ever asked for. And I'm praying…we're all praying, that she makes a complete recovery." When his friend turned,

James added, "I can't imagine what we would have done without you, the Montgomery's, or Shane." He shook his head. "We can never thank you all enough."

"Well, we're old friends and Eric and Ashley have done some good work for me before but that young man, Shane." The Admiral cleared his throat and smiled. "He's the real hero in this. He used his head, his ability to reason, and local knowledge to find out where Charles was being held. All the covert operators and technology couldn't find him. He used what we call humint—human intelligence—to find your grandson."

"I know, and I won't forget it. Samantha has found herself quite a young man," James agreed giving his old friend a pat on the back. "Please call and tell me how Jeanie is, Brian," James repeated.

The Admiral nodded and hurried out the front door.

****

The remainder of the night passed in a blur for Samantha.

When they arrived back at their house, Charles was rushed inside. He hugged Poppy for a very long time. Then, before anyone could corral him, he ran up the stairs to see their mother. After Charles spent a few moments assuring her that he really was all right and had not suffered any at the hands of his kidnappers the FBI politely asked him to come downstairs, took him into Poppy's study, then closed the door. Yet despite trying to glean information from him, the only thing he could offer was his recognition of the man tied up on the floor of the kidnap house. Even the vehicles his captors had driven were destroyed in the explosion.

Eric and Ashley returned with them as her grateful grandfather opened his best bottles of Champagne and more than one of twenty-year-old Single Malt Scotch to fuel the celebration.

While the Dennis police attempted to pick up and packed their equipment they were treated to Poppy's generosity and exuberance.

"You are top shelf and cannot leave this house before at least one generous pour," he told the officers and technicians. "Maybe two!" he added with a wink.

Misha and the security team went back to their posts but even the ever-vigilant head of the Edgerton's Security Team allowed himself the luxury of a tall glass of Single Malt.

But the one person absent from the ongoing celebration was Shane.

****

The Admiral's driver knew his passenger's situation. He drove like a man possessed along the sparsely traveled side roads and up to the entrance of the Cape Cod Hospital. When he stopped abruptly the Admiral threw open his door and ran inside.

When he stepped off the elevator on the third floor the same two doctors met him and directed him into a conference room. Both looked somber and the Admiral closed his eyes and steeled himself fearing the worst.

But after sitting down heavily when he opened his eyes, he felt a wave of relief. He saw the senior surgeon, Dr. Alison, smiling. "There are still no guarantees, sir. But..." He looked at Dr. Alvarez who was nodding. "It's looking like she may be out of danger."

"That's...that's wonderful," the Admiral whispered. "After the last time I saw you I was so afraid that the news might not be positive." He struggled to compose himself.

"Yes, Ms. Flynn's condition has made a marked improvement in the last few hours," Dr. Alison added. "Far more so than we had any right to expect."

"She's a very strong woman," the younger doctor added.

The Admiral nodded. "Could I…sit with her for a while?"

The two doctors exchanged glances.

Dr. Alison nodded his approval.

The Admiral pumped both their hands and followed them to Jeanie's suite in the ICU.

They gestured for an orderly and spoke to him in a whisper. In a matter of seconds two more attendants appeared with a state-of-the-art automated recliner. They nodded and wheeled the impressive apparatus inside and placed it very close to Jeanie.

"Can you reach her hand from here, Admiral?" one of them asked.

He sat and nodded, amazed that they knew who and what he was. He bent and kissed her hand gently then sat down taking it in his.

"We're all praying for her, sir," the head attendant said quietly, touched the Admiral's sleeve, and left him alone with Jeanie.

"Thank you, son," he told the attendants as they nodded and left.

He tucked her warm limp hand inside his and closed his eyes then sighed deeply, finally feeling at peace.

****

After leaving four voicemail messages for Shane without a reply Samantha was so angry, she was sure smoke was coming out of her ears.

As she left a fifth message filled with mild profanity, she heard knocking at the front door. She went to see who else could be invading the welcome home celebration for her beautiful younger brother. "Who is it?" she asked as two of their security people and several of the police who'd remained stood poised.

When no one answered Sam opened it very slowly and there Shane stood in the doorway.

"Oh...my...God! Where have you..." she began but before she could finish Shane took her in his arms so tightly, she could barely breathe, pulled her onto the front porch, and kissed her so hard it hurt. Then he backed away looking sheepish.

"On my way here, I realized I'd left my phone on the hill where we watched the house from." He shrugged and blushed, looking embarrassed. "I need it for my job. All my contacts and emails are on there, so I went back to find it but no luck. When I got back here one of the Dennis cops had found it! I saw you'd called me a lot and were so angry at my..."

Sam's anger had already melted away. "Shhh." She put her fingers to his lips. "You saved my brother's life tonight, Darling. For the second time." She sighed deeply. "I was never angry. Simply worried." Sam put her hand on the back of her neck and groaned softly. "It's been quite a day."

Shane stood watching her, nodding. "Yes. It has."

No one and nothing had ever looked so special. So kind. So caring. "Would you like to come in," she asked then grabbed his hand and giggled feeling delicious, sexy, and full of energy despite the endless afternoon and evening.

"Love to," Shane replied.

They walked down the long hallway and out onto the back deck, doing their best to avoid the small crowd rejoicing and enjoying James' Champagne and Single Malt.

"Shane, I want to talk with you later. I have something I think might interest you," James called out after they sped by laughing deliciously.

Sam raised her eyebrows and grinned. "He mentioned something about needing a talented and dependable young man for one of his nautical enterprises."

"Actually, I'd kind of like to just unwind for a while. With you," he whispered. Finding the seclusion of the back porch they ran out and across the back lawn to the dock.

"Hmmm," she purred in her most provocative voice. "Sounds like a plan to me," Sam agreed while they boarded the small launch tied to it.

Shane looked at her and beamed a smile her way. She nodded and threw the cushions on the floor of the small vessel then laid down opening her arms. "Have I ever told you I love you?"

"Hmmm," Shane said in a contented whisper. "Not that I remember, Darling," he whispered, then lay down beside her pulling off his T-shirt. He put his arms around her tightly.

"Well I do," she whispered gently caressing his back and shoulders.

Shane beamed his most tempting smile finding her neck with his lips. "Well the feeling is mutual…"

****

"Has anyone seen Samantha and Shane?" James

340

asked half an hour later when he walked out onto the large screened-in porch.

"No, I...I haven't," Misha told his employer doing his best to hide a smile while sneaking a look toward the dock and watching the gentle rolling of the launch. "I'm sure they're in the house somewhere."

"Well, yes. I'm sure they'll turn up somewhere." James nodded, the glow of several single malts obvious in his eyes and speech. "I'd never worry as long as Sam is with Shane," he added heading back inside to rejoin the festivities. "I believe those two are really quite fond of each other!"

Epilogue

It took more than two months and a lot of support, but Jeanie Flynn made a complete recovery. By Labor Day she had returned to her job at NIRA. She wore a small diamond pendant around her slender neck since it was explicitly against NIRA policy for two staff members to engage in "fraternization." And since Brian Turner, aka the Admiral, was the one who had written that policy it would have been rather clumsy for he and his lovely assistant to hold hands or show their affection for each other in the hallway. But Brian had decided it was time to turn the reins over to a younger person, so after his retirement in December he would augment Jeanie's meager jewelry collection with a ring to accompany the necklace. He had been invited to continue consulting for the Department of Defense and the White House on matters of National and International Security.

Charles Edgerton had some difficult times over the summer of 2016. He would awaken terrified and sweating when his dreams took him back to those long frightening hours of his captivity. But as the summer days grew shorter and the shadows longer his difficult times grew fewer and fewer helped greatly by an unexpected ally—his mother Millicent who in her boy's needs had found new purpose in her own life while helping her son overcome and assuage his fears.

Eric, Ashley, and Kylie continued to help the Edgerton family enjoy their Cape Cod summer. When James left to lecture at Harvard in September, he had decided to keep the house on Pleasant Street. At least through New Year's 2017. Sam found the idea of celebrating another New Year's Eve—this one with her new fiancé—quite delightful.

The family estate in Cornwall had been a remote place. So as Charles gradually overcame his fears and the bad memories faded James was convinced to allow his grandson to enroll in the Cape Cod Academy in Osterville. Charles had to take a complex battery of tests. He passed them with flying colors, and it did not hurt in the admission conference that Charles was also a first-rate soccer goalie who had participated on several club teams in the UK. Over the summer he had made many friends amongst the local teens—especially several young ladies who found his recent frightening experience demanded their utmost sympathy and affection!

Samantha had been offered the opportunity to enroll in several courses at Harvard in reciprocation for her grandfather's agreement to lecture there, but since she had graduated a Summa from the London School of Economics and Political Science, she found something more to her liking—a local position as an instructor at Cape Cod Community College in entry level microeconomics.

And since the person he wanted to marry had decided to stay on the Cape for the near future Shane also found something more to *his* liking than the position of Dennis Harbormaster or the possibility of working for James in one of his businesses. In July he was approached by a fellow Coast Guard veteran who had read about the Edgerton kidnapping and discovered that Shane was once again the hero of the tale. Commander Ellis Alden, who years before had been the executive officer on the Raymond Evans, the cutter Shane had served on, approached his old shipmate and asked if he had any interest in teaching at the Mass Maritime Academy, one of the country's finest undergraduate institutions for young men and women interested in a career in maritime related fields. Shane was thrilled at the opportunity.

The FBI and Dennis Police were unable to discover any credible evidence or information about who the perpetrators in the Edgerton kidnapping case were, where they came from, or if any members of the plot had escaped. The explosion which Ilya Romanov triggered just after releasing Charles did its job well. Too well. Though the Admiral suspected that both Lassiter and Derrick Muldoon were involved it was nothing more than a case of interesting speculation and made no difference since the remains of the men and any usable forensics remaining inside had been incinerated beyond recognition.

The three men who escaped through the prohibition tunnel returned to their former lives, Lassiter continued to prosper in his illicit pursuits, Ivan and Nicolai disappeared into oblivion. However, each year on the anniversary of their deaths the simple headstones of a mother and two children of the St. Petersburg Romanovs were adorned by a new floral bouquet.

And by Labor Day Kylie Montgomery had finally managed to master her Argo sailing dinghy!

A word about the author...

Kevin Symmons has written five novels for The Wild Rose Press. He has been a college faculty member and served four terms as President of the Cape Cod Writers Center.

His 2012 novel, *Rite of Passage,* was a RonCom Reader's Crown finalist and a #1 Amazon best-seller. His 2013 release, *Out of the Storm,* is a romantic thriller set on Cape Cod. It's gathered dozens of 5-star reviews and has also been a #1 Amazon best-seller. Both novels were selected for Amazon's elite Encore Program. His 2014 novel, *Solo*, is a mainstream best-selling novel that's gathered critical acclaim, and *Chrysalis*, his 2015 tense YA thriller, is set on Buzzard's Bay during the summer of 9/11.

His latest novel, *Eye of the Storm*, is another romantic thriller, the sequel to *Out of the Storm*, that should be released in mid-2020. He is a member of NY's prestigious Authors Guild and a sought-after lecturer and public speaker. He has collaborated with an award-winning Boston Screenwriter-Playwright creating a screenplay for his earlier novel, *When Summer Ends*. Visit Kevin at:

his FB Author Page
@KevinSymmons on Twitter
Goodreads, Amazon, and his website:
www.ksymmons.com

CPSIA information can be obtained
at www.ICGtesting.com
Printed in the USA
LVHW081930301020
670187LV00023B/862

9 781509 229741